A Place in Time

WENDELL BERRY

A Place in Time

Twenty Stories of the
Port William Membership

COUNTERPOINT

BERKELEY

A Place in Time: Twenty Stories of the Port William Membership
Copyright © 2012 by Wendell Berry

Library of Congress Cataloging-in-Publication data is available.

ISBN: 978-1-61902-049-8

Cover and interior design by David Bullen

The cover painting "Springdale" by Harlan Hubbard is used courtesy of
Dr. Robert and Charlotte Candida, with thanks to Meg Shaw.

Map and genealogy designed by Molly O'Halloran.
Genealogy prepared by David S. McCowen.

Counterpoint Press
1919 Fifth Street
Berkeley, CA 94710
www.counterpointpress.com

Printed in the United States of America
Distributed by Publishers Group West

10 9 8 7 6 5 4 3 2 1

In memory of James Baker Hall,
who was the first friend
of the fiction of Port William

Contents

Acknowledgments

In my work I always need help. I have often asked for help, and as often have received it. But being helped, for me, has not been merely a necessity. It is half the pleasure of doing the work.

This book's dedication to James Baker Hall acknowledges a debt that has been accumulating interest for nearly sixty years. My late dear friend Don Wallis read most of these stories and wrote me letters about them that not only improved my writing but were happy events in themselves. Tanya Berry listened to every story in first draft, made the first typescripts, and as always helped me along as critic, editor, and consultant. David Charlton typed the computer versions of every story, and kindly endured my second thoughts, revisions, and additions for what must have seemed to him a time much longer than it actually was. When I became unsure about some technical matters in "The Dark Country" and "A New Day," David Kline and Jason Rutledge led me to solid ground. And I am grateful indeed for this further step in my long collaboration with Jack Shoemaker of Counterpoint, and with David Bullen.

I give my thanks also to the editors of the magazines in which the stories were first published or reprinted: "The Girl in the Window," "Fly Away, Breath," "Andy Catlett: Early Education," "Drouth," and "Not a Tear," in the *Threepenny Review*; "Down in the Valley Where the Green Grass Grows," "A Burden," and "Who Dreamt This Dream?" in the *Oxford American*; "Burley Coulter's Fortunate Fall," "The Dark Country," "A New

Day," "Mike," and "An Empty Jacket" in the *Sewanee Review*; "A Desirable Woman" and "A Place in Time" in the *Hudson Review*; "Misery" in *Shenandoah*; "Stand By Me" and "Sold" in the *Atlantic*; "The Requirement" in *Harper's*; and "At Home" in *Orion*. "Drouth" also appeared in *Farming*. "A New Day" and "Down in the Valley Where the Green Grass Grows" also appeared in *The Draft Horse Journal*.

There is as much in that little space within the heart, as there is in the whole world outside. . . .

What lies in that space, does not decay when the body decays, nor does it fall when the body falls.

The Ten Principal Upanishads,
Put into English by Shree Purohit
Swāmi and W. B. Yeats

Tell ye your children of it, and let your children tell their children, and their children another generation.

JOEL 1:3

A Place in Time

The Girl in the Window (1864)

They might as well all have been the same bunch, although they weren't. Sometimes there would be enough gray uniforms or uniform pieces among them to permit them to be identified (perhaps) as Rebels. Sometimes they would be more formally recognizable as Yankees because they would all be dressed in uniforms that would be blue. Sometimes, because of their unlikeness to one another and to any living thing ever before seen in Port William, you couldn't tell who they were. Whoever they were, the town shut itself against them like a terrapin closing its shell. From the yards and porches and storefronts along the single street, people withdrew behind doors. People who had ridden into town in a wagon or on horseback got themselves and their animals out of sight, if they could. Otherwise, they were apt to have to get away on foot, their mules or horses "requisitioned," and if the younger men could get away at all before being arrested or "recruited."

The Yankees would be looking for persons disloyal to the Union, a category not clearly defined, or for revenge against perpetrators of disloyal acts, which also were not well-defined or perhaps even definable. The Rebels would be on the lookout for recruits. The others, the self-described irregulars or guerillas, would be actuated, as like as not, by some local grudge going back a long time before the war. All of them, always, were looking for any livestock that could be ridden, worked, or eaten, *anything* that could be eaten, anything usable as a weapon, anything portable that was worth carrying away, any opportunity for amusing themselves by any of the cruelties available to those who had abjured, seemingly forever, the laws of kinship and friendship and neighborhood.

And Port William was isolated, beyond the reach of official help, too small and divided even to consider defending itself, both too Southern and too near the Ohio River.

Doing freely, beyond constraint or compunction, the things that it seemed men would do if they got the chance, they all were trouble, trouble when they were present, trouble when they were gone, no end of trouble. She feared them all, and therefore she hated them all.

She was Rebecca Dawe, daughter of Maxie and James John Dawe, sister of Galen Dawe who had been killed by a neighbor as he was leaving to join the Confederate army at the start of the war. Her two older sisters were at home on the river bottom farm down by Dawe's Landing where their father had a store, and where the family and their handful of slaves provided more help in fact than was needed. She could be spared. And so she had come up to Port William to help her aunt Dicey, her mother's sister, with her young children, to help with the work of the household, for her greater safety as her parents saw it, and as she herself saw it for relief from isolation in the great space of the river valley and from her parents' grieving.

And Dicey needed her. Until Rebecca came, walking barefoot up from the river, carrying her shoes and extra clothing bundled in a shawl, Dicey had been alone with her three children, the oldest almost still a baby, and what she called her little dab of livestock: a milk cow, two shoats, and by now a bare dozen hens. Like some of the other houses in Port William, the Needlys' fronted a small farm, theirs going narrowly all the way back to the woods on the river bluff. Dicey's husband, Thomas Needly, the town's only blacksmith, was in the federal military prison in Louisville for an "act of disloyalty." One evening past dark, working mainly by feel, he had reset a shoe on a stranger's horse. He had charged nothing. The stranger, who was in a hurry, had not asked what he owed, and Thomas, in the circumstances and from experience, was afraid to name the price. But the stranger had been the wrong one to help out with such a favor. He was a wanted man. He was caught, and on his testimony Thomas Needly was charged with aiding him in his attempt to escape.

A small band of federal soldiers came in the night, arrested Thomas, and carried him away. Dicey did not know why they had taken him or where, or if he was alive, until she received a long-delayed letter somehow smuggled out of the prison. It was a letter much beyond Thomas's powers of writing, written for him in a determinedly beautiful flowing script by a fellow prisoner:

> Mrs. Needley
> dr. Madam:
> Thos. Needley your houseband was put in here the fed. mil. jail at Louisvle on yesterday charged with aiding a Rebble. He says say he is well & alrite & fully abled of body & mind & send cloths, &c if poss.
>
> a Friend

Dicey did send a packet of his clothes and a few other things that, not knowing, she thought might be of use. This he never received, nor did she hear from him again. Until the war ended nearly a year later, for all she knew, he had fallen off the edge of the world.

And it had been, she would think, a kind of world's edge that he had been to, for he had come back from the helplessness and powerlessness of the dead. When he stood again at his anvil in his strength, in the fierce heat and exactitude of his old work, he had, it seemed to her, the aspect of one who had returned from the grave.

In Thomas's absence, lacking his offering to the community of his needed work and its return of money, the household had become oversimplified and poor. Dicey, who had married late, was thirty, Rebecca just sixteen. They watched over the children. They kept house sparely and neatly. They gardened and foraged and traded for food, and accepted gratefully the food sent up to them from the Dawe household down in the river valley, always in small amounts as a precaution against theft and because, even at the Dawes' place, food was hardly abundant.

The dab of livestock pertained to the two women and their household only conditionally. The two shoats, their ears notched, had been turned loose in the woods, and they were Dicey's own still if they were not caught or shot by some band of soldiers or bushwhackers, and if ever she could get them penned and slaughtered when the time came. The chickens, too easily stolen from the henhouse, had been allowed to go half wild, roosting in trees and hiding their nests in the weeds or the barn, at the mercy of predators. The cow they had saved from theft or slaughter, so far, by confining her in the farthest pasture. Thomas had built in a corner next to the woods a pen of split rails and a small shed where some hay could be stored. To this pen Rebecca carried the milk bucket every morning and every evening, the children following along. And then she carried home again enough milk to drink fresh and to keep them in cream and butter and clabber. "The cow," said Dicey, who liked to say things well, "is our luck and our luxury."

This was late in the summer of 1864, and their luxuries were in fact lucky, and rare. But they were living in what Rebecca was learning fast to recognize as the human condition, in which things are most clearly known by their opposites. She and the others were most touchingly and dearly living because Galen Dawe and so many others were dead, because so many boys even as young as Rebecca had been killed in battle, cut down like weeds. They were most movingly, most consciously and thoughtfully free, because Thomas and so many others were in prison. They ate with relish their frugal meals because of the lively possibility that even they, before the coming winter would be over, could be hungry. They were gathering in and preserving and putting away, even hiding, every surplus scrap of food. There would be stuff yet from the garden. In the fall they would gather walnuts and hickory nuts from the woods. They might, with help, catch and slaughter the two hogs. But the prospect was neither bounteous nor certain.

There were times when their thoughts were carried round and round by hope and fear, courage and resignation. Dicey said, "Lord, I reckon the pore human race has come to a many a fall such as this one. We'll make it, maybe, if those creatures don't steal the food right out of our mouths."

At the start of the war she had been openly in sympathy with the Confederacy, like the rest of her family. By now all the violent ones in their bunches she called, without distinction, "creatures." It was a vital, reverberant word when she said it, for as she acknowledged with frank reluctance the belonging of all creatures to God she pointedly refused to these the classification of "human." Even at the height of her resentment and indignation she did not curse them. But she made no distinction between them and the other creatures—"supposedly," as she would say, "lower"—who conducted themselves in bunches. The state was occupied officially by the Union army. She did not indulge herself by supposing that official occupation by the Confederate army would have been better or, for that matter, different. Power—and for how long? —was the power of the bunch.

The bunches had been with them from the beginning. In the summer of 1861 a company of recruits of each side had drilled in Port William on the same day, and by their taunting back and forth had come close to a shooting scrape right there in the road. "It was almost history," Dicey said. "It would have been known as the Battle of Port William." If it had happened, it would have been as intimate an engagement almost as a family quarrel. No strangers would have been involved. Everybody in each company knew everybody in the other one. It would have been Port William's own. The town and the countryside were divided most cruelly, for the division was not among strangers but among neighbors and kinfolk. That was why in the Port William neighborhood the violence peripheral to the official war was never entirely at rest. In addition to the almost routine recruiting or kidnapping, arresting and stealing, there were barnburnings and other acts of vandalism. Threats were shouted from the darkness, or delivered openly to housewives standing in their doorways. And there were rumors, groundless as often as not, but grounded firmly nonetheless on experience.

The effort of the day was all but over, though the sun was still well up in the sky. Rebecca and the children had walked back to attend to the cow and walked home again with the milk, giving Dicey time to set the house to rights and have a little quiet. Rebecca then had come upstairs to her bedroom, for she loved the stillness of the ordered house at the day's end, and she too needed her quiet. The house, especially the upstairs rooms, was warm beyond comfort, but she sat still by the open front window for the touch of a breeze that was there, and looked out as she liked to do. In a while they would have a supper of milk and cold biscuits and other leftovers from dinner, and then she and Dicey would sit on the front porch in the gathering dusk while the children played in the yard. By full dark all of them would be in bed—"to save light," Dicey would say, meaning candles and lamp oil.

The shadows of the house and the trees beside it had reached all the way across the road to the Feltner house shut and quiet on the other side. And then the murmur of voices from down along the few storefronts of the town became briefly louder and then ceased altogether. She heard the hoofbeats of one horse galloping away along one of the paths that led out from the town into the fields. A shiver passed over her as shivers do when somebody has stepped on the place that will be your grave. She leaned in her chair to look, and saw coming down the hill from the schoolhouse, toward the stores and the bank and the church in the town's middle, a little band of riders. They rode at a walk, looking around. When they came among the business places, now evidently shut and deserted, they stopped, bunching together, and then began riding erratically back and forth, leaning now and again from their saddles to test a latch or to pound a fist on a locked door. One of them fired a pistol into the air. They were well-armed, with holstered pistols and long guns scabbarded or lying across the saddle bows. One of them had a sheathed saber dangling at his side.

That the one had so reasonlessly fired his pistol suggested to Rebecca that they were there without a purpose, looking merely for whatever they might find. But watching them was in fact like watching creatures of another species, a flock of blackbirds or a school of shad. Everything they had done seemed to her familiar and unsurprising, but she could not in the least anticipate what they would do next. It was this sense of their oddity, their utter strangeness, that made her afraid of them. Her fear was a palpable tremor inside her, but even though she was alone she did not allow any visible sign that she was afraid. She stayed as she was, quietly watching. The breeze bore up to her window the warm smells of horse sweat and dust, and now and again the voices of the riders.

She had no idea who they were. They clearly were not Yankees of the force of occupation. But there were several other possibilities. They could have been strayed Rebels or members of the so-called Home Guard or irregulars or bushwhackers, who could have been anybody with any cause or intention. In Port William the war had a lot of sides; it was hard to tell how many or which was which. Worse, it was sometimes hard to tell who in Port William was on which side. This had made the town cautious, and as a result far less talkative than it had been before the war and would come to be again years after it ended. During the war Port William found it hard to keep to its old way of talking to itself about itself. As nearly everybody seemed to know, there were great men at the top of the contending governments and armies who foresaw and even desired that eventually the war would have an official end, but at the bottom were men who did not care if it never ended.

She would remember all her life the threatful or wanton or heartless things she saw during the years of the war, and in fact during many years following—unofficial acts of violence as surely permitted by the war as if they had been determined by policy. The war also had given her two visions of such acts which she had not seen, but which she saw in her mind in such detail that she might as well have seen them with her eyes.

She could see, she would see all her life, her brother Galen on the bay gelding known as Rex, starting to a place near Smallwood where a company of Confederate volunteers was known to be gathering. He was senior to Rebecca by eleven years and therefore, to her, a mature man. But in her vision of him, as she grew older, he became younger, until the day when, in her never-finished sorrow, the realization would come: "He was just a boy!"

He sat well on his horse. He rode alone and—as she saw, as in her vision she increasingly understood—his face had a certain solemnity as if, the hesitance and effort of his decision now behind him, he felt himself a man fated to war—though not, surely, a man fated to be killed in that moment, before he could breathe again.

The family knew who did it, though there was no witness, no avowal, no evidence that was indisputable. And so the story she knew was not the story only of her brother, but in her vision he was alone, and when she heard the shot it surprised her. Every time the vision returned to her in the night or in the daytime when she sat alone the shot surprised her—for she saw each time that Galen anticipated nothing, was aware perhaps of nothing but himself and his horse passing on their way. It seemed to her that Galen did not hear the shot. He fell at once and cleanly from the saddle, delivered out of time without even a suspicion of the cause. The ones who happened upon his body found the horse nearby, grazing along the roadside.

The second vision was from the fall of 1863, more than two years after the first. Several slaves, five or six of them, both men and women, were cutting and shocking corn by moonlight out on the Bird's Branch Road, not far from the church. In her vision she saw them plainly, working steadily along to the rhythm that their corn knives hacked into the rustling of the dry corn. They were singing. They were singing, "Freedom! Oh, freedom!" That was all the song, but they sang it back and forth among themselves. Sometimes they would fall silent, and then the song continued unsung to the beat of the knives. And then a solitary voice would lift into the moonlight, "Oh, freedom!" and then they would all sing, "Freedom! Oh, freedom!" a cry that was old and creaturely and human. Later she would imagine that there had rarely been a time, and in Port William after slavery perhaps never again a time, when the word "freedom" had been so under-standingly sounded. As the singers sang, they worked. As they worked, the rows of standing corn slowly became fewer and the rows of shocks increased. Over the striking of the knives and the steady rustling of the corn and the singing, the moonlight fell as if a greater silence were thus made visible.

And Rebecca saw too, following the narrow road up the rise from the church, another of the little bands of hostile men that in those years criss-crossed the neighborhood, leaving it each time, it seemed to her, worse than it had been before, just as they crisscrossed also her own mind, leaving it each time sadder and yet stronger and less to be fooled.

There was no question who these were, for the people of Port William had come by various ways to know for certain. These were Confederate cavalry, six men and an officer. Their presence was perhaps accountable by some minor event or accident of the war, and yet, to her own mind, it was factual without being explainable. They simply were there, alien and unbelonging, as they had been wherever they had come from, as they would be wherever they would go, like all the others who had been displaced by the unaiming destiny of the bunch.

As they came up along the corn rows and into the sound of the Negroes' singing and understood it, that word rising as if by nature out of bondage, the officer abruptly spurred his horse, put him to the rock fence beside the road, and neatly cleared it. He rode in among the crew of workers—they were scattering, running like quail into the standing corn. Drawing his pistol, he shot the eldest of them, a slave man named Tucker, point-blank in the side of the head.

It was no wonder that her time to marry came late for a young woman of Port William. It came when she was twenty-four, seven years after the formal, the "historical," ending of the war. The nighttime reprisals of vengeful men—the unofficial violence set loose and still nominally justified by official violence—were still terrorizing the country. Her own repugnance and disdain persisted in those years of official peace. She would not be wedded, she could hardly bear to be looked at, by the young men of her own place, every one of whom seemed to her to bear the taint of what she called ever after "that awfulness." She married instead an Irish immigrant who, to escape the bunch-violence that ruled his own land, had come to America and, hearing that a "shoe cobbler" was needed, finally to Port William.

Though she was old enough in that summer of 1864 for a Port William girl to be married, the awfulness already had driven any thought of courtship or marriage from her mind. She had instead taken a defensive stand on the side merely of the helpless and the threatened. On their behalf she distrusted all the creatures of the bunches and the weapons. That was why she sat still in her fear and watched as the alien riders, in the absence or invisibility of the entire membership of the town, occupied and ruled over the empty road.

And then, seeing nothing easily to be taken or enjoyed, they began to give the place up. They gathered again in the road and formed raggedly a line, resuming the direction that would carry them on through the town and finally into the river valley.

Looking away then in the direction they were going to go, she saw hanging over the river a single small white cloud just touched by the gold of the weakening sun. And then she saw, as if wonder must now be added to the new normality of outrage, the figure of a walking man emerge into the open concavity of the road as it came up out of the valley and turned toward the town. She knew immediately who it was, as she might have recognized at a distance too far for reading the character of her own script. It was Eli, her mother's slave, with a split basket on his arm, bringing to her and Dicey, she supposed, some gift of food. Alone, old and ambling, visible against the bare horizon as the chimney of a burned house, he would be at the mercy of the riders, who had not yet seen him, though they would see him as soon as they looked. They would surround him on their horses. They would point their guns at him for the pleasure of seeing him frightened. They would demand the basket. Or worse. They could do worse. They could do as they pleased.

In her mind a thought like a prayer cried out: "Eli! Get out of sight!"

She looked quickly at the line of riders now coming up even with her window, and then quickly back at Eli. For another wonder, he had seen them first. Exactly as if he had heard her unspoken warning, he had vanished.

Relieved, she now looked only at the line of riders as one by one they straggled by. Their horses were fairly fit and of fairly good stock. The men in general rode them well enough, with an evident sense of their power, even maybe of pomp, and yet still she felt their strangeness, the strangeness of their ability now, in their bunch, to do as they pleased. They were like biting dogs. Emboldened by the fear they had caused, they longed for pursuit, but they had found as yet nobody to pursue.

They had almost gone by. She had almost relaxed her strict vigilance over her fear—her courage, though she had not called it so, that had kept her sitting and watching. She was ready to stand up, shake herself, and go to find Dicey and the children, when the last of the line of riders glanced up and saw her.

He stopped his horse, turned him to face the house, and sat looking up at her. Having recovered her stillness, pressing firmly downward within herself the physical tremor of her fright, she looked back at him. He was a young man with a curly, sand-colored beard. To somebody else, or in different circumstances, he might have seemed even, in his fashion, a handsome young man. But she feared him and she hated him, and without flinching she looked back at him.

She thought, and the thought was familiar to her, how easy it would have been, if she had had a gun, if she had placed herself a few feet back in the shadowy room, to have shot him dead. And then she thought immediately, for this thought also was familiar, of the endlessness of such an act, or of its many ends multiplying unforeseeably forever. Maybe it was that thought that kept most people out of the way of such acts, when they could keep out of the way of them.

She knew she was daring him. She meant her facing him, her looking back, to be merely a refusal to be cowed by him. But she knew, she felt, the boldness even of so quiet a refusal. The deliberate impassivity of her face he would see as impudent. He would be challenged by it. He could, if he wished, shoot her and get clean away, unwitnessed, his shot not necessarily causing his companions even to look back.

His reprisal, though not violent, though it did not cause her to move or change expression, was nonetheless shocking to her, for it was just as unexpected as she expected it to be. He said without raising his voice, in perfect contempt, "Get your ugly face out of that window."

Though for some time she continued to watch him, defying him, for she trembled now with the knowledge that she gladly would have killed him, he went on and did not look back.

Finally she allowed herself to look away. She willed herself free of her anger and her fear. She allowed the familiar room and all the house, quiet and warm and shadowy, to come round her again. Old Eli, wherever he was out there in the dimming country, was safe. The household and the town still were silent. Chances were there would be no human sound again until morning.

She got up from her chair. She would go now to find the others. They would fix supper and eat. They would let another evening come upon them. They would sleep.

As she went by the mirror on her dresser, she paused a moment and looked in. Unlike her mother, but as her daughter Margaret would be in her turn, she was a young woman of principled modesty. She would not have liked to catch herself thinking of herself as beautiful, though she was. But she did think, articulating the words deliberately as if saying them aloud: "That is not an ugly face."

Fly Away, Breath (1907)

Andy Catlett keeps in his mind a map of the country around Port William as he has known it all his life and as he has been told about it all his life from times and lives before his. There are moments, now that he is getting old, when he seems to reside in that country in his mind even as his mind still resides in the country.

This is the country of his own life and history, fragmentary as they necessarily have been. It is his known country. And perhaps it differs also from the actual, momentary country insofar as time is one of its dimensions, as reckonable in thought as length and breadth, as air and light. His thought can travel like a breeze over water back and forth upon the face of it, and also back and forth in time along its streams and roads.

As in thought he passes backward into time, the country becomes quieter, and it seems to grow larger. The sounds of engines become less frequent and farther apart until finally they cease altogether. As the roads get poorer or disappear, the distances between places seem to grow longer. Distances that he can now travel in minutes in an automobile once would have taken hours and much effort.

But it is possible, even so, to look back with a certain fondness to a time when the sounds of engines were not almost constant in the sky, on the roads, and in the fields. Our descendants may know such a time again when the petroleum all is burnt. How they will fare then will depend on the neighborly wisdom, the love for the place and its genius, and the skills that they may manage to revive between now and then.

The country in Andy Catlett's mind has assuredly a past, which exists in relics and scraps of memory more or less subject to proof. It has presumably a future that will verify itself only by becoming the past. Its present is somewhat conjectural, for old Andy Catlett, like everybody else, cannot be conscious of the present while he is thinking of the past. And most of us, most of the time, think mostly of the past. Even when we say, "We are living now," we can mean only that we were living a moment ago.

Nevertheless, in this sometimes horrifying, sometimes satisfying, never-sufficiently-noticed present, between a past mostly forgotten and a future that we deserve to fear but cannot predict, some few things can be recalled.

In all the country from Port William to the river, one light shines. It is from a flame on the wick of an oil lamp, turned low, on a little stand table at the bedside of Maximilla Dawe in a large unpainted house facing the river in Glenn's Bottom between Catlett's Fork and Bird's Branch. The old lady lies somewhat formally upon the bed, seemingly asleep, in a long-sleeved flannel nightgown, clean but not new, the covers laid neatly over her. Her arms lie at her sides, the veined and gnarled old hands at rest. She is propped, in the appearance at least of comfort, on several pillows, for she is so bent by age and work that she could not lie flat.

She has been old a long time. Though "Maximilla" was inscribed in her father's will, by which he left her the farm in the river bottom, the family of "the slave woman known as Cat," and his stopped gold watch, and though it was signed in her own hand at the end of two or three legal documents, she was never well known even to herself by that name. Once upon a time she was "Maxie"—"Miss Maxie" to the Negroes and some whites. For at least as long, to herself as to all the neighborhood of Port William, she has been "Aunt Maxie." To her granddaughter, who was Andy Catlett's grandmother, she had always been "Granny Dawe," as to Andy she still is known.

Andy's grandmother, born Margaret Finley, now Margaret Feltner, sits by the bedside of Granny Dawe in that room in the dim lamplight in the broad darkness of the river valley in the fall of 1907, a hundred years ago.

Margaret Feltner is a pretty woman—or girl, as the older women still would have called her—with a peculiar air of modesty, for she knows she is pretty but would prefer not to be caught knowing it. She is slenderly formed and neatly dressed, even prettily dressed, for her modesty must contend also with her knowledge that her looks are pleasing to Mat Feltner, her young husband.

With her are three other young women, also granddaughters of the old woman on the bed. They are Bernice Gibbs, and Oma and Callie Knole. Kinswomen who know one another well, they sit close together, leaving a sort of aisle between their chairs and the bed.

Their voices are low, and their conversation has become more and more intermittent as the night has gone on. The ancient woman on the bed breathes audibly, but slowly too and tentatively, so that they who listen even as they talk are aware that at any moment there may be one more breath, and then no more.

But she is dying in no haste, this Aunt Maxie, this Granny Dawe, who lived and worked so long before she began to die that she was the only one alive who still knew what she had known. She was born in 1814 in the log house that long ago was replaced by the one in which she now is dying. At the time of her birth, the Port William neighborhood was still in its dream of itself as a frontier, "the West," a new land. The chief artery of trade and transportation for that part of the country then was the river, as it would be for the next hundred years. When the time came, she bestowed her land, her slaves, and herself upon a man named James John Dawe, whose worldly fortune consisted of a singular knack for trade and the store and landing, the port of Port William, known as Dawe's Landing. He left the care of the farm to her. With the strength and the will and the determined good sense that have kept the farm and household in her own hands until now, she ruled and she served through times that were mostly hard.

The Civil War had its official realization in movements of armies and great battles in certain places, but in places such as Port William it released and licensed an unofficial violence also terrible, and more lasting. At its outset, Galen Dawe, on his way to join the Confederate army, was shot from his horse and left dead in the road, no farther on his way than Port William, by a neighbor, a Union sympathizer, with whom he had quarreled. And Maxie Dawe, with the help of a slave man named Punkin, loaded the dead boy onto a sled drawn by a team of mules. Looking neither right nor left at those who watched, she brought home the mortal body of her one son, which she washed and dressed herself, and herself read the great psalm over him as he lay in his grave.

The rest of her children were daughters, four of them. Her grief and her bearing in her grief gave her a sort of headship over daughters and husband that they granted without her ever requiring it. When a certain superiority to suffering, a certain indomitability, was required, she was the one who had it. Later, when a band of self-denominated "Rebel" cavalry hung about the neighborhood, she saved her husband, the capable merchant James John, from forcible recruitment or murder, they never knew which, by hiding him three weeks in a succession of corn shocks, carrying food and water to him after dark. By her cunning and sometimes her desperate bravery, she brought her surviving family, her slaves, and even a few head of livestock through the official and the unofficial wars, only to bury her husband, dead of a fever, at the end of the official one.

When the slaves were freed in Kentucky, when at last she had heard, she gathered those who had been her own into the kitchen. She told them: "Slavery is no more, and you are free. If you wish to stay and share our fate, you are free to stay, and I will divide with you as I can. If you wish to go, you are free to go."

There were six of them, the remaining family of the woman known as Cat, and they left the next morning, taking, each of them, what could be carried bundled in one hand, all of them invested with an official permission that had made them strange to everything that had gone before. They left, perhaps, from no antipathy to staying, for they arrived in Hargrave and lived there under the name of Dawe—but how could they have known they were free to go if they had not gone? Or so, later, Maxie Dawe would explain it, and she would add, "And so would I have, had it been me."

She and her place never recovered from the war. Unable to manage it herself, and needing money, she sold the landing. She hired what help she could afford. She rented her croplands on the shares. After her daughters married and went away, she stayed on alone. To her young granddaughters, and probably to herself as well, the world of the first half of her life was another world.

No more would she be "Maxie" to anybody. Increasingly she would be "Aunt Maxie." She was respected. By those who lacked the sense to respect her she was feared. She held herself strictly answerable to her necessities. She worked in the fields as in the house. Strange and doubtful stories were told about her, all of them perhaps true. She was said to have shot off a man's ear, only his ear, so he would live to tell it.

And now her long life, so strongly determined or so determinedly accepted by her, has at last submitted. It is declining gently, perhaps willingly, toward its end. It has been nearly a day and now most of a night since she uttered a word or opened her eyes. A younger person so suddenly moribund as she would have been dead long ago. But she seems only asleep, her aspect that of a dreamer enthralled. The two vertical creases between her brows suggest that she is raptly attentive to her dream.

That she is dying, she herself knows, or knew, for early in the morning of the previous day, not long before she fell into her present sleep, her voice, to those who bent to listen, seeming to float above the absolute stillness of her body, and with the tone perhaps of a small exasperation, she said, "Well, if this is dying, I've seen living that was worse."

The night began cloudy, and the clouds have deepened over the valley and the old house with its one light. The first frosts have come, hushing the crickets and the katydids. The country seems to be waiting. At about dawn a season-changing rain will begin so quietly that at first nobody will notice, and it will fall without letup for two days.

When midnight passes through the room, nobody knows, neither the old woman on the bed nor the young ones who watch beside it. The room would seem poor, so meager and worn are its furnishings, except that its high ceiling and fine proportions give it a dignity that in the circumstances is austere. Though the night is not quite chilly, the sternness of the room and the presence of death in it seemed to call for additional warmth, and the young wives have kindled a little fire. From time to time, one or another has risen to take from the stone hearth a stick of wood and lay it on the coals. From time to time, one or another has risen to smooth the bedclothes that need no smoothing, or to lay a hand upon the old woman's forehead, or to touch lightly the pulse fluttering at her wrist.

After midnight, stillness grows upon them all. The talk has stopped, the fire subsided to a glow, when Bernice Gibbs raises her hand and the others look at her. Bernice is the oldest of the four. The others have granted her an authority which, like their grandmother perhaps, she has accepted merely because she has it and the others don't. She looks at each of them and looks away, listening.

They listen, and they hear not a sound. They hear instead a silence that reaches into every room and into the expectant night beyond. They rise from their chairs, first Bernice, and then, hesitantly, the others. They tiptoe to the bed, two to a side, and lean, listening, at that edge which they and all their children too have now passed beyond. The silence grows palpable around them, a weight.

Now, as Andy Catlett imagines his way into this memory that is his own only because he has imagined it, he is never quite prepared for what he knows to have happened next. Always it comes to him somewhat by surprise, as it came to those who remembered it from the actual room and the actual night.

In silence that seems to them utterly conclusive, the young women lean above the body of the old woman, the mold in which their own flesh was cast, and they listen. And then, just when one of them might have been ready to say, "She's gone," the old woman releases with a sigh her held breath: "Hooo!"

They startle backward from the bedside, each seeing in the wide-opened mouths and eyes of the others her own fright. Oma Knole, who is clumsy, strikes the lamp and it totters until Bernice catches and steadies it.

They stand now and look at one another. The silence has changed. The dying woman's utterance, brief as it was, spoke of a great weariness. It was the sigh of one who has been kept waiting. The sound hangs in the air as if visible, as if the lamp flame had flown upward from the wick. It stays, nothing moves, until some lattice of the air lets pass the single distant cry of an owl—"Hoo!"—as if in answer.

Callie Knole turns away, bends forward, and emits what, so hard suppressed, might have been a sob, but it is a laugh.

And then they all laugh, at themselves, at one another, and they cannot stop. Their sense of the impropriety of their laughter renews their laughter. Looking at each other, flushed and wet-eyed with laughter, makes them laugh. They laugh because they are young and they are alive, and life has revealed itself to them, as it often had and often would, by surprise.

Margaret Feltner, when she had become an old woman, "Granny" in her turn, told Andy of this a long time ago. "Oh, it was awful!" she said, again laughing. "But the harder we tried to stop, the funnier it was."

And Andy, a hundred years later, can hear their laughter. He hears also the silence in which they laugh: the ancient silence filling the dark river valley on that night, uninterrupted in his imagination still by the noise of engines, the great quiet into which they all have gone.

The laughter, which threatened to be endless, finally ends and is gathered into the darkness, into the past. The night resumes its solemn immensity, and again in the silence the old woman audibly breathes. But now her breaths come at longer intervals, until the definitive quiet settles upon her at last. They who have watched all night then fold her hands. Her mouth has fallen open, and Bernice thinks to bind it shut. They draw the counterpane over her face. Day whitens again over the old house and its clutch of old buildings. As they sit on in determined noiselessness, it comes to the young women that for some time they have been hearing the rain.

Down in the Valley Where the Green Grass Grows (1930)

You would think a fellow whose paunch was bigger than his ass would take the precaution of underdrawers. Or suspenders. Or bib overalls. Big Ellis didn't, of course. He never thought of precautions until too late. After it was too late he could always tell you what the right precaution would have been if only he had thought of it. "Burley," he would say, "I see the point. I've got my sights dead on it." But he saw it going away, from behind. And so when he was a young man, and had grown to his full girth, his pants as a rule were either half on or he was holding them with one hand to keep them from falling off.

Big was late getting married. Marriage was a precaution he didn't think of until his mother died and left him alone to cook and housekeep for himself. And then he really began to hear the call of matrimony.

He was quite a dancer in his young days. You would think at first it was the funniest thing you ever saw. The fiddle music would carry him clean out of his head, and there he would be, swinging his partner like she didn't weigh anything, with his hair in his eyes, his shirt tail half out, sweating like a horse, his pants creeping down, and that one hand from time to time jerking them back up. But if you paid attention to him, you would soon see that he really was a dancer. He was a smooth mover, a big man but light on his feet. His feet had ways of going about their business as if he himself didn't know what they were up to. They were answering the music, you see, and not just the caller. He could really step it off. He could cut a shine.

He did all right in his socializing until he got his eye set on a girl, and then he would get shy and awkward and tongue-tied. He would figure then that he needed to get her cornered in some clever and mannerly way that would be beyond his abilities. And he would come up with some of the damnedest, longest-way-around schemes such as nobody ever thought of before and were always well worth knowing about. He edged up to a girl one time at the Fourth of July and said, "I know a girl's about the prettiest thing ever I looked at," and was struck dumb when she said, "Who?" He wrote one a love letter in his outrageous pencil-writing and signed it "A Friend." He brought one a live big catfish and held it out to her like it was gold-plated, and never offered so much as to skin it. Those times, I have to say, he was not very serious. What he had in his mind then was sport. As you might call it.

When he began to shine up to Annie May Cordle with the honorable intention of marrying her if she would have him, he outdid himself for judgment. She was about as near the right match for him as he could have found. But he went about the business as perfectly hind-end-foremost as you would have expected. For a while he just hung around her every time he got a chance, looking as big-eyed and solemn as a dying calf. If she looked at him or said anything to him, he turned red and grinned with more teeth than a handsaw and hitched up his pants with both hands.

After he got his crop sold that winter, Big did what he usually would do. He took it in his head to trade off the team of mules he already had, maybe adding a few dollars to boot, for a better team. He always thought he got "a good deal" on "a better team," and that was why he never in his life owned a team that was better than passable. In fact he was too big-hearted and generous, especially if he'd had a drink or two, to be any account at all as a trader. Somebody always took his old team and his money, and he wound up with a team just a teensy bit better or worse than what he had before. And so of course he was always wanting to trade.

By springtime sure enough he had his new team, a rabbity pair of three-year-old red mules, not above fifteen hands. Dick and Buck. They sort of matched, and he was proud of them, though they were not hardly what you would call well broke.

The weather got warm. We needed rain, and then we got a showery day that was about what the doctor ordered and made us feel good. The next day it faired up. The ground being too wet to work and the day fine, I walked over to Big's to see what I could put him up to. He was a good one to wander about with on such a day. He was a good companion, always ready for whatever you needed him for. I thought we might drop down to the river and fish a while, maybe.

But when I got to his place he was hitching his new team to the sled. He was going to take a bunch of broken tools to the blacksmith shop in town to get them fixed. It was never any trouble at Big's to find broken tools, which wasn't because he worked all that hard. He just *used* things hard, or he used them for purposes they weren't meant for. He treated wood the same as steel. He had piled onto the sled a plow with a broken handle, a hoe with a broken handle, a grubbing hoe with no handle, a broken doubletree, and other such, too big a load to take in his old car.

"Why don't you use the wagon?" I said.

"Oh," he said. "I forgot. Here. Hold the lines a minute."

He went into the wagon shed and came back rolling a wagon wheel with two broken spokes.

So there was nothing for it but the sled, which wasn't the best vehicle on a gravel road, and with no tongue, behind a team the least bit touchous. And especially that little Buck mule, if I had pegged him right, was just waiting for a good reason to demonstrate his speed. He was the reason Big asked me to hold the lines while he went to get the wagon wheel.

Big had left himself a place to stand in amongst the load. I made myself a place and turned up a five-gallon bucket to sit on. Big told the mules to come up, gave the lines a little flip, and we started off with pretty much of a jerk.

When we hit the gravel, which we would be on all the way to town, you could see that both mules became deeply concerned. They got into a little jiggling trot and backed their ears so as not to miss anything that might be gaining on them. And the runners did screech and batter something awful. But Big was stout enough to hold them and two more like them, if his old lines and bridles held together. Just looking at the back of him, I could see how pleased he was with his team, showing spirit the way they were. And they matched, you know. To some people, and Big was one, a bad team that matches is better than a good team that don't.

So we went stepping pretty lively into Port William. I unloaded the sled at the blacksmith shop while Big kept hold of the lines. And then we started back. There was no chance of loafing a while in town, for the mules couldn't be trusted to stand tied. One backfire from somebody's automobile and they might've disappeared off like two mosquitoes.

But when we got to the mouth of our lane, Big drove right on by. I saw then what he had on his mind. His real business for that morning wasn't to take a bunch of broken tools to town. He was going on out by the Cordles' place. If Annie May was where she could see, she was going to have the benefit of a look at that well-matched, high-spirited team of mules, and of old Big standing there holding the lines, calm as George Washington, everything under control.

The trouble was, by the time we were closing in on the Cordles', after the extra mile or so, the mules had lost their fine edge. They had worn down to a civilized manner of doing business. They were walking along, nodding their heads and letting their ears wag like a seasoned team. Looked like they both together didn't have an ounce of drama left in 'em, and the large impression Big was wanting to make had fallen by the wayside.

So without making a sudden motion I got on my knees and skimmed up a rock about the size of a pocket watch and settled back onto my bucket.

Big, among other things, was a lucky creature. For when we came in sight of the Cordles' house down in the pretty little swale where their farm was, there was Annie May, sure enough, looking sweet as a rose, right out on the front porch. She was churning, working the dasher up and down at a steady gait. She looked patient, gazing off at the sky. Maybe the butter was slow to come and she had been at it a while.

I was wanting to help Big all I could, of course. I waited until I was sure Annie May had seen us coming, until we could almost hear the dasher chugging in the churn, and then I shied that little rock almost under the Buck mule's tail where he felt it the most.

He lost no time in taking offense. He clamped his tail down and humped up in the back, which notified the Dick mule that the end of the world was at hand. They shot off both at once like their tails were afire.

I swear I had no idea I was going to need a handhold as quick as I did. Just as I was starting backwards off of my bucket, I grabbed a double handful of Big's pants, and down they came.

He said very conversationally, "Burley Coulter, damn your impudent hide."

But he stood to his work. He had to, of course. He made the drive past the Cordles' as magnificent as you please, proudly and calmly in control of his spirited team that was plunging on the bits, with his pants down around his ankles and his shirttail flying out behind. As we went past, I glanced up at Annie May and, so help me Jesus, she was smiling and waving—a good-hearted, patient, forgiving, well-fleshed girl, just right for Big.

Well, old Big did keep his team in hand. He never let them out of a short lope. Pretty soon he stopped them and got his pants back up more or less where they belonged, and took the long way home so he wouldn't have to pass the Cordles' again. He never looked at me or said a word. He wasn't speaking.

But when we finally got back to his place and had put away the mules, which were a good deal better broke by then, I felt obliged to have a serious talk with him.

"Big," I said, "you're going to have to ask that woman to marry you, after you've done showed yourself to her the way you have."

You couldn't beat him for good nature. He just grinned, clean back to his ears. He said, "All right. I reckon I will."

So he was speaking to me again. And afterwards he told me all about it. He was giggling, red in the face, and absolutely tickled almost to death.

He gave up all his clever notions about courting, and was forthright. When he saw Annie May in town next time, he said, "Come here. I want to talk to you."

She followed him out of earshot of the other people, and he said, "Well, you've done had a look at my private life. Don't you reckon me and you ought to get married?"

She looked straight back at him and laughed. She laughed right into his face like the good old gal she was.

She said, "I would like to know why *not!*"

Burley Coulter's
Fortunate Fall (1934)

It has been a long, long time since old Uncle Bub Levers was called on to pray at the Bird's Branch church for the first and last time in his life, and he stood up and said, "O Lord, bless me and my son Jasper. Amen."

The Lord must have thought that was a good idea. For with His help, maybe, Jappy Levers grew up and got himself educated for a lawyer. When he hung out his sign in Hargrave, he wasn't Jappy Levers any more. He was J. Robert La Vere, Attorney at Law. That might not have been all put-on. Some say that La Veres was what the Leverses were before they turned up around Port William. People in Port William don't say things they haven't heard of. They never had heard of La Veres. They had heard of levers.

With the Lord's help maybe, maybe not, Mr. La Vere got to be a rich man. Getting rich, you know, does not always meet with everybody's approval. There was always somebody, or several bodies, in Port William who would tell you confidently that Mr. La Vere got rich by finding out where the money was and helping himself to a good deal more than his share. In fact they didn't know, and I don't know. To find out how such things are done, you will have to ask somebody besides me. Maybe you can do like Mr. La Vere, who gaveth the credit to the Lord, at the same time keeping a good deal of it for himself, the Lord maybe not minding, maybe.

Anyhow, the Lord either did or didn't bless Mr. La Vere with the money he scraped together by the time he was forty-five or so, when he bought the biggest house in Hargrave with a front porch two stories tall. After Uncle Bub died, Mr. La Vere kept the old Levers home place out on Bird's Branch, and as the chances came he bought other farms hither and yon.

So he was right smart of a big deal and on the downward slope when he topped himself off by taking to wife, as Wheeler Catlett put it, the elegant, accomplished, and beautiful Miss Charlotte Riggins. Miss Charlotte was from somewhere off. She could have been rich herself for all I know, maybe, maybe not, but she did come up in the world by changing her name from Riggins to La Vere and setting up housekeeping behind the tallest front porch in Hargrave.

How Mr. La Vere and Miss Charlotte hit it off as a loving couple is anybody's guess. I somehow never quite could imagine it myself, so I will leave it to you. But Mr. La Vere lived long enough that by the time he died, Miss Charlotte had taken on all his dignity and become a great lady.

By the time Mr. La Vere departed, Miss Charlotte's hair had turned mortally blue, but she wasn't exactly an old woman yet. If widowhood hadn't suited her so well, and with all her goods and money, surely somebody would have married her. I reckon I might have married her myself, maybe, if she had ever asked me.

Mr. La Vere died at about the start of the Depression or a little before, and Wheeler Catlett, who was a wingshot of a young lawyer then, settled the old man's estate, nearly all of it directly onto Miss Charlotte. At about the same time the tenant on the old Levers place gave it up, and Wheeler traded with Grover Gibbs to be the new tenant. And so Grover and his wife, Beulah, and their children moved into the old Levers house that was the Gibbs house then until Beulah's mother and daddy had gone from this world and left her the little piece of it where she was raised.

Grover was one of my old running mates, a little younger than I am, but it seems like I was young a long time. So from then on I was party to the doings of Miss Charlotte and to her, what do you call it? relationship, I guess, with Grover. Grover was probably the ideal man for the place—Wheeler probably couldn't have done any better. The Levers place was run down but still a pretty good farm, and Grover was a pretty good farmer, so it was a fit. Being a pretty good farmer was good enough for Grover. Now and again, when he was a little down in the mouth, he would make the usual complaints about farming on the halves, but being a tenant farmer suited him really well enough. He had several other things he needed to see to: fishing and hunting, and drinking a little whiskey from time to time for his health, and holding up his end of the conversation out at town. Well, he held up his end along with the ends of several others in case they couldn't make it.

And, too, he took a particular pleasure in his relationship with Miss Charlotte. Miss Charlotte, you might say, was an enjoyable lady. I don't believe she was as enjoyable a lady as Beulah Gibbs, fact is I know she wasn't, but she was in her own way enjoyable. Wheeler, who was Miss Charlotte's lawyer for the next thirty or so years, had the gift of enjoying her for her own sake. Which was fortunate for Wheeler, for after she died her relatives decided that her estate was beyond the powers of "a country lawyer." So Wheeler was paid for in fact a lot of bother mostly by a little pleasure. But Grover enjoyed the idea of himself as her tenant, and the idea of her as his landlady.

While she was still a widow in mourning, Miss Charlotte took over the supervision of the farms, and I don't believe there has been anything like it in the history of the world before or since. She would come riding in, always unexpectedly, in the back seat of her long green car that was about the same color as folding money. It would be shined so slick, Grover said, that a housefly couldn't stand up on it. She would be wearing a dress that was like a cloud or like a flower bed in full bloom or like a pool with goldfish—this is Grover talking. And she would have on white gloves and a hat with a veil, and if the weather was the least bit cool she would have a fox or a mink fur piece around her neck and her hands stuck into a fur muff with every hair standing on end. And she would be sitting straight up like a queen in a picture, in reference strictly to herself.

Driving her would be Willard Safely, of the black branch of the Hargrave Safelys, wearing a black coat and an official little black chauffeur's cap, Willard being a whole nuther item of interest himself. When he wasn't wearing his black coat to be Miss Charlotte's chauffeur, he would be her butler or table waiter wearing a white coat. His wife, Bernice, was Miss Charlotte's cook and housemaid, always starched and white and waiting to be told what to do next. Willard's life was in a way glorious, for who else anywhere around drove such a car? But it was difficult too, and not

just when Miss Charlotte joined forces with Bernice in regard to several
of his pleasures. I know some of what I know, not just from Grover, but
also from Wheeler.

I don't mean to give you the idea that Wheeler Catlett went around
gossiping about his clients. But when his boy Andy got big enough to be
some account at work, he would tell us things. At that age, Andy wasn't
always on the best of terms with his father, but he enjoyed Wheeler's
knowledge and his language. So when we were all together at work and
the stories would get started, Andy sometimes had good things to pass
along. It's a mystery how the voices gather. Our talk at row ends or in
the barn or stripping room would call up the voices of the absent and the
dead. Somebody maybe would wonder what old Uncle Bub would think
of Miss Charlotte, and though we never knew him and he never knew her
he would say about her what he said about everybody of wonder. "Hell
and dammit, boys! She's a ring-tailed twister!" About everybody knew of
Miss Charlotte and took some interest in her. She was surrounded, you
might say, with observation. And of course also, as Wheeler said, with
her own glitter.

Grover said he could tell when she was coming because first he would
see Willard in his chauffeur's cap driving around the corner of the rock
fence along the driveway and then, well behind him, Miss Charlotte would
come into sight in the back seat. They would drive up in front of the feed
barn. They would look around. If they didn't see Grover, Miss Charlotte
would tell Willard to blow the horn, and he would give forth a toot. When
Grover appeared, if he did, Miss Charlotte would roll her window down.

Grover, you would think, might have gone over and leaned down to
speak to her at a respectful level through the window, but Grover never
felt dressed for the occasion. So he stood back at some distance, requiring her to raise her voice to, as he put it, his level to speak to him, and he
would holler back to her. She took herself too seriously to notice that he
took her unseriously.

"Grover, are you giving milk regularly to the cats?"

"Yes *mam*, Miss Charlotte."

"Grover, you aren't looking well. Are you well?"

"I *was* feeling pretty well, Miss Charlotte, but I got over it."

"I see you have a nice automobile, Grover," she said once, pointing to one of Grover's semi-wrecks that he said would roll down any hill it couldn't pull up. "What *kind* is it?"

"A small Packard, Miss Charlotte."

Grover liked that remark so well that every old car he had from then on he always called it a small Packard.

But maybe more often than she came, Miss Charlotte would send Willard by himself. When she sent Willard it was usually with a message she didn't want to deliver in person.

Neither one of them ever said so, but Willard and Grover saw eye to eye on a lot of things. They enjoyed a lot of the same pleasures without ever so much as a look or a wink passing between them.

Willard's natural laugh was something to see and hear. He would bend way forward and then rear way back and give out a great bellow that would loosen shingles. But when more was going on than met the eye he had a little pecking laugh, "heh-heh-heh."

Miss Charlotte was maybe the president of the widows and old maids of the Hargrave aristocracy, and she made a big thing of giving all her constituents an old ham every Christmas, a big ham to the widows with families and a little ham to the old maids. How she got the little hams was a matter of some embarrassment to Willard, and a matter of artistic pride and satisfaction to Grover.

Every fall when the nights were getting cold and hog-killing time was getting close, Willard would come driving in by himself. He would say, "Trim them shoulders round, Mistah Grover, heh-heh-heh."

Miss Charlotte's hogs, you see, were the only ones ever known to have hams at both ends. "They had hams coming and going!" Wheeler Catlett said.

Sure enough, Grover could trim a shoulder so anybody who didn't know the difference would take it for a ham. And the aristocratic old maids at Hargrave didn't know the difference.

When it was coming Christmas there would be Willard again, by himself. He would back the big car up to the smokehouse door, Grover would hand the yearling hams out to Willard, and every time Grover handed him one of the little hams Willard, never looking at Grover, said, "Heh-heh-heh."

What made Willard laugh his big true laugh was for instance this.

One afternoon Willard was driving Miss Charlotte and a lesser widow or two and Miss Agnes Heartsease home from some function, and they were overtaken by a big storm of rain at the same time that Miss Heartsease, full of coffee, was overtaken by an urge to uncork herself that she was powerless to resist—this is Wheeler talking.

Miss Heartsease was a schoolteacher and a lady of the strictest religion. Her virtue, Wheeler said, was a mighty fortress that she had successfully defended against every assault, as many maybe as one.

Anyhow, and this was probably something else new in history, Miss Charlotte made Willard stand out in the rain to hold an umbrella over Miss Heartsease, looking away, while she peed I'm sure a genteel little trickle on the gravel.

The only one who would have told that was bound to be Willard, so I guess he told it. And of course it got back to Grover. And if it happened to be raining, Grover, who liked to make Willard laugh, would say perfectly serious, "Willard, I hate to ask it of you, but that coffee's working on me. Have you got your umbrella?"

When Miss Charlotte came to supervise the farming, she never got out of the car. Her need to supervise was fulfilled just by making the trip, passing a few words with Grover, and looking lovingly across the hollow behind the house at the roof of what she called "Father La Vere's tobacco barn."

"Father La Vere" was what with deep respect and daughterly love she called Uncle Bub. It had been Uncle Bub's barn, sure enough. And hard telling whose before him. It was old. Part of it was log. It went back maybe to the time of D. Boone. It had been pieced out and added to by later generations until it sprawled all over the hillside. Sometime toward the end of his earthly passage, Mr. La Vere had got a good deal on, it must have been, a barrel or two of blue paint, and he hired some brave fellows to brush it onto the rusty roof of that old barn. So when Miss Charlotte looked at Father La Vere's barn, what she saw was half an acre of blue roof that made Chicken Little look like a true prophet. You could say, and maybe Mr. La Vere did say, that a barn is no better than its roof. But Miss Charlotte's philosophy on barns was that if the roof is all right then the barn is all right.

In fact, under the roof, the barn was just a collection of splices and patches. It was tiered off with old fence rails and locust poles, all nailed and wired up every which way. All of us who ever worked in it fell out of it at least once. And there was a big old cedar tree grown up on the downhill side with its limbs bushed out until they touched the wall. The tree had no business there, but way before Grover some tenant had let it get started, and every one since had left it, maybe as a comment on the barn that said more or less "To hell with it!"

Well, after Grover had been there must have been four or five years, the rust began showing through the blue paint to where it was visible even to Miss Charlotte. And faithful to tradition, she wanted it painted again with blue paint.

She put the proposition to Grover, but Grover couldn't do it. He couldn't work high off the ground. It made the world whirl. It made him so dizzy and sick he couldn't hardly hold his dinner he was so scared he would fall. This was either true or it wasn't, but it saved Grover a good deal of trouble along with maybe his neck.

So Miss Charlotte authorized Grover to see who would take the job, and Grover put the proposition to my brother, Jarrat, who took him up. Out of generosity he took him up on my behalf as well as his own.

"Hang on!" I said. "I don't want to paint that damned roof. I can't spare the time. And high places make me sick like they do Grover."

Jarrat, a man of few words, said, "You could use the money."

Matter of fact, I could. But like Jarrat I also could have done without it, and unlike Jarrat would have been glad to. But I was in and I knew it.

Jarrat had traded with Grover for two dollars a day and our dinner, dinner to be furnished by Beulah Gibbs, which was the best part of the deal, for Beulah was a fine cook, paint and brushes and so on to be furnished by Miss Charlotte.

So as soon as we got our crops laid by we gathered up ladders and ropes and everything we thought we'd need, and we got started. We had a long job of it. That roof *must* have been half an acre, give or take a tenth or two, and in them days nobody had thought of spraying paint or rolling it on. We *rubbed* it on with brushes, making sure to cover the nailheads and the rust, doing a thorough good job.

We did the uphill side first because that was the bigger side. But also we wanted to get ourselves well used to the job before we got to work on the downhill side which was all of it steep and almighty high at the eave. To tell the truth, I didn't have Grover's problem with heights, but I knew that if you fell from so high onto that old ledgy hillside you wouldn't get up again maybe until resurrection morning.

Finally we did conquer the uphill side. We passed our ropes over the comb of the roof then and tied our ladders on the downhill side. And we were keeping our feet always on the ladder rungs. We weren't taking any chances. We started each one on a side and worked toward the middle. After it seemed like forty days and forty nights we were working pretty close together, which back then wasn't always the ideal arrangement for Jarrat and me.

We came back onto the roof one day after dinner and went at it again. We were meaning to get the job over with that day if it took us till dark. I don't know why it is, but even when you're getting paid by the day, you want to get done. You're *eager* to get done, just as you'd be if you were working for yourself at no wage. And it did seem like we'd been there nearly forever when there were better things to do. Looked back at, it was beginning to seem like a waste.

And my Lord it was *hot*! You couldn't touch that roof bare-handed, and you could barely see for the sweat. It was pure punishment. By the middle of the afternoon I began to feel unhappy with Jarrat for including me in the deal. I began to put on a little speed, laying that paint on slappity-slap, knowing he couldn't help but hear. I had to keep it up quite a while before he said anything.

Finally he said, "What's your hurry?"

"Well, you *said* it's time we were getting done with this," I said, no matter that we clearly were getting done with it. "I'm just taking your word for it, that's all."

He didn't answer. But I knew he was getting mad. It would make him mad when you were being unserious about work. I went on, slappity-slap, loading my brush with paint and making it pop against the roof. Jarrat was commenting by not saying anything. I was cooking him on a slow fire, and I ought to've had my ass kicked, for the poor fellow all his life had a harder time of it than I did, but being a man of weak character I couldn't stop.

I said, "And I got places to go and things to do."

He went ahead, serious about his work, and didn't say anything for another while. And then he said, "Well, don't *slobber* it on."

I straightened up and unseriously rolled a cigarette and stuck it in the corner of my mouth and lit it and picked up my bucket and brush. I hadn't hardly more than just started painting again when we heard this low buzz way off in the sky, and it got louder. We looked where the sound was coming from, and directly out of the heat haze and the shimmer this airplane just appeared.

Back then an airplane was a rare sight, and this one was a four-winger flying lower than we'd ever seen one. The idea that some *body* was in that thing flying through the sky seemed to come somewhere between prime idiocy and a miracle. It passed right over the top of us.

And then several events took place so fast they almost happened at the same time. While I was looking so straight up that my hat started to fall off, I stepped backwards to see better and threw my whole weight right onto the wet paint. I grabbed for my hat with my right hand that had the loaded brush in it and only painted the side of my face, the hat was gone. And so was I, of course. I dropped bucket and brush both to try for a handhold in the thin air, and didn't find one.

Half a gallon of spilled paint makes a tin roof uncommonly slick. I hadn't had time to fall over, so I was going down that roof standing up, like a boy sliding on ice, and I was saying very clearly in my mind, "Well, this is the end of you, old bud." I shot off the roof right into the top of that old cedar tree, and that's how come I'm here to tell about it. I never could make my mind up whether it was Providence or luck, so I split the middle and thanked Providence for my luck.

A tree like that, you know, grows its top branches upwards and its lower ones outwards. As I was flying in among them, the top branches raked some skin off here and there, and I reckon that slowed me down. When I came to the outreaching lower branches, they just bent and tumbled me from one to the next, sort of gently, maybe gracefully, until the bottom one dropped me without too much of a thump onto the ground. And there I sat, spraddle-legged in the shade, cooler than I'd been since dinner.

When I got reorganized enough to look up at where I'd come from, there was Jarrat holding to his rope and looking over the eave of the roof to see what was left of me. We looked back and forth at each other what seemed a long time, and it was awfully quiet.

After a while he said, "Well, are you practicing up for something, or was that it?"

It came to me I was alive. That cigarette was still stuck in the corner of my mouth, still lit. I didn't answer. I sat there with half my face painted blue and finished my smoke. Jarrat watched me until I reckon he was satisfied, and then he got back to being himself.

"Long as you're on the ground, how 'bout getting us a fresh jug of water?"

A Burden (1882, 1907, 1941)

"Me and Teddy Roosyvelt, we rode through hair, shit, blood, and corruption up to *here*." Uncle Peach used the stick he was whittling to mark a level across his nose about an inch above his nostrils.

"You did not," Wheeler said, but all the same he was laughing. He was seven years old, and sometimes just looking at Uncle Peach made him laugh.

"The hell you did," said Andrew, who was Wheeler's brother, five years older, because to Uncle Peach he could say anything he wanted to, and he did. Andrew, as Wheeler understood, was practicing to be a grownup. An ambitionless boy would not say "The hell you did" even to Uncle Peach.

The boys supposed, because everybody else appeared to suppose, that Uncle Peach had been somewhere in the Army during the war with Spain. But they knew from their own observation that Uncle Peach's shotgun, "Old Deadeye," was an instrument of mercy to all creatures that ran or flew as well as to some that were sitting still.

The three of them, the two boys and their uncle Peach, who was their mother's baby brother, were sitting in the shade of the tall cedar tree in front of the house. Uncle Peach was whittling a small cedar stick, releasing a fragrance. His knife was sharp, and he was making the shavings fine for fear he would use up the stick and have to go look for another. One of his rules for living was "Never stand up when you can set down," and he often quoted himself.

None of the three of them wanted to get up, for the day was already hot, and the shade of the old tree was a happiness. It was happier for being a threatened happiness. A sort of suspense hung over them and over that whole moment among the old trees and the patches of shade in the long yard. Maybe that was why Wheeler never forgot it. They did not know where the boys' father was. They did not know how come he had forgotten them. They knew only that if Marce Catlett came back from wherever he was and found them sitting there, they would all three be at work before they could say scat.

"Yeees sahhh," Uncle Peach said, drawing out the words as if to make them last as long as his stick, "them was rough times, which was why we was called the Rough Riders. Hair, shit, blood, and corruption up to the horses' bits, and you needed a high-headed horse to get through it atall. When it was all over and we was heroes, Teddy says to me, 'Leonidas, looks like one of us is pret' near bound to be the presi-dent of our great country, and if it's all the same to you, I'd just as soon it would be me.' And I says, 'Why, Teddy, by all means! Go to it!'"

"The hell you did!" Andrew said again. "You couldn't tell the truth if it shit on your hat."

And that made Wheeler laugh so much he had to lie down in the grass.

At the age of seven, Wheeler was already aware of a division of his affection between his father and Uncle Peach that he could not resolve, and he felt the strain. He loved Uncle Peach because he was funny and was interesting in the manner of a man who would do or say about anything he thought of, and because Uncle Peach loved him back and treated him as an equal and was always kind to him. Uncle Peach's trade was carpentry, which he was more or less good at, more or less worked at, and made more or less a living from. When he made more than a living from it, sooner or later he spent the surplus on whiskey and what he called "hoot-tootin" in Hargrave or Louisville or wherever he could get to before he got down and had to be fetched home.

Uncle Peach was in fact a drunk, which at the age of seven Wheeler pretty well knew and easily forgave. Once, thinking to change his life after a near-lethal celebration of the heroism he had shared with by-then President Roosevelt, Uncle Peach had gone so far as to plan a migration to Oklahoma, which he actually carried out, and had persevered there for one year, to which he ever afterward referred as "my years in the territory." While there, he said, he had been adopted into a tribe of Indians with whom he had lived and hunted and fought, which Wheeler even at the age of seven knew he had not done. Uncle Peach called Indians Eenjins. His Eenjin name was "See-we-no-ho," which in English meant "Friend of Great Chief." Though Wheeler knew that Uncle Peach was just storying, he could see nevertheless in his mind's eye Uncle Peach feathered and painted, riding his Indian pony named "Wa-su-ho-ha" which in English was "Runs Like Scared Rabbit." Uncle Peach loved to tell how he had hunted buffalo with his Eenjin friends, how well he had ridden, how accurately he had shot with his bow.

And Andrew would say, "You got enough damn wind in you to blow up an onion sack."

Uncle Peach had about him the ease of a man who had never come hard up against anything. All his life he had been drifting. All his life he had followed the inclination of flowing water toward the easiest way, and the lowest. Wheeler may always have known this, in the way an alert boy picks knowledge out of the air without asking. And with a boy's love for even the appearance of freedom, he loved Uncle Peach for his drifting.

He loved his father, as eventually he would know, for precisely the opposite reason. Marce Catlett was a man who lived within limits that he had accepted. He did not drift. Year after year he had been hard up against the demands of farm and family, the weather and the bank. He had known more hard times than good ones. In the winter of the year Wheeler was six, his father had sold his tobacco crop for just enough to transport it to the market and to pay the commission on its sale.

But he was not a one-crop farmer. His rule was "Sell something every week." This, as Wheeler would come to know, meant economic diversity; it required a complex formal intelligence; it was good sense. Marce was a man driven to small economies, which his artistry made elegant. He once built a new feed barn exactly on the site of the old one, tearing down the old one, reusing its usable lumber, as he built the new one, and his work mules never spent a night out of their own stalls. His precise fitting of force to work, his neat patches and splices, his quiet transactions with a saddle horse or a team of mules—Wheeler learned these things as a boy, and all the rest of his life he thought and dreamed of them, as of precious things lost.

As he grew in understanding, Wheeler more and more consciously chose his father over Uncle Peach. He chose, that is, his father's example, not his life. For when the time came, and out of plain economic necessity, for there was not a living for him at home and he could not afford to buy a place, Wheeler went to school and became a lawyer. And yet he never abandoned his inheritance from his father. Marce Catlett's love of farming lived on in his son, as later it would live on in his grandsons. And all his life Wheeler felt his father's good ways aching in his bones, for he remembered them in palpable detail and loved them, though in his own life he had given most of them up for others less palpable.

Because after law school Wheeler did not go to any place offered him as "better," but returned to set up his practice at home, he came into an inheritance that was, as he knew, in many ways desirable, but was also complex and in some ways difficult. That he had deliberately made himself heir to his father's example did not prevent him also from inheriting Uncle Peach, as an amusement but also as a responsibility and a burden.

Uncle Peach was in truth amusing. He always had been—"in his way," as his sister, Dorie Catlett, often felt called upon to add.

As a boy of seven, wanting to "do like the old mule" who drank directly from the water trough, he tried to drink buttermilk from a stone churn and got his head stuck. Dorie had to break the churn to get him loose.

"Damn him, I would have left his head right where he put it," Marce would say. He would be growling, also laughing.

He would pause then, to allow her to say, "Yes, I reckon you would have let him drown."

And then he would say, "Something gone, nothing lost."

Once, exasperated by his daily resistance to washing and going to school, Dorie told her brother, "I ought to let you grow up in ignorance."

And he replied, *"That's* it, Dorie! Let me grow up in ignorance."

As Wheeler would tell it much later, his Uncle Peach did grow up in ignorance. And even before he had finished growing up, he shifted from buttermilk to whiskey, which also he drank, while it lasted, as freely as the old mule drank water. He seldom had enough money to make it last very long, "And that," Dorie would say, "was his only good fortune, poor fellow."

But his sufficient surpluses of money, seldom as they were, gave him a sort of fame. His reputation as a drinker far exceeded his reputation as a carpenter, and stories of his exploits were still told in Port William and Hargrave half a century after the beginning of television.

One afternoon Burley Coulter came upon Uncle Peach in front of a roadhouse down by Hargrave. Uncle Peach had been drinking evidently a lot of whiskey and also eating evidently a lot of pickled food from the bar. He had just finished vomiting upon the body of a dead cat, at which he was now gazing in great astonishment.

"Well, what's the matter, old Peach?"

"Why, Burley," Uncle Peach said, "I remember them pigs' feet and that baloney, but I got no recollection whatsoever of that cat."

Sometimes Uncle Peach found drunkenness to be exceedingly hard work. Dancing to keep standing, he would pronounce solemnly, "Damn, I'm tard! My ass is draggin' out my tracks."

Sometimes he found himself in a moral landscape exceedingly difficult to get across: "I got a long way to go and a short time to get there in."

Wheeler's own favorite story was about, so far as he knew, Uncle Peach's only actual fight.

Standing at the bar of a saloon in Louisville, Uncle Peach discovered, to his great disgust, that the man standing next to him was drunk.

"If they's anything I can't stand," Uncle Peach confided to the man, "it's a damn drunk."

At which the man confided back to Uncle Peach: "You ain't nothing but a damn drunk yourself."

Upon which Uncle Peach, grievously offended, took a swing.

"It is generally understood," Wheeler would say, "that when one man aims a violent blow at another, he had better hit him."

But Uncle Peach missed. Whereupon the previously offended flew at Uncle Peach and thrashed him not hardly enough to kill him, but thoroughly even so.

When Wheeler came later to rescue Uncle Peach from the Stag Hotel where he lay, as he said, "bloodied but unbowed," Uncle Peach was already referring to his opponent as "them gentlemens."

"Them gentlemens sholy could fight. They sholy was science men."

When Uncle Peach had decided to become a carpenter and showed some inclination to settle down, Marce Catlett helped him to find and buy a place with a few acres for pasture, a garden, and a little tobacco crop over by Floyd's Station. It was ten miles away, a distance that ought to have kept Uncle Peach "weaned," as Marce conceived it, from Dorie. But when Uncle Peach was on the downslope of a binge and in need of help, he would show up, intending to stay until he wore his welcome out—and longer, if he could.

On a certain night in Wheeler's childhood, perhaps not long after their conversation under the cedar tree, Uncle Peach showed up and, to the immense happiness of Wheeler and Andrew, drank copiously from a pan of dirty dishwater, complaining all the while of the declining quality of Dorie's soup. He proceeded to get sick, and then, shortly, to disappear. There must have been a passage of strict conversation between him and Marce at that time. Uncle Peach continued to show up now and again, but he never again showed up except sober.

Wheeler inherited Uncle Peach from his mother, who had inherited him from her mother, who had died soon after his birth. Dorie had pretty much had the raising of him, and it was she who named him "Peach," because it was handier than "Leonidas Polk" and because as a little fellow he was so pretty and sweet. That this Peach may have been a born failure did not mitigate Dorie's sense that he was *her* failure. With exactly the love that "hopeth all things," she did not give up on him.

Marce, on the contrary, gave up on his brother-in-law as a condition of his tolerance of him. It was a tolerance that worked best at a distance. With Peach in view, it was limited. After he had met its limit, Uncle Peach was always sober when in view. For Peach Wheeler drunk there was no longer room within Marce Catlett's horizon.

And so Wheeler inherited, along with Uncle Peach, two opposite attitudes toward him, and was never afterward free of either. As he grew into the necessary choice between his father and his uncle, and made the choice, Wheeler found that he had not merely chosen, but, by choosing his father, had acquired in addition his father's indignation. Wheeler could at times look upon his uncle as an affront, as if Peach had at conception or birth decided to be a burden specifically to his as-yet-unborn nephew.

But as he grew in experience and self-knowledge, Wheeler also grew to recognize in himself a sort of replica of his mother's love and compassion. He was never able quite to anticipate and prepare himself for the moment at which the apparition of Uncle Peach as nuisance would be replaced by the apparition of Uncle Peach as mortal sufferer. This change was not in Uncle Peach, who never changed except by becoming more and more as evidently he had been born to be. The change was in Wheeler. When the moment came, usually in the midst of some extremity of Uncle Peach's drinking career, Wheeler would feel a sudden welling up of love, as if from his mother's heart to his own, and then he would pity Uncle Peach and, against the entire weight of history and probability, wish him well. Sometimes after telling, and fully delighting in, one of his stories about Uncle Peach, Wheeler would fall silent, shake his head, and say, "Poor fellow."

Andrew, the firstborn son and elder brother, despite all his early practicing to be a grownup, did not manage to grow much farther up, if any, than Uncle Peach. Andrew, as it turned out, did not inherit attitudes toward Uncle Peach so much as he inherited Uncle Peach's failing. For Andrew in his turn became a drinker, and he too would say or do about anything he thought of. He would do so finally to the limit of life itself, and so beyond. As Andrew's course of life declared itself more or less a reprise of Uncle Peach's, that of course intensified and complicated the attitudes of the others toward Uncle Peach. Their stories all are added finally into one story. They were bound together in a many-stranded braid beyond the power of any awl to pick apart.

When Wheeler came home and started his law practice, he bought a car, for his practice involved him in distances that needed to be hurried over. But the automobile also was a fate which, as it included distance, also included Uncle Peach. The automobile made almost nothing of the ten miles from the Catletts' house to Uncle Peach's. Because of the automobile, Dorie could more frequently go over to housekeep and help out when Uncle Peach was on one of his rough ascents into sobriety, when, she said, he needed her most.

Uncle Peach most needed Wheeler when he was drunk and sick and helpless and broke and far from home. The automobile made this a reasonable need. No power that Wheeler had acquired in law school enabled him to argue against it, though he tried. Because he had the means of going, he had to go.

If Uncle Peach had the money to get there, his favorite place of resort was a Louisville establishment that called itself the Hotel Stag. From the time of Wheeler's purchase of the automobile until the time of Uncle Peach's death, Wheeler, who would not in any circumstances have taken Uncle Peach to the Stag Hotel, went there many a time to bring him home.

At the Stag Hotel and other places of refreshment Uncle Peach would encounter commercial ladies of great attractiveness and charm. Sometimes when Wheeler would be bringing him home, and despite his pain and exhaustion, Uncle Peach would still be enchanted, and he would confide as much to Wheeler: "Oh, them eyes!" he would say. "Oh, them eyes!"

Many a good and funny story came of Wheeler's missions of mercy, and also many a story of real pain and suffering that moved Wheeler to real pity, and also many moments of utter exasperation at the waste of time and effort when Wheeler, mocking himself and yet meaning every word, would cry out against "the damned Hotel Stag and every damned thing involved therein and pertaining thereto." Or he would say of Uncle Peach indignantly, "He's got barely enough sense to swallow." And then he would laugh. "Burley Coulter told me he'd seen Uncle Peach drink all he could hold and then fill his mouth for later." He would laugh. And then, affection and hopelessness and sorrow coming over him, he would shake his head. "Poor fellow."

In his turn, young Andy Catlett, namesake of his doomed uncle Andrew, also inherited uncle Peach from his grandmother's lamentation and his father's talk, from trips with his father to see that their then-failing Uncle Peach was alive and had enough to eat, and from various elders who remembered with care and delight Uncle Peach's sayings and doings.

One Christmastime, when he was about six, Andy overheard his father tell Uncle Andrew, just home for the holidays, that Uncle Peach, "sleeping it off in his front yard," had frozen several of his toes, which had then needed to be amputated.

"Toes!" Uncle Andrew said, laughing his big laugh. "Anybody can spare a few toes. He better be glad he didn't freeze his *pecker* off." In the midst of his sadness and exasperation Wheeler also laughed, and they went away, leaving Andy, whom they had not noticed, with a possibility he had never considered before.

Andy had gone with his father to visit Uncle Peach after the surgery. Uncle Peach was sitting by the drum stove in his bare, bad-smelling little house with his foot wrapped in a soiled white bandage. He was talking in his old, slow voice about the hospital in Louisville, which he pronounced "Louis-ville." Though Andy, who had seen inside a hospital, could not picture him in one, Uncle Peach had enjoyed his stay. He had admired the nurses. "Damn pretty, some of 'em," he said to Wheeler.

And then, studying Andy, he said, "This boy'll be looking at 'em, 'fore you know it."

When Uncle Peach died in Andy's seventh year, and they all knew that he was dead, Andy overheard his father and mother saying what a story it had been. His father said with regret and sorrow and amusement and, instead of indignation, perhaps relief, for Uncle Peach had died sober in his sleep in bed at home: "Like Jehorum, poor fellow, he has departed without being desired." Wheeler was capable of feeling some things simply, but he never spoke of Uncle Peach with unmixed feelings.

And then when they were all in Wheeler's car, driving home from the graveyard on the hill outside Port William where they had laid Uncle Peach to rest, they were silent until Wheeler said, "Well!"

He let the silence come back, and then he said, "The preacher takes a very happy view of Uncle Peach's prospects hereafter."

Wheeler was lining out a text that would be clearly printed in his son's memory, where it would wait a long time for interpretation.

When his father again let the silence come back, Andy understood that his mother wasn't saying anything because she felt that the fate of Uncle Peach hereafter was none of her business, and his grandfather wasn't saying anything because he didn't want it to be his business, and his grandmother wasn't saying anything because it *was* her business. It came to Andy then, for the first time, that his father was still relatively a young man.

The preacher had said Uncle Peach was going to Heaven, or was there already, because his soul had been saved when he gave his life to Jesus and was baptized at the age of twelve. His baptism, so many years ago, in another century, was still in force. Andy imagined that baptism had left on Uncle Peach's soul a mark like a vaccination scar to show that he had been saved. When he got to Heaven he was to be let in.

Andy had stood in church beside his mother, had heard her singing with the others,

> While I draw this fleeting breath,
> When mine eyes shall close in death,
> When I rise to worlds unknown,
> And behold Thee on Thy throne,
> Rock of Ages, cleft for me,
> Let me hide myself in Thee,

and he had thought, "*She*? *She* will?" And so he knew that in the soul's bewildering geography there was a Rock of Ages. In his mind it looked like the Rock of Gibralter cleft like a cow's foot, and you could hide in the cleft and be all right.

But from other songs they sang he knew that this geography had a shore too from which the dead departed to cross a wide river, and another shore beyond the river, a beautiful shore, that was Heaven. He had seen in his mind a picture of people on the far shore waving to people coming across in a boat who were waving back. They were calling each other's names and they were happy.

But Wheeler wasn't finished. He was always concerned with fittingness, which was maybe a kind of honesty. Those were words he used: "fitting" and "honest." He was always trying to get the scattering pieces of their history to fit together in a pattern that made sense. He wanted to find the right words and to say things right. "Right" was another of his words, as was "sense." His effort often made him impatient. This also Andy took in and remembered.

"If Uncle Peach is in Heaven," Wheeler said, "and Lord knows I hope that's where he is, then grace has lifted a mighty burden, and the preacher ought to have said so."

And then he said, as if determined in his impatience to capture every straying piece, "And as an earthly burden it wasn't only grace that lifted it"—meaning it was a burden he too had borne. Even at the time, Andy caught that.

So did his grandmother. She said one syllable then that Andy later would know had meant at least four things: that his father would have done better to be quiet, that she too had borne that earthly burden and would forever bear it, that Uncle Peach had borne it himself and was loved and forgiven at least by her, and that it was past time for Wheeler to hush.

She said, *"Hmh!"*

A Desirable Woman (1938–1941)

For Tanya and David Charlton

She was not beautiful according to the standards of the magazines and moving pictures of the time, and she knew it. But by any standard she was a desirable woman, and she also knew that. She knew it from what she had seen in the eyes of certain men, to which from time to time she had felt something like an echo in herself.

That she was desirable was acceptable to her as a part of the liveliness and also the goodness of the world. It was a gift. But that she was desirable and knew it and accepted it unfitted her somewhat for her role as a minister's wife. It was not expected. She had not expected it herself until her own wits told her it was so. Part of her desirability was her look of knowing more than she was saying, and of being amused by the difference. That, and the utter frankness of her presence. There was in her, even in old age, a declarative force of being that was unhesitating and without disguise.

She was born Laura Stafe. She became Laura Milby. She was in love with her husband and would remain so. Another gift. This was not just because she knew she was desirable to him, as he to her—they had settled that soon enough—but from the beginning she had sensed a goodness in him that she knew she could trust. Later it seemed to her that she had not known such trust was in her until he called it from her and she gave it.

They met at a small denominational college where her parents had sent her because they thought it a safe place to send a girl, and where he had come, after an interval of employment in his father's small lumberyard, to prepare for the ministry. His name was Williams Milby. When they were introduced, she laughed. "Oh! Do they call you Bills?"

His reply, the grin subtracted, she thought was elegant, even courtly: "Not yet, mam. But if *you* call me that, that's my name."

He was a good-looking young man, regular of feature and curly-haired, his countenance so open and unassuming that it might have passed for naïve except for a self-knowing good humor that sometimes lighted it. He attracted her also because the seriousness, even the solemnity, of his vocation already hung about him as a kind of obscurity, and she loved her own power of drawing him forth, in person, out of that shadow.

"What do you want? What do you want for your own self?" she asked. "Oh, that! Oh!" She looked straight at him then, and her laugh undisguised them both.

The day after they graduated they were married. That was 1938.

They went in the fall of the same year, not having known for a whole summer where they would go, to serve a small church known as The Little Flock at a place called Sycamore on the south side of the Ohio River. Sycamore had once been a river port of some note, but was by then merely a ferry landing, two general stores, two churches, a blacksmith shop, a bank, a loose assemblage of houses, and three shantyboats tied up to trees along the river.

The church paid in money "not much more than you could put in your eye," as one of the members forthrightly told them. But it provided also a parsonage of three rooms, with a cistern and pump conveniently at the back door, a garden spot, and at the back of the garden a privy. Thus they were saved the necessity of living out the rest of the Depression on love alone.

They were neither passive or incapable, neither careless nor low-spirited. They made the most of their garden. Their house was cooled by a huge elm that threw its shadow over it on summer afternoons; in winter it was snug. And the little they were paid in money was aboundingly supplemented in kind: a sack of fresh sausage or an old ham, a dressed chicken, jars of fruit or vegetables or pickles or preserves, baked goods or fresh fish or wild honey. These gifts were sometimes brought to them openly for their commendation and their pleased surprise, sometimes left on their back porch when they were not at home.

There was little enough of money at large in Sycamore at that time, but it was rich in the produce of its fields and woods and the river, and to their young preacher and his wife the church members in general were free-hearted to a fault.

The town accepted the arrival of the young strangers, "Brother Milby" and "Mrs. Milby," without surprise. It had expected that they would come, as it expected that they would eventually go. It accepted them formally when the congregation of his church sat down on Sunday morning and listened respectfully to Williams Milby's inaugural sermon. It accepted them less formally by helping them to settle into their house and by giving them things they needed. It accepted them in fact by admitting them into the flow of its talk, the unceasing meandering of its story of itself by which it diverted, amused, and consoled itself.

Small as it was, the town seemed to them to be inundated with self-knowledge. This knowledge moved over it in an unresting current, some of it in stories told openly that eddied with variations from teller to teller and place to place, some of it more darkly and quietly in an undertow of caution, sometimes fraught with the unacknowledged pleasure of malice, sometimes bearing a burden merely of anxiety or concern. It was to this subsurface current of gossip that Williams Milby learned to listen with greatest care, for it told him where needs were.

Needs were everywhere. Sycamore had suffered the depressed agricultural economy of the 1920s. It had been hit hard by the Depression of the 1930s, by the severe drouths of 1930 and 1936, and by the great flood of January 1937. But it was a community of farm people and of people related to farmers and dependent on farming. They had never expected to live independently of the weather or to be free of hardship and struggle. They suffered as they had to suffer and did as they had to do. They also knew of one another's struggles, and as they could they helped.

Also, by their own modest standards and by their skills and thrift, they throve. Because none of them had ever been overly prosperous, their losses were never great. It was not the sort of place where people took large economic risks or contracted large debts. It says much for the hardiness of the place that its population increased during the Depression, as young Sycamoreans who had gone to the cities to prosper returned home to survive.

There were the Wallis twins, Goebel and Noble, elderly sons of an ancient mother, bachelors forevermore, good farmers, both independent and neighborly, who did according to their reasons, which often were both unexpectable and unobjectionable, and who drove into town every Saturday afternoon in their like-new Model A, in which they sat side by side, dressed in like-new tan work clothes starched and ironed as stiff almost as tin.

And there was Mrs. Etta Mae Berry, an elderly widow for whom the truth was ever too tame. One day, as she was scattering corn for her hens, a big airplane flew over so low that it blew her dress practically over her head and she could hear the passengers talking. And she was never sick because she always looked for germs in the dipper before she drank, and any she saw she skimmed them out with a spoon.

There was Uncle Lute Wisely, born a slave, who remembered every-thing, and now, too old to work, he moved, as he said, in winter from fire to fire and in summer from shade to shade. There had never been many of his race around Sycamore, and now, all the younger ones gone north, he was the last. If there was prejudice against his race in Sycamore, and their certainly had been and still was, by now it was not openly applied to solitary old Uncle Lute, whom the town treated more or less as a pet.

There was the family of Bernice and Red Callahan, who were sitting at dinner when a big snake fell through the ceiling onto the table, caus-ing, but only indirectly, much breakage of chairs and other furniture and some bodily injury.

On one of the shantyboats lived the perhaps married couple, Lizard Eye and Zinnia Creed, joyfully Frenchified by the Sycamoreans as "Mr. and Mrs. Lizzard." Zinnia Creed was widely esteemed for her language, which was purely her own. When she picked blackberries, the chiggers broke her out all over in whelps. Sometimes the summer apples got all swiveled up before they could be eaten. There was a famous day when she had come to town for a gallon of coal oil, and the lecrik went off and every light bug in Jones's Merchandise went out all to-wunst. She had seen two cars meet in a headlong collusion. She loved, moreover, to refine her pronunciation by adding r's to words such as "crush" and "crunch" and "push" so that they came out "crursh" and "crurnch" and "pursh." Virtually everybody in Sycamore had learned Zinnian and spoke it on every appropriate occasion.

Of these and others, as church members or as not-members, the Milbys were given knowledge.

You could usefully think of the consciousness of Sycamore as the continual, continually wandering story that in one way or another included everybody, carrying them through time like the current of the river.

Or, usefully also, you could think of it as graduated depths in that flow. At the top was the convivial talk, open and unembarrassed. Below that, quieter and darker and less free, was the talk that issued from fear and envy, cherished grudges and resentments, meannesses, suspicions, unforgiven or unregretted wrongs. This was not so readily heard by newcomers, but the Milbys stayed long enough (they stayed until after the end of World War II) to hear most of it, if not all. It proved itself continually to be present, to be regrettable, and sometimes to be worried about.

Below that, much quieter and darker, and yet to the conscience of the young minister most present of all, was the depth at which the community suffered its mortality, error, pain, and grief. How many among the older wives or widows had buried a child struck down by a winter illness or an epidemic or a bullet in France, who now remembered in silence?

As the knowledge of this depth of suffering grew upon her, Laura understood, as she had not before, the gravity of her husband's calling, for she saw that it was to this suffering that he was called. As he sank inevitably into it or as it rose inevitably out of its depth, its quietness and darkness, to meet him, she saw not only the gravity of his calling but its authenticity. For Williams Milby had the gift of comforting. He carried with him, not by his will, it seemed, but by the purest gift, the very presence of comfort. And yet even as it was a comfort to others, it could be a bafflement and a burden to him. His calling, and the respect accorded to it, admitted him into the presence of troubles he could not mend. When old Uncle Jones McKinney, who had been sick for a long time, finally died, and afterwards his old wife, Aunt Ruth, would hear him calling her in the night and would get up and go to his bed and again find it empty, what could any living mortal do for her that would be of any use at all? A living mortal could do only as Williams Milby did: go and sit with her while she mourned, and then leave her in her mourning, for no living mortal could sit with another time without end. It was plain to him—and Laura knew this—that he was always hopelessly in debt to his own ministry, for he could not give all that he wanted and longed to give. He was needed, even so, and what he had to give, and more, was continually asked of him. People were glad to see him coming. They called him to come. They were glad to have him around when they did not need him, just for the assurance that he would be at hand when they did need him.

And as Laura had earlier given him her trust that until then she did not know was hers, now she granted him a sort of honor that was not personal, not hers or his, but honor to his vocation that he had not surely known was his until he began to fulfill it.

At Sycamore, then, Laura grew with her husband into a life that probably neither of them had expected. She grew also into knowledge of the church's function of iteration. The church house itself, she now saw, was a place consecrated to the proclamation over and over again of things in which most of the members more or less believed but in which they generally were not greatly interested, and which they helped to make uninteresting by their lack of interest. It was a place where nearly all of the women seemed to feel at home, and where many of the men clearly were not at home. In bearable weather the men were likely to stand outside before the service began, holding themselves until the last minute in one another's company and the unconfined light and air of mere day.

And there was the rigid, humorless, never-forgiving piety of Old Man Elbert Stump who believed devoutly that all of whom he disapproved were destined to fry upon the griddles of Hell. How was Williams Milby to treat him kindly, how minister to him, without appearing to agree with him? How, more urgently, was the preacher's wife, Mrs. Milby, to listen to Mr. Stump's dooming and damning for two minutes in a row without *dis*agreeing with him—without, in fact, flying into his face like a hen defending her chicks?

For nearly the whole congregation, or for all of them, and especially the men and children, there was a disconnection between the little white clapboard church with its steeple and bell, its observances and forms of worship, and the world's daily life and work. It was as though the building itself, in its emptiness between services, contained along with its smells of old paper and stale perfume a solemnity that the people entered into and departed from, quickening it for a few hours a week with the stirrings and smells of living flesh, but could neither inflect with the tone of their daily preoccupations nor transpose into their actual lives. This was a disconnection perhaps exactly coextensive with the disconnection they felt between Heaven and Sycamore, eternity and time. Laura recognized these disconnections in the people because she felt them, and labored over them, in herself.

Thus she mapped in her mind the cracks and flaws in the lives of the church and the place. She had been a studious girl, and beyond that a thoughtful one. Since before she'd had much to ponder, she'd been in the habit of pondering. She was a conscious, thoughtful believer in the Gospel that her husband had bound himself to offer and defend, even to obey and enact—that is, to suffer. But the things that she struggled with he seemed to accept with a silence that included a measure of resignation. He could be quiet because in some depth of himself he *was* quiet. She recognized this as his strength, his very faith, at the same time that it fretted her.

Of the pair, hers was the mind that was restless and questing, enticed and disturbed by mysteries. That the world was as it was did not save it from her sense that it might in many ways be different and certainly better. It seemed to her both tentative and final, unshakeable and woefully fragile.

Her husband's ministry, as he conceived it, was not only to the church but to the whole community, and this often involved a thanklessness hard for her to bear. Not only did he stand up week after week to say and to offer again what he and generations of ministers before him had said and offered before, with no dramatic amelioration of this world as a result, but also he made himself answerable to any and every sufferer within a radius of five or six miles. Any sufferer who was in need or want of him could summon him, even by the ringing of the telephone in the middle of a stormy or frozen night, and he would go.

And when, having done all he could do to help a family through a quarrel or an illness or a death, performing services he was not paid for and could not have been paid for, he might never hear from them again, let alone see their faces even for the courtesy of one Sunday among his hearers, Laura felt herself wounded with sorrow for him and anger at them for their ingratitude.

"It's not right!" she cried to him once, breaking for that once into his silence about it. "It's *just not right!*"

"No. It's not right," he said quietly, and he gave her his smile with which he sought to quiet her. "But it's all right."

And yet she knew his own need for comfort, for shelter, for her herself, and for the welcome it was her need, in turn, to offer to him. They did not fit together like the two halves of one apple. Sometimes they were flint and steel, and the sparks flew. But they needed to fit together, and they were trying to. Often they did. They were a good couple. Out of the sometimes far estrangement of their differences, their need to fit together would draw them back to each other again. That was their desire. And desire would then freely have its way with them.

And so desire, her own and his, was one of the subjects of her thoughts. She saw the danger of it. She saw the beauty and the preciousness of it. She saw even the necessity of it, for it imparted beauty and motion, life itself, to the whole world. The desire to be at one with another, the desire to be pleased in living together, seemed to her at times to infuse with light the bedrock of the earth.

To know this was a passion with her. She felt herself to be most alive when she felt it alight within herself. It was this light in herself that strangely made her self matter little in comparison. It had the power, in fact, to cause her self entirely to disappear. And so she was mortified, most deeply thwarted in her instinctive tenderness toward the life and light of this world, when she was confronted, as she often was, with the belief, at large among their church people and in Sycamore itself, that desire merely was lust. It was not an adequate mitigation that she knew surely that desire sometimes was lust, and that the dearest, pleasantest desire, especially for the women, sometimes led to suffering.

"But they think desire is no different from lust," she said to her husband. "Think of the loneliness of that. Think of the terrible loneliness of it!"

"Where do they get that idea?" Williams asked, though he knew.

"They think Jesus said so. 'Whosoever looketh on a woman to lust after her hath committed adultery already in his heart.'"

That a history of shame and loneliness did surround that saying they then acknowledged in the look they gave each other.

Williams Milby laughed, and his laughter granted standing to this acknowledgment, and it made room for her dissent that he knew was coming. He said, "If he meant desire, he has caught us all. I speak of course only for us men."

"Speak for us all!" she said. And now to her own surprise she felt her tears, for suddenly it was to her as if she were lifting from herself a nearly unbearable weight. "Speak for us all! If he meant desire, he has caught every one of us."

When Williams spoke again he spoke quietly, but his voice had changed, borne upward and unsteadied in his throat by an emotion like hers, for now he felt his great love for her, his great desire for her, pressing like a wind at his back. "You don't think then"—he was testing, teasing her, beckoning her forward—"you don't think then that desire is necessarily the same as lust?"

"No! Lust is selfish. It seeketh its own. Desire without selfishness, with self-denial, is only praise. It is even love."

She had more to learn of the cost of self-denying desire.

In those days, in Sycamore as in all the country around, there was an honored practice known as "feeding the preacher." The housewives of the church, or most of them, held it as an unbreakable law, for they had never known it to be broken, that the preacher and his wife, and their children if any, would be fed dinner and supper in some household of the congregation every Sunday. It was as though the preacher's lesson, which was never altogether learned, and his comforting, which could not sufficiently be given, were to be compensated by this hospitality in earnest of a tribute never adequately paid. Part of the organization of the church was the order in which the duty of feeding the preacher was passed around from household to household.

This ceremony of Sunday hospitality was a dear privilege to Williams and Laura, for it opened the countryside to them as it was opened otherwise only to the veterinarian. And the veterinarian certainly never received anything like the hospitality that was accorded the Milbys. It was as if they perhaps were angels who appeared in the guise of a young minister and his wife. Whatever their hostess had that was best was laid before these strangers, who would always be strangers to some extent because set apart by the minister's calling, which required that he and his wife should be sheltered, so far as they could be, from whatever was harshest in the speech and thought and experience of their hosts. The same compunction withheld also knowledge of the extremer pleasures. The list of things the Sycamoreans did not do "in front of the preacher" granted to the preacher a front as wide as a three-horse team. It took the Milbys a long time to learn of the community's music-making and its dancing, about which it was a mark at least of decorum to say nothing to the preacher.

Whatever was set on the table at those Sunday meals thus was offered somewhat in apology, but also with the unspoken confidence and pride that it was the best available, and the Milbys learned to expect with about the same confidence that whatever was set before them would deserve the praise they would give in return. The food was heaped on the table and they were urged to eat as if they were being fattened for slaughter, or as if it were the known practice of ministers and their wives to eat only on Sundays.

In the hours between the big dinner and the lighter supper after which they would return to church for the evening service, Williams and Laura discovered two difficulties that they had to exert their ingenuity to deal with. The first was the onset of drowsiness after the noon meal. The second was the possibility that in trying to fulfill their hosts' expectation of a proper Sunday conversation they would run flat out of anything to say.

"I hate to say *anything* to keep from saying nothing," Williams said. "I look at you for help, and you say for the tenth or twentieth time, 'What a wonderful dinner!' and I say for the tenth or twentieth time, 'Oh, yes, it was wonderful!' It's funny now, Miz Milby, and you can laugh, but it wasn't funny then."

Both of these dangers they learned to avoid by the one expedient of asking to be shown something outside the house—and usually, since most of their congregation were farmers, they would ask to be shown something on the farm. For this they learned always to bring their overshoes. And it was this that brought them into the presence of the place, the country itself, and that taught them their people's ways of belonging to it and living upon it. They found that the farmers generally were proud of their farms, whether justifiably or not, and were ready, often eager, to speak of what they knew. Williams and Laura asked questions and learned and remembered, for they realized that they were being taught where they were, and more profoundly than they had expected to know.

They were not city people exactly, but they both had come from big towns. They had never known before a whole community in which everybody knew everybody, and the life of which went all the way to the ground. The community or neighborhood known as "around Sycamore" was a small place divided into many smaller places—farms and fields and woodlands—each of which, if you asked or if you waited to hear, had its unique, inseparable attachment of memories and stories.

On those Sunday afternoons in their unending sequence, when the weather was fit and sometimes when it was not, the Milbys followed their guides through barns and lots, fields and woods, and along the wild streamsides. They were shown flower beds, gardens, crops, and animals in all the stages of the year. Within a year or two they came into the intimate geography and life and worklife of the place. On the Kentucky side of the Ohio there at Sycamore the bottomland was rather narrow, and the farms were not large. The primary intent of the farm families they visited was to live from their land. Every farm produced a few acres of tobacco. Almost every farm had a small herd of beef cattle, and many had a flock of sheep as well. But invariably, and primarily for their own use, the farmers had vegetable gardens, milk cows, hogs for meat and lard, and poultry flocks.

The Milby's interest in the place and its community fed upon their understanding and upon their failures to understand. Williams's ministry carried him always along the seams of the community where the people were joined to one another and to the place, and he carried his realizations and his mystifications to Laura. There was always much that needed talking about. They began to know the farms they visited not only familiarly but also critically. From the comparisons that were inevitable, from comments overheard or casually made, they saw that some farms were more kindly and thriftily used than others. They learned to recognize bare ground as a danger. They began to see that the best farms were much grassed and little plowed. When Ernest Russet told them one day, finally breaking his rule against speaking critically in front of the preacher, "You can't *plow* your way out of debt," they knew what he meant.

*　　*　　*

Those Sunday afternoons afforded occasionally a benefit to Laura that she waited for and prized. When the after-dinner talk involved Williams in a way unusually needful or private, she gladly excused herself and went out alone. She was free then to walk at her own pace, following in silence her own direction and the line of her own thoughts. The only requirement was to get back on time, and for that she carried her husband's watch.

Sometimes on these walks her direction would be one she prescribed to herself. Sometimes her direction seemed to be required by the place, and she went where it beckoned her to go. Sometimes she felt complete in herself and separate, walking in the place. Sometimes the place seemed to occupy her and to have its being within her, and she forgot herself.

At the end of a cloudy day in full spring the sun suddenly came out. Along the edge of the woods, the thrushes began to call. A mockingbird sang from a dead treetop nearby; a cardinal sang and a wren; in the distance a bobwhite whistled and was answered. Laura felt herself carried up into the freshened light where she seemed to have no life except that which now sang all around her.

On a rainy winter day, just at sunset, she saw the sky divided by the leftward stroke of a rainbow, the other side hidden by trees. Within the visible arc the sky glowed with a vibrant pinkish light, while outside it night was falling.

Walking one frozen afternoon in a wooded hollow of the valley side, she realized suddenly that her own steps made the only sound in that place. She stopped. And then absolute silence came over her, absolute stillness. Every tree, the wooded slope, the world itself, stood as if in the very nothing from which it had been called out.

At such times as these she felt that the great, mute creation was trying to speak to her. This disturbed her, it moved her almost to tears, for it seemed to intimate the nearness of some consolation—forever imminent and unreachable, almost knowable—for everything that was wrong.

As would be bound to happen, there came to be some farms, some couples, that they preferred above others. Of them all, Ernest and Naomi Russet were the most interesting and the most congenial.

Ernest Russet was in his late fifties, beginning to speak of growing old, but still straight and hard-fleshed. He was, as he said, a true-born farmer, who loved eagerly his well-husbanded farm. He loved the work and the care of it, and the abundance that by his passion and his skill he drew from it. He was a humorous man with a hearty, emphatic way of talking, a little too loud, as if his hearers were a little farther away than they actually were. He had only one eye, but a bluer, more intense, more seeing eye than that one never looked out of a man's head. He quickly became an indispensable counselor to Williams Milby, for not only did his seniority and humor make his advice easy to hear, but Ernest Russet was a man of sound, practical judgment. He was likely to know what needed doing and how to do it.

Naomi, a famous cook at that time in that country where good cooks were commonplace, was an ample, round-cheeked, cheerful woman of great sweetness, who from the first always greeted Laura with her arms opened. Her energy and industry matched her husband's. Together, they made their farm a place of abundance and generosity. They loved to eat the food they had grown, and they loved feeding it to others. They took delight, when it was their turn to do so, in feeding their young preacher and his wife. Sometimes, as their friendship grew, the Russets would invite the Milbys out for dinner on a weekday when they had something especially good to offer.

"Eat, now," Ernest Russet would say as soon as Brother Milby had offered thanks. "Ask for what you can't reach."

The Russets understood that the minister's vocation was in a way a hardship, a cross to bear, and they tried to ease the burden. The Milbys rarely left the Russet place without something good to eat stowed away in their old car. Laura came to depend on Naomi much as Williams depended on Ernest. The Russets became, in fact, the parents the young couple needed in a place unlike any other they had known. Sometimes when an extra hand was needed, Williams would work a day or a few days for Ernest Russet.

The Russet place, the Milbys thought, and not just because of their affection for its owners, was the most beautiful farm in all the country around Sycamore. It was in a valley tributary to that of the great river. The house, standing on a shady rise of the ground well back from the road, was white-painted, with steep gingerbreaded gables, a wide front porch, and a second porch of two stories running along the ell that contained the kitchen and a bedroom above.

Behind the house were the garden and henyard, henhouse, and privy. And then, joined by lots and pens for the handling of livestock, were two barns, a corncrib, a granary, and various other outbuildings, all in good repair and painted white like the house.

From this steading the fields spread away on three sides, the bottom-land sloping gradually downward to a winding stream bordered with tall white-limbed sycamores. Beyond the stream the land rose gradually again, steepening to permanent pasture on the valley side, and from there, as it steepened more, wooded to the hilltop. On the pastures were Ernest's four work mules, a small herd of beef cows, a larger flock of sheep, a few pigs, and three Jersey cows whose surplus cream went to the cream station in Sycamore and whose surplus milk went to the pigs. Because it was orderly and well-kept, this farm, even when Ernest was hard at work upon it, seemed somehow to rest within itself.

Always, as the Milby's knowledge grew or as Williams's gift of sympathy apparently summoned it, the underlayer of suffering or sorrow would be revealed. The sorrow of the Russets was that they had had no child. Their expectation of a child had almost gently graduated into a wish for one, and thence into a doubt that there would be one, and later into the certain knowledge that there was never to be one, and then into resignation of a sort and an ever-deepening commiseration with one another, for never had a place been more lovingly made ready for in inheritor, of whose absence it itself was a daily reminder.

To this place in the spring of 1941 came a young man, hardly more than a boy in age, but to all intents and purposes and by reputation a man: Tom Coulter, from the next county down the river. Ernest Russet, as he said, was getting on in years. He and his place were needing a young man. Tom Coulter was available. He and the Russets had worked out a satisfactory "trade," and Tom had come to them, moving with his few belongings into the room over the kitchen. The room opened onto the upper porch from which an outside stairway went down to the lower porch and the kitchen.

When Tom Coulter came to the Russets, he came with a story and a reputation both of which were well known to Ernest Russet. When he was sixteen years old Tom had left home after a fight with his father, and he had been on his own ever since. The fight had been over a small thing—a contest of work in a tobacco patch—but it had been a small thing in which everything was at stake. It could not be got over, and Tom had gone away.

"I've known Jarrat Coulter all his life, about," Ernest Russet told the Milbys. "He was all right—hell for work, excuse me, but all right—until his wife took sick and died when Tom and his brother were just little, and then he sort of turned in on hisself. He got unreachable, you might say. Jarrat's folks were on the adjoining farm, and they took the boys and raised them up. They and Jarrat's brother, Burley. That Burley, now, he's in a class by hisself. There's stories about him that nobody's going to tell you, Mrs. Milby, or anyhow I ain't, but I wish you could know him. He done right by them boys, and he's a good man."

After he left home, Tom raised a little crop and worked by the day for some people by the name of Whitlow. He proved satisfactory, and things went well until Mr. Whitlow died in the summer of 1940. Tom stayed on, finishing the crop and his year's work after the farm was sold and Mrs. Whitlow settled with her daughter in town. And then he got word that Ernest Russet, who was looking for a good young man, wanted to talk to him.

Tom had the reputation of a prime hand, and he was respected for his industry and honesty. He had come up under good teachers, his grandfather and father and uncle, who had taught him from before the time when he knew he was learning. By 1941, when he was nineteen, he was not only a good hand but also a good farmer, a young man with initiative and judgment, fully in charge of himself, needing and eager to know what Ernest Russet could teach him, yet needing no boss. To his elders he was a boy who had come to be honored as a man, and was said to be "promising."

He had the benefit of a proper upbringing too, as Naomi Russet soon was pleased to say. He accommodated himself considerately and quietly to the Russet's life and household. He quickly learned their ways and the ways of the farm. He needed less and less to be told what to do. Beyond his instructions and duties, he looked for ways to be useful, doing on his own various jobs the Russets had not yet thought to ask him to do, and some that they would not have asked him to do. He sometimes accompanied them on their trips to Sycamore or the county seat, and he was always with them when they came to church. Sometimes on Saturday nights he would find a ride to Hargrave, which was the seat and commercial center of his home county, and which was widely known as a "Saturday night town." He could be fairly sure of seeing his brother there, and perhaps his uncle too. And though the Russets never asked, they assumed he knew girls whom he would see there. He did not go too often, and he did not stay too late. His handsomeness, which was considerable, involved not just his looks but also an emanation, an almost visible luster, of intelligent, exuberant strength.

There was a day in the late spring when his brother and uncle came to see him. They were invited to dinner on a Sunday when, as it happened, the Russets were feeding the preacher, and so Laura did meet the storied Burley Coulter, who was, as promised, in a class by himself. He was then in his forty-sixth year. The marks of time and weather were on him and his hair was gray, though he was still a man unusually attractive, which he seemed to know both frankly and modestly. Though he carried a much-abused felt hat in his hand and his blue suit shone with wear at points of stress, he had made himself presentable for what he clearly thought an important occasion. And on this occasion his obvious gift for sociability wore a sort of patina of formality. He was being conscientiously correct for the sake of his nephews. And yet when he was introduced to Laura he gave her an openly appraising look, which communicated both a compliment and his amusement that she had caught the compliment and liked it. She offered her hand. With fine discrimination he shook it *almost* too long, and she laughed.

Nathan Coulter, who had driven them over in his father's much-muddied automobile, seemed younger than his brother by more than the two years between them. He was a nice boy, in looks a little dreamy perhaps, and by nature much quieter than Tom, though obviously a product of the same teaching and upbringing. To everybody's relief, the group of them went together fine, as Ernest Russet later said. It was at first a pleasant and then a happy meal, at which much was eaten in verification of the many praises that were passed over the food. And afterward, to the Russets and the Milbys, it seemed that their acquaintance with Tom Coulter had been enlarged and even lengthened. They knew him better, from farther back, than before.

By the fall of that year two changes had come about that, in Laura's mind, had assumed the standing of facts, and facts moreover that she pretty well understood: The Russets had come to love Tom Coulter as the son they had longed for but never had, and Tom Coulter had come to love Laura Milby as a young man loves a woman forever beyond his hope.

The first of these facts may not yet have come into speech between the two Russets, but Williams and Laura, who had watched it happening, had talked of it, and to them it was merely obvious. On the one hand there was an absence long unfilled, and on the other hand, now, a presence that might exactly fill it. They thought it only a matter of time, another year perhaps, until the beautiful farm would have its designated heir. "That Tom," Ernest Russet said, "he's a born stockman if ever there was one."

The second fact was known only to Laura herself. If it was plain to her, it was in no general way obvious. Tom was not forward. In the presence of women, even of Naomi Russet, he was somewhat shy. But when he looked at Laura and looked away, his face was marked by a thought she recognized. That he wished to be near her she knew, because when it was possible for him to be near her he would be, though then he would hold himself a little apart and look away. And when, at the Russets' or at church, there was something that could be done for her, something such as a load to be carried, he would be first to see it, for he would be watching, and he would do for her what needed to be done. But even without these visible signs, it seemed to Laura that she would have known his feeling for her by the mere force of it passing to her through the air.

And she knew fairly well what to make of it and how seriously to take it. She was then twenty-five years old and in the fourth year of her marriage. In her thoughtful way she had parsed out the kinds of love and its changes. There was love as mere attraction, mere feeling, not of which as a girl she had known enough of the power and the giddiness. By now she had seen how such love could gather knowledge to itself and become different, and how it was changed again, profoundly this time, when it made the solemn offer of trust and submitted to vows. Love and trust, that vow "until death," had carried Laura and Williams into an abyss of sorts, lighted only by the light they could find within and between themselves. They were passing on and on into the unknown life of plighted love. Behind them, committed and unchangeable, was the history of their love, which was changing it and would change it.

She necessarily regarded this love of Tom's as young, younger by far than any love of hers would ever be again. And yet, though she could not return it in kind, she was moved by it. She granted a certain respect to it. She saw moreover that, as it was unaskingly given, it was a gift to be honored, and she did honor it. She would not withhold from it even the name of love, for all love must begin without knowledge. Perhaps, as she thought, it is itself a kind of knowledge.

At that time there already was war in Europe and war in Asia. Though war had not, so to speak, yet shown itself above the horizon around Sycamore, neither was it any longer ignorable. To the ones who were living there in those days, war had become a thinkable possibility, a premonition, like a distant mutter of thunder on a clear day.

And then after the seventh of December 1941, war was present among them. Around Sycamore it was as if the people had turned away from the distant thunder, distracted from it by their workaday lives, and had turned back again to find a black cloud covering half the sky. As the magnitude of the opposing forces became manifest to her, it seemed to Laura that the whole sky darkened, and an unsourced light illuminated creatures and objects on all sides so that they stood out in sharp relief against the darkness. The young men in particular looked to her that way. Tom Coulter looked that way to her, as if a dark fate was gathering around him, and he was lighted, not by daylight at all, but by his own small life shining within him.

The realization grew upon them all that everything would be changed. No life would be immune. No life now would be changed merely by time and mortality. Now history was outrunning time.

January came. Though the lengthening of the days was hardly apparent so far, it was felt. The year was beginning. On the floor of Ernest Russet's tobacco barn, now partitioned and bedded and furnished with mangers, the lambs of the new year were being born. Now the Russet household never completely slept. To give help to the laboring ewes when help was needed, to save a wet newborn lamb from the cold, Ernest or Tom would be going to the barn by turns all through the nights, sometimes staying for hours, busy with a difficult birth or a weak lamb, or just sitting and waiting, warming their hands over the lighted lantern between their feet.

At that time knowledge, fear, and sorrow were descending also upon the Russets. For them, the great fact of the war was coming to bear with a singular pointedness upon what was now their dearest hope. The war, as they had tried not to know but nonetheless knew, was going to require Tom Coulter. It would take him away. That it would destroy him they did not yet know, but they knew it could destroy him. Knowledge had begun to shudder in their hearts. The change that was coming had already begun to come, and they felt themselves impaired.

On a Sunday near the end of the month, when the Milbys again came for dinner, sorrow was in the air undeniably—partly because of the Russets' palpable need to deny it. The effect of the presence of Williams Milby, the comforter, was to make grief evident. The Russets were smiling and genial as usual, but there came relentlessly a moment when Naomi lifted a corner of her apron to wipe an eye, and when Ernest, seeing her do that, stopped twice in the midst of a story to clear his throat.

As soon as the meal was over, according to her custom at such times, Laura excused herself and left the table. She put on her warm overcoat and scarf, her gloves and galoshes, and began one of her solitary walks, leaving the old ones in their sorrow, Tom in his embarrassment, Williams in his helpless standing by that was yet a comfort.

Her departure had its usual excuse of discretion; Williams was the needed one, not her. But today, as she knew and told herself, there was cowardice in it too. She did not want to bear what in that house that day was to be borne. The place, which normally would have seemed to welcome her, today seemed to exclude her. She felt its indifference to whatever might happen in it. Its quietness, as if waiting or expectant, which usually would have comforted her, she felt now as indifference.

Though it did not comfort her, she continued her walk for some distance, going as far as the little stream under the sycamores, which was flowing too full to cross by stepping stones, and then turning back toward the barns.

The tobacco barn, now the lambing barn, opened front and back into two pastures. In the pasture behind it were the ewes whose lambs were now safely born and strong; in the smaller pasture in front were the ewes still to lamb. Laura walked up the long slope among the ewes with their new lambs, and here she felt a kind of pleasure at last. Here was a small success, even a small triumph, of the kind the world most dependably allows. The ewes moved out of her way as she passed, their lambs following. She walked to the wide-open doorway and went into the barn.

When she had blinked away the outdoor brightness, she saw Tom busy by the row of lambing pens along one wall.

"Hello," she said.

He answered, "Hello."

The barn no doubt had needed to be visited, but no doubt also, like her, he had welcomed an excuse to leave the house. She felt then how strongly his life claimed him, how he needed for his place and being the whole outdoors.

She went to the row of pens. In the second one a ewe was nuzzling and muttering to a lamb as it stood unsteadily to nurse. Almost at her feet her suckling lamb's twin lay on the straw, still slimed and bloody from its birth, marvelously formed to live, except that it was dead and now to the ewe a thing of no importance.

"I should have got that out of there," Tom said.

"No," she said. "It's all right."

He had lifted from a nearby pen an orphan lamb and was holding it, its long legs dangling, in one hand, a nippled bottle of cow's milk in the other.

And suddenly she was filled with knowledge of him that was like love, or was love. In him, as he stood before her then, she saw the ancient unthanked care of shepherds. The sheep merely suffered what was to be suffered, living the given life, dying the given death. They did not ask for care or appreciate it when they received it. And yet the care was given. The flocks throve by no care commensurate with a price, but by an overplus of love, filling a known need in the shepherd, passionate and beyond memory old.

What Laura said then she said as if merely in answer: "You're in love, aren't you?"

He gave back her look. He grinned. She could see the boy in him then— the boy, anyhow, that he had been not long ago.

"I thought you knew it," he said. "I didn't look for you to say so."

She said, "I would like to thank you."

Their held gaze seemed then to be one thing to which their two beings were for the moment incidental. It was a moment that had to pass. And it did pass. Time carried them from the moment before to the moment after.

She smiled. "I don't think we'll talk of this again."

He nodded, and the boy he had been was nowhere near him now. "No. We won't again."

There was in fact no more to say. Because they said no more, for the rest of his life, which would not be long, she shone in his mind as she had been that day: "I would like to thank you." And to the end of her own long life she was grateful to him because with his young heart, never old, he had loved her.

Misery (1943)

The house where my father's parents, Dorie and Marce Catlett, spent their long marriage was not a happy one, though I was often happy in it. It was regulated by the seasonal order of all farmhouses of its time and shared in the comeliness of that order. Even so, it was not a happy house because my grandparents' marriage had been so often a collision of wills. Opposites attract, but this can be so only within limits, and Grandma and Grandpa's story had the contending themes of attraction and conflict.

To all of us younger ones in the family and some who were not in it, Grandpa in his old age referred to Grandma as "your mammy," thus acknowledging their fundamental difference: She, and not he, had borne their two sons, a fact that he held in awe. This was the honest, insoluble awe of a livestockman and farmer who had been preoccupied all his life with the fecundity of the world. *She* had borne their children, had suffered their births—and how far this set her apart from him! But in telling of a time he went to see her during their courtship, a time he returned to often in his last years, he would conclude, "And your mammy came out to meet me—the prettiest *formed* little thing." He would gaze away, seeing her again as she was, and again he would be moved. "Ay Lord!" Thus he acknowledged the attraction.

It had been mutual. She had thought him in those early days "the best-looking man on the back of a horse that ever I saw." In the first years of their marriage she would hear him away in the distance, calling the cattle. His call was beautiful, and she would think, "Oh, that such a voice should ever cease!" He remained a good-looking man on the back of a horse almost to the end of his days. Grandma came to take that as much for granted as he did. That he was as he was she saw as a condition of her life, and their fundamental difference, the difference of dam and sire, grew between them.

There were other differences, some issuing from that primary one, some that were differences of character.

Grandpa, burdened as he was by things as they were, suffering as he had and did from the circumstances of this world, accepted them nevertheless with the finality of a tragedian. This was in no sense "stoical," for he was a passionate man, but was simply a disposition to see the world as a matter of fact. The deity he most spoke of he called "Old Marster," and this was a world-making, weather-making, fate-making deity, not effectively to be pled with, who revealed his purposes by what happened.

Though she faced with equal candor the things that were, Grandma resisted and protested. Some things that were should not have been. I don't think Grandma ever reconciled herself to mortality—or, for that matter, to humanity. Her mourning of her losses, which were ever on her mind, always involved an unrelenting objection. She objected to growing old, which she felt as a wrong imposed upon her. "Oh, Andy," she would say to me, "it's awful to get old," and she said this, I felt, pitying not only herself but also the old man that I would one day be. Of humanity in general she was skeptical. She had a few favorites, of whom I was one, but even of those she could be suddenly and peremptorily dismissive, unsurprised at any outrage they might commit.

And yet, going wide of Christian charity and forgiveness as she sometimes did, she adhered to her church and served it. She was one of the pillars of the little white clapboard Bird's Branch Church, to which Grandpa did not adhere and of which he was not a pillar. Like, I believe, a good many others of his kind, who like him deferred to Old Marster in their ultimate unknowing, Grandpa felt excluded, and perhaps according to doctrines made to exclude him and his likes. And so religion had come between them. Grandpa told me once in the presence of Grandma, and for her benefit, that he was thinking of buying the church and tearing it down. This was a joke surely, and just as surely a provocation, a blow dealt in an established conflict.

Grandma replied, "Yes. I reckon you would."

Her domain was the house and household, the domestic economy. The house, in the course of her time with Grandpa, had been under the influence of hard times from the depression of the 1890s to that of the 1930s, and it bore everywhere the signs and marks of economic constraint. Until well on in my childhood, when the electric lines and our brief heyday of cheap fossil fuels finally reached it, the most modern thing in it was the coal oil stove sometimes used for cooking in hot weather.

The matching set of furniture in the dining room was of oak and oak veneer, not fine. That room was heated only by a grated fireplace, was mostly unused, and smelled unforgettably of the spices and brown sugar that Grandma kept in the sideboard. The parlor, also rarely used, offered the luxuries of a sofa and easy chair identically upholstered, an upright piano, and a glass-fronted bookcase containing a collection mainly of old textbooks and old popular novels. Except for that in the dining room, all the furniture in the house—even in the parlor, with its air of determined and deserted refinement—had a way of being mismatched. There were a few truly fine old pieces, perhaps left over from the time of Grandpa's parents, but those were odds and ends along with the rest, not so fine, that appeared to have been acquired randomly, a piece at a time, from hard telling where. Except in the parlor, the floor coverings were of linoleum, with a few worn scatter rugs. There was a general character of make-do. And yet the house afforded the common luxuries of deep feather beds that made for delicious sleeping on winter nights, and a wealth of good food, nearly all of which came from the place.

The household economy included a milk cow or two, meat hogs, a flock of chickens, a few turkeys, a big garden. There was a grape arbor, a pear tree, a cherry tree, a few scattered old apple trees, and wild berries for preserves and pies. The surpluses of cream and eggs provided Grandma a small money income of her own, of which she was watchful and proud. She deposited it in the bank and used it sparingly, except that once in a long while she would indulge herself by ordering from Sears, Roebuck something she didn't really need. This often would be something that looked good in the catalogue but odd in reality. Once she ordered a pair of toeless white shoes that clearly, even to my eye, were made for a much younger woman. Once she ordered a small metal bed with a baked-on, imitation-wood finish. The bed, as pictured in the book and in her mind, was undoubtedly pleasant, but it could have matched nothing in the world but itself.

She was, on the contrary, an infallible cook. Her kitchen and pantry and smokehouse and cellar were places of abundance. One of the happinesses of the place, for me, was in observing her intricate housewifery, her economizings and small savings, her mendings and patching. But she was never stingy with food. She put meals on the table that were luxurious.

Grandpa belonged to the farm, the barns and fields, the pastures and crops, the animals. The farm had been his life, his passion and his trial. The economy of the farm, depending as it did on markets and the money economy, had been during most of his life far less stable and secure than the household economy that depended almost entirely on the place itself. Grandpa's long effort to possess and thrive on a place whose economy he did not in the least control had been inevitably a trial. But insecurely as the farm had belonged to him, he had belonged absolutely to it. He had been ruled absolutely by his vision of pastures deep in grass, abundant crops, good animals well fed.

When the farm was handed on to him, one of the back fields was scarred by gullies. Working with a breaking plow and a slip scraper, Grandpa dug a pond in a swale of that field and used the extracted soil to fill the washes, and so he healed them. Driven by debt, he planted another field all to corn, plowing more than he knew he should, and it washed badly in a hard rain. He put it back in grass and never plowed it again, and he grieved to the end of his life over the hurt he had given it. And yet the farm, past all losses and griefs, called him to imagine it as good as it was, and better than it was.

He had been a man of notable hardiness and strength. A neighbor woman told me in her old age that she remembered him disking ground with a team of mules, wearing only a pair of pants. She was carrying water to her father on the adjoining farm. Grandpa called to her, "Sally Ann, when you bring your daddy another drink, would you bring me one?" Was he working a young team he could not leave? He was thirsty, anyhow, and he had not stopped to drink. He had come by then into responsibilities and lean times. He did not afford himself clothes he could do without.

Once he was leading a brood mare from home to the Forks of Elkhorn beyond Frankfort. He had arranged to breed the mare to a stallion at that place. She would have been a standardbred, not saddle broke, and he had set out to walk the forty or so miles, leading her. But she was not well broke even to lead, and she was wearing him out. Finally he stopped at a farm and borrowed a saddle, not doubting that if he could saddle her he could ride her. He saddled her, straddled her, and went his way. Presumably she was well broke by the end of the trip. This was told to my father, after Grandpa's death, by the man who had loaned the saddle.

Late in his life, when he might have considered himself old, his teeth began to bother him. He got on his horse, rode the five miles to Smallwood on the railroad where Gib Holston, the atheist doctor, was then living. He told Doc Holston, "Pull 'em out! Ever' damned one of 'em!" And Doc Holston did so, one after another. When all were pulled, Grandpa got on his horse again, rode home, and ate his supper. Teeth had become incidental to him, a bother gone, and he was toothless then until his death, which was still a long way off.

At some time before I came along he ceased entirely to wish to be anywhere but where he was. His mind belonged as entirely to the place as its rocks and trees. Grandma, though, remained always curious about distant places, treasuring the postcards she received from traveling friends and relatives. She went once to South Carolina to visit her eldest son, my uncle Andrew, who was then working down there. She walked beside the ocean, and brought back a big seashell in which, holding it to my ear, I could hear the ocean for myself. She and some neighbors once made an excursion to the Cincinnati Zoo, from which her most persistent and delighted memory was of Uncle Eb Markman who, scouting ahead, had come rushing back in a state of near-death excitement: "They got a hippopotaymus!" She had gone also, with the ladies of the church, on a visit to Mammoth Cave, and had brought back as souvenirs from deep in the earth several crystalline rocks that she prized.

Grandpa was the creature, not only of his own place, but also pretty exclusively of its surface. His curiosity about the underground was fully satisfied at the depth of an end post hole. He did not aspire into the air beyond the height of a barn roof. On the only "trip" of his life, when my father coaxed him to the top of the overlook at Cumberland Gap, Grandpa took one look over the edge at the "view" and shrank backward—"like a dog," said my father—and would not look again.

When I was a child I had not traveled as much even as Grandpa. For a long time I had not gone farther from home than Louisville. And so, like Grandma, I was enchanted by the thought of places I had not been. I could sit with her and be carried away by her collection of picture postcards. But I observed also Grandpa's local travels on horseback, on some of which I rode with him behind his saddle, holding to his waist, or following along on Beauty the pony. Grandpa loved to eat, and sometimes it suited him to show up at a neighbor's house at noon and get himself invited to dinner. He was perfectly convinced, at least by that stage of his life, that the highest compliment a man could pay a woman was to eat her cooking and praise it. Those fortunate women evidently thought so too, for they were kind to him. In hot weather he also would visit the good springs, which were scattered about the neighborhood, in order to know again the varying tastes that the cool waters bore up from the darkness.

Within the little world of the farm, Grandpa's sense of the right kind and the right way was unshakeable. It amounted to a local propriety, complex and fierce, that determined his expectations of my brother, Henry, and me. He taught us, I think, much that we needed to know, but we didn't learn it willingly or quickly. His standards were high, and his teaching, like our father's, could be peremptory. If we backtalked him, he would say, "Shut your traps!" And if we were face to face with him, or in reach of his cane, we did shut our traps. When we were out of reach, we found ample room for impudence, also disobedience.

But there were forces from the greater world outside the farm that could shake him, and had, and did. The weather of course could shake him, but like all his kind he suffered the weather as a matter of fact. As large almost as the weather, and even less to be trusted, the money economy that limited the economy of the farm had shaken him for most of his life. That economy could not be suffered as a matter of fact, for it was less subject to expectation, more arbitrary, more surprising, than the weather. And entirely surprising to me, when finally it hit me, was the realization that the expectations of his grandchildren also had the power to shake him.

Christmas for our immediate family was a progress lasting several days, involving a big dinner, a Christmas tree, and presents at various houses, including the house of Granny and Granddaddy Feltner, my mother's parents, and that of Grandma and Grandpa Catlett. Granny and Granddaddy Feltner's house was a happy one. By various turns of fortune it had been a house less subject to economic hardship than that of the Catletts. But also, and unlike the Catletts, the Feltners were at one in their marriage. Their mutual consent to their life together had been generous. Christmas at the Feltners' in my earliest years was a horn of plenty poured out, with no fear of emptying. In the parlor would be a beautiful Christmas tree that reached all the way to the ceiling, and presents would be heaped up among its lowest boughs. The table in the dining room would be stretched to its full length. It was Christmas to the limit of possibility.

And then there came a year when I saw beyond doubt that Christmas at Grandma and Grandpa Catlett's was nothing like so fine. Their tree was small and spare, sitting, not in the parlor or the living room, but in the cold front hall, and with only a few presents under it. And I knew, as if I had seen her do it, that Grandma alone had fixed it there, and only for us children, according to an idea, not familiar or congenial to her, of what we children expected or would like. But what most touched me was the further realization that Grandpa had seen in my face, or in all our faces, some hint of judgment and disappointment. His attentiveness to us bore the tone of apology for what he felt was poor by a standard he did not know but nevertheless applied on our behalf.

They were growing old, he and Grandma, in their estrangement from each other and in a time that made them strange to themselves. Theirs was an afflicted marriage, and originally the affliction must have been sexual. In a time with little understanding of "birth control," without a telephone or good roads, when a doctor might be hours away, pregnancy was something to fear. I know from enough that was said that Grandma learned by the hardest way to fear it. And so at the heart of their life together was a terrible paradox. They lived by the fertility of the world and the farm, but their own fertility had been "a cross to bear."

"Your mammy said, 'That's all,' and ay God I knew what she meant."

Their marriage was unhappy, and that unhappiness was present in their house, just as happiness was present in the Feltner house. And yet the unhappiness of Grandma and Grandpa's house was not exclusive or unqualified. Love was in it also, however balked and disappointed, however much it had been a cause of the unhappiness. But above all the household embodied and was sustained by an agricultural order, resting upon the order of time and nature, that was at once demanding and consoling. Because this order was the order of the house, a child could be happy in it. But the time was coming, was already arriving, when that order would be disvalued and taken apart piece by piece.

I had come along just in time to glimpse the old order when it was still somewhat intact. I had played or idled in blacksmith shops while the smiths shod horses or mules, and built from raw iron and wood many of the simple farming tools still in use. I had gone along with the crews of neighbors as they followed the binder in the grainfields, gathering the bound sheaves into shocks, stopping to catch the young rabbits that ran from the still-standing wheat or barley. I had watched as they fed load after load of sheaves into the threshing machine and sacked and hauled away the grain. And I had been on hand when the sweated crews washed on the back porch and sat down to harvest meals equal to Christmas dinners, even in wartime with no sugar for the iced tea.

And then there came a threshing day when Grandma, old and ill and without help, was not up to the task of cooking for the crew, and my father could see that she was not. He had taken time off from his law office to splice out Grandpa, who also was not equal to the day.

"It's all right," my father said, comforting Grandma. "I'll take care of it."

And he did take care of it, for he was a man who refused to be at a loss, and he was capable. He went and bought a great pile of ground beef and sacks-full of packaged buns. He fired up the kitchen stove and, overpowering Grandma's attempts to help, fried hamburgers enough, and more than enough, to feed the crew of hungry men and their retinue of hungry boys. It was adequate. It was even admirable, in its way, I could see that. But I could see also that something old and good was turning, or had turned, profoundly wrong. An old propriety had been offended. I could not have said this at the time, but I felt it, I felt it entirely. There was my father in the kitchen, cooking, not like any cook I had ever seen, but like himself, all concentration and haste, going at a big job that had to be done, nothing lovely about it. And there was the crew sitting down, not to a proper harvest meal, but to hamburgers that I knew they associated, as I did, with town life, with hamburger joints.

Grandma and Grandpa had achieved their threescore years and ten and more; their strength had become labor and sorrow. The life they had lived, the old season-governed life of the country, was passing away as they watched. No threshing machine or threshing crew would come to their place again, and there would be no more big strawstacks for a boy to climb up and slide down. The combines had arrived, their service to be purchased by mere money.

It must have been at about the same time that Grandpa's "misery" began to come upon him in the night. I would be asleep in that little metal bed in the corner of Grandma's bedroom upstairs when suddenly the whole house would fill with Grandpa's crying out from his folding bed down in the living room. His cries were the sounds, unmistakably, of misery: "Ohhhh! Ohhhh! Ohhhh!"

Grandma would get up. In her nightgown, barefooted, she would go out into the hall and down the stairs, turning on lights as she went, for by then the electric line had come. The cries would continue a while, after a while they would stop, and after a further while Grandma would come back up the stairs to bed, turning the lights out as she came.

I said nothing, but I never ceased to wonder: What was his misery? And how was it eased?

Only many years later, when my father was getting old, and maybe I wanted to ask while there was time, I asked him, "What was the matter with Grandpa that would have made him cry out at night?"

And my father said only, "I don't know." If he did know, it was hard knowledge and he did not want to talk about it. But maybe, in fact, he did not know. For the first time I realized that I may have known my father's parents in their old age better than he did.

Still later, my brother, Henry, told me that he too had heard those outcries in the night, and had said nothing. And we wondered, as we often have, at our silence, our mere acceptance as boys of events and conditions that to our adult minds would have seemed urgent. Apparently it never occurred to us that the world, or any detail of it, might have been different. To us, as boys, as if we too deferred to Old Marster, things were as they were. Grandpa was as he was.

What was his misery? That question has been one of the themes of my life, and for most of my life I had not a glimmer of an answer. But now maybe I do. Maybe I have aged at last into the knowledge I lacked before, for now I have heard in my own heart in the deep night that outcry of misery. "What is it?" I have asked myself. And I believe I know.

Time is said to flow like a river. I have said so myself, and perhaps it does. But time is a great mystery, not to be declared by one simile, or by several. It flows also like molten metal, cooling and solidifying even as it passes. The past is as it was. As it was it is forever. It cannot be changed, not by us, not by God. No doubt it is forgettable. We do surely forget some of it, and surely all of it in time will be forgotten. Maybe we can forgive ourselves, or be forgiven, for our wrongs that we remember, but they remain nonetheless wrong. This is the true rigor mortis, this rigidification of all that is past. Under the rule of time, the past is as it was.

And so Grandpa, reduced to himself alone in the darkness, dwelt upon wrongs done and forever undoable, of limits met and unsurpassed, of understanding come too late. His strength had become labor and sorrow, and from his bed lonely as a grave he cried out.

When I think now of his cries, I think also of the scientific braggadocio of human longevity, and of the selfishness, or the deficiency of experience, of those who wish to live forever in time. Did we, as some improbably would say, invent eternity? If so, we invented it because we needed it as the air we breathe. So for mercy. So for grace.

Grandpa's misery, great as it surely was, belonged entirely to the darkness and to his sole self within it. When daylight returned, he was delivered out of the dark confinement of himself. After the night's displacement, he became again a living soul, familiar to himself. His place, lighted, again laid before him its infinite promise and demand. And again he recognized it, anciently made and still being made, partly by him who had been made by it, who was still in his moment alive upon it. He ate his breakfast, went to the barn, saddled his horse, and rode out into the fields. Or, increasingly as he aged, he sat on an inverted bucket in the barn door and went to sleep again, secure in the light.

And yet the return of light was not what ended his nighttime misery. When he cried out Grandma heard him and got up and went to him. She was his opposite, the other side of his life, so prettily formed and so lost, that had attracted him and fended him away. But when she heard him in his misery, crying out, she went to him, and after a while he was quiet.

What did she do? I can only give my father's answer: I don't know. Having been carried back now all the way into the perfect darkness of ignorance, I can only form the vague outline of a wish.

I will begin by stepping back a little into the light of what I know. I know that Grandpa enjoyed a drink of whiskey. He especially enjoyed a drink, as I have been told, if he had not paid for it himself. He saw nothing wrong with it in terms of his own thirst for it, which was limited. He could stop. He did not need to drink it all, as a friend of mine once said of himself, just to get rid of it.

But Grandma—and this, I think, was another critical opposition—Grandma was a principled teetotaler. She belonged to the Women's Christian Temperance Union, and by "temperance" she meant abstinence—not a drop, none. And for this she had substantial reasons: her brother whom we knew as Uncle Peach, Grandpa's older brother Will, and my uncle Andrew who was her own first born son—drinkers all, who could not stop, or who did not know when to stop, or who did not want to stop. Uncle Peach, who managed to be an epical nuisance to everybody, including himself, capped his career one winter night with an impromptu nap in his front yard, from which several of his toes never woke.

I suppose, had she been less intelligent or less inclined to doubt, Grandma might have been fanatical on the subject of liquor. But she was no fanatic, and she could make do with what the world afforded. And so I can imagine her bringing the problem of Grandpa's misery to Doc Holston, who by then had the house next door to my parents' house in Hargrave.

To do this, she would have had to face the scandal of Doc's boastful athiesm. Doc was a small man who aspired to higher standing by looking down upon God. He would have been astonished to know that his blasphemy did not offend her nearly so much as his absurdity.

"Marce is having a terrible misery in the night. What can I do?"

"Does he have the misery in the daytime?"

"No."

"Why, damn it to hell, woman, when he wakes up that way, give him a drink!"

"A drink?"

"Of whiskey, damn it! Put a little water in it. Sweeten it a little if you want to."

And I can imagine her asking my father—who else could she have asked?—to get her a bottle of whiskey. She would have blushed.

He would have laughed. "An old white-ribboner like you? What do you want it for?"

Such impudence would have made her secretive. "In case I get a cold."

So then I can see her, on the nights of Grandpa's misery, going down the stairs and straight back to the kitchen, where she had hidden the bottle. For I know she would have hidden it. Grandpa, she said, could smell out candy and find it, no matter how well she hid it. But he could not have smelled whiskey in a stoppered bottle wiped clean, even though he would know she had hidden it somewhere.

She would have poured the whiskey into a table glass with some water, perhaps a little sugar. And then, holding it well away from her for the harm in it, determined to do good with it, she would have carried it to his bedside.

"Sit up, Marce. Drink this."

He would not have needed to be invited twice.

I can see her standing and watching as he drinks. After the first swallow, he says, "Ah! Ay Lord!" He drinks slowly, with pleasure. When he has finished she takes the glass. He lies down, and she draws the cover over him. She sits down in the rocking chair by the bed. Holding the empty glass, gazing away into her thoughts as she would often do, she sits by Grandpa, patting his arm, as she would have sat by a wakeful child, until he goes to sleep.

That is my vision. I would like to think it might have happened so, and maybe it did. It is probable enough, credible enough. But what is the good of it? Perhaps none at all. But on my own now, from my imagination and my sorrow for them, I offer them nevertheless, out of time, this wish.

Andy Catlett:
Early Education (1943)

In grades one and two I was a sweet, tractable child who caused no trouble. I was "little Andy Catlett," the second of that name, the first being my uncle Andrew who had raised more than his share of hell and mowed a wide swath among the ladies. My own public reputation so far was clean as a whistle. But in grade three I learned of the damage that could be done to a strict disciplinary harmony by a small discord, and I was never the same afterwards.

In grade four, Miss Heartsease, abandoning her premature hope that I might be educable, brought stacks of *National Geographics* to keep me quiet. In one of them I found several pictures of a chemistry laboratory, and I fell into what I can only call an infatuation. I had no idea what was done in a chemistry laboratory. What captivated me was the intricate plumbing of glass pipes, some of them in coils; the vials, tubes, beakers, and retorts; the neat rows of bottled powders and fluids; the bunsen burners. The thought of working in such a room with such equipment sent me into urgent fantasies. I would be a chemist when I grew up. I would be a chemist *before* I grew up. I entertained seriously the possibility of becoming a child prodigy. I could see a picture of myself in my white coat in my laboratory in *National Geographic*, pouring a fuming green liquid from one container into another.

My scientific bent led me in that same year to the discovery of afterimages. One of the bare lightbulbs in the ceiling of our classroom was of clear glass and much larger than the others. Inside it was a filament in the shape of a horseshoe that glowed with a white incandescence. I learned that I could stare at that lightbulb for a while, and then, by blinking, send a flock of brightly colored horseshoes flying all over the room. But my experimental looking around and blinking proved too violent for Miss Heartsease, and she soon forced me back into my chemical fantasies.

I asked for a chemistry set for Christmas, and got one. But it was a disappointment. It was deficient in apparatus and drama, and too obviously intended to be "educational." I mixed up a concoction that smelled bad but was otherwise uninteresting, and gave up chemistry.

I went instead into the business of candle-making. Since it was not long after Christmas, candles were on my mind and the makings readily findable. I made a colorful collection of candle drippings and butt-ends. For good measure I added one whole candle that didn't match any of the others in the pantry, and I knew my mother wouldn't want it if it didn't match. I had read in a book about pioneer days that you could make a candle by dipping a string into melted tallow, and I knew from looking at lighted candles how to go about melting them.

And so I waited until I was at home by myself, to avoid disturbing others, before I started my candle-making business. It was in fact going to be a business, for I fully intended to sell my candles at a profit, and I thought I could count on my grandmothers to buy at least two apiece.

I put my drips and fragments into a small pot, cutting up the nonmatching whole one so it would fit, measured a piece of string to about the right length, and turned on the burner. How what happened next happened I can't say, for I soon found that I didn't have time just to stand around watching a pot, but it did happen that a fairly spectacular tall flame was standing on top of the stove. Pretty quickly it burnt up all my wax and went out, and I soon got the kitchen back to rights and no harm done. There was no sign of fire except for the faintest little cloudy smoke stain on the ceiling that you wouldn't see if you didn't look close. If my parents ever looked close they must have wondered, but they never asked me.

So I went out of the candle business with no profit, but also with no loss except for the burnt wax, which I no longer needed.

My parents were very much afraid that my brother, Henry, and I would not live to be grown. This fear, when it manifested itself, could be oppressive. But we were fortunate, Henry and I, in having a father who was often busy at his office and a mother whose attention was often required by our two younger sisters. This state of things bestowed upon us boys a latitude of freedom that we knew exactly what to do with.

As a result, a secondary fear haunted particularly our mother—namely that the behavior of her sons would deviate so far beyond the known human range that an apocalyptic embarrassment would fall upon the family. This too could be oppressive. When my mother said to me, "I don't know what's going to become of you!" I could hear the squeak of the hinges of the jailhouse door. In her worst moments, I fear my mother too could hear those hinges, and she also could see in her mind's eye the raw opening of an early grave for a boy drowned or burned or run over by a car or kicked in the head by a mule.

To save us from ourselves—and herself from the anguish she knew she would feel at the shutting of that iron door or the opening of that grave, if she had not done all she could have done by way of prevention—at certain extremities of our self-education and of her tolerance, she resorted to the use of a switch. The switch would be one of the sprouts that grew up from the roots of our lilac bush, and it would be keen, lithe, and durable. Our mother's use of it was fiercely honest. She dispensed the "good whipping" she had promised, no fun for the recipient, though the pain was soon over. What was not soon over was my sense of her own reluctance and regret, which stayed with me and made me sympathize with her as maybe nothing else could have done.

I sympathized with her; in my sympathy, as I can see now, I greatly loved her, and yet her punishments wrought no significant change in my behavior. Her influence over me at that time did not extend many feet beyond the end of her lilac switch, whereas my quest for knowledge extended limitlessly round about.

Probably because of my early gift for science, I was eager to learn in school. But I was not intellectually stimulated by the schoolbooks or the established curriculum. What I wanted to learn was the precise line between what my teachers would put up with and what they would not put up with. And to draw a line of this sort required much experimentation.

My curiosity about the limits of, for instance, Miss Heartsease was extraordinarily keen. I probed the coastlines of her patience and sounded its estuaries like an early navigator mapping the New World. When school let out, I shifted my interest to other continents as handily as an astronaut.

It may have been in the fall of my year of Miss Heartsease that I applied myself to a critical textual examination, and ultimately to the scientific debunking, of *The Night Before Christmas*.

At that time my sisters' upstairs bedroom still had an open fireplace with a grate that, before our time, had been used for burning coal. I had never paid it much attention until one night after supper, when I was loitering in that room, enjoying maybe the strangeness of its feminine prettiness, one of my earliest quandaries attached itself to that fireplace as if by magnetic attraction. It was far yet from Christmas, still warm. And by then I'm sure I "knew about Santa Claus." But my quandary was a Christmas quandary of long standing, and it had to do specifically with Santa Claus.

I knew from my close observation of falling bodies, and from having been a number of times a falling body myself, perhaps as much as one needs to know about gravity. And so I saw no great problem in the alleged descent of chimneys on the part of Santa Claus. If the chimneys had been big enough, and if he had no more graceful way of doing so, he could have got down them by falling.

How he got back up them again was my question. I was going, you see, by the book. As a critic, from the beginning I held the text in great honor, and the text did not say that he came down the chimney, left the toys for the children, and let himself out by the door. The text said in plain English: "up the chimney he rose."

In those days I was a true pure scientist. If the subject of my inquiry had been the nature of gravity itself, I would not have minded whether the falling body had been an apple or a bomb, or upon what or whom it might have fallen. I was hard driven in my quest for truth.

And so, being alone, and having therefore full intellectual freedom, I stooped into the fireplace, inserted my head and shoulders into the chimney, and did a passable job of standing up. Such was my objectivity in regard to the chimney that I would not have been surprised if I had been able to go right up it.

But it was not a roomy chimney. I could not raise my arms to feel for a handhold, and except for the grate there was no foothold. And so I absolutely knew something: If I couldn't get up it, Santa Claus couldn't get up it. I wasn't entirely objective at this point, for I was truly sorry. It would have been extraordinarily pleasant to go up the chimney and climb out onto the peak of the roof. From there I could have gone down onto the roof of the back porch, from there into the branches of our big old apple tree, and from there to the ground.

But I accepted disappointment, shrank out of the dark chimney, and stood up again in the lighted room. And that, I think, must have been the occasion upon which I discovered soot. Coal soot is exceedingly black and exceedingly light. I was covered with it, which I only found out by using one of the curtains to wipe what felt like cobweb out of my eyes. I was a living pencil, for on everything I touched I left a mark.

And then I saw that the soot, in addition to being on me, was coming off. It was drifting loose in chunks and flakes and floating to the floor, where it broke into pieces that fled away on tiny currents of the air, insidious little breezes which I also discovered at that time.

The Christmas quandary I had started with, despite its scientific interest and the seriousness with which I had taken it up, began to look like a pleasant sort of ignorance. I would gladly have gone back to it, except that it had now evolved into an insistently present problem for which there was no present solution. In fact, every attempt I made at a solution reliably worsened the problem. Even when I merely rubbed my head the better to study the situation, I loosened more soot. I saw a flake of soot levitate from the top of my head and land on a bedspread, white to match the curtains. When I took a swipe at it to knock it to the floor, I made a broad dark streak. It began to seem to me that I needed to be going.

I started to the door and only then saw that my mother was standing in it, having just arrived. We paused and looked each other over. I saw from her stance and demeanor that the situation was not as she would have preferred it to be.

I managed to dodge past her, maybe because she was dazed, not having as quick an eye for the truth as I did, or maybe she was reluctant to touch me. She hadn't even thought of anything to say.

Once I was safely past her, I ran to one of the windows at the back of the hall, "threw up the sash" (as *The Night Before Christmas* says), and flung myself out onto the porch roof. Thereupon, displaying a presence of mind I had never given her credit for, my mother shut the window. I heard her lock it. I heard her go to the window on the other side of the hall and lock that one.

Laying low seemed to be called for, and like Brer Rabbit I laid low. For a long time I didn't make a sound, and I didn't hear a sound. I thought hard, and I didn't come to a satisfactory conclusion. I was safe as long as I stayed on the roof. My mother, I knew, would not climb onto the roof. But then there was a limit to how long I could stay there. There was no bed or blanket on the roof, and there would be no breakfast. I could go down by the apple tree, but where would I go then? I didn't know where everybody else was, but I knew my mother was at home. Sooner or later my father would come home, and that did not brighten my prospects.

The idea of running away from home in case of need had been ready-made in my mind for a good while, but to do that I would have to be on the ground. Once on the ground and safely gone, I would maybe think of a place to go, some place an orphan boy might find welcome and shelter. So I got up ever so quietly, and slowly so as not to make a sound I eased down the slope of the roof. I went so far as to step from the roof into the apple tree before I looked down and saw my mother.

She was sitting on the ground with her back against one of the tree's three trunks. She looked comfortable. A lengthy switch was lying across her lap beneath her folded hands.

She looked strange. I had never before seen her or anybody else look as she did then. It took a long time for my education to catch up with the vision of her I had then, for though she was a Christian woman she was sitting down there looking positively Buddhist. She was sitting perfectly still. She was not going to move in so much as I could imagine of the future. She was not looking left or right, let alone up into the tree where I was. But I knew she knew where I was. I felt illuminated as if by omniscience. She was at peace down there. She was using up all the peace there was. There was none at all up in the apple tree where I was.

Without making a sound I eased back out of the tree and onto the roof again. Though I knew she was not looking at me and was not going to look at me, I moved back out of her line of sight, where at least I was relieved of looking at her.

My mind was breaking new ground and was working hard. It was working so hard I could spare no energy for standing up. I sat down. For quite a while I thought methodically and strenuously. I saw that I did not have many options. I had, in truth, only three options: I could climb down that tree, which, with precise reason, I was afraid to do; or I could kick the glass out of one of the hall windows and go back into the house, which, on second thought, did not seem to be an option; or I could jump off the roof, and then, if able, run.

To avoid thinking again of the tree, I gave a lot of thought to jumping off the roof. If I did that successfully, with no damage to myself, the option of running away would be renewed. But if I jumped it would be a long way to the ground, and I would have a fair chance of breaking a leg. This was a possibility not entirely unattractive, for if I broke a leg my mother surely would feel sorry for me and forget to whip me. On the other hand, I might kill myself, in which case I would lose the benefit.

And so I was driven back by my thoughts to the first option of climbing down the tree. But I lingered on a while to give my mother a reasonable opportunity to depart, an opportunity which she did not receive with favor. When I got up and eased back again to look for her, there she was. She had not moved. She looked exactly as she had before.

I was really getting to know my mother. I am many years older now than she was then, and I can easily imagine how knowingly she was amused. But I could imagine then, for I *saw*, how perfectly she was determined. It was getting dark. It was time to bring this story to an end.

Making no longer an effort to be quiet, I stepped back into the tree, slid down, and stood in front of my mother. I felt as if I were presenting myself to a bolt of lightning. It was somewhat like that: swift, illuminating, and soon over.

Drouth (1944)

Early in my childhood when the adult world and sometimes my own experience easily assumed the bright timelessness of myth, I overheard my father's friend Charlie Hardy telling about the drouth of 1908. I liked hearing the grownups talk, and when I wanted to I could be quiet. By being more or less unnoticeable, I heard a lot. Some of the adult conversations I listened to ended with a question: "How long have *you* been here, Andy?"

Charlie Hardy, anyhow, grew up on a rough little farm on Bird's Branch. Charlie, as he said, "came up hard," though that phrase, by now, has lost much of the meaning it still would have had in the early 1940s. At the time of Charlie's boyhood, except for the railroad and the little packets that still carried passengers and freight up and down the river, there were no machines in the country around Port William, no electricity, no "modern conveniences" or not many. Now, when electricity, indoor plumbing, and many personal machines have become normal, people generally assume that a hundred years ago life was "hard" for almost everybody, though few still have the experience needed for a just comparison. It is perhaps impossible for a person living unhappily *with* a flush toilet to imagine a person living happily without one.

Like every child of his time and in his circumstances, Charlie grew up working. One of his jobs was to carry water for the household from a spring at the bottom of the hill. It was a good spring, with a reputation for never going dry. It was known as the Hardy Spring, and people spoke of its "deep vein," and of its fine-tasting water that ran cool through the hot weather. It didn't go dry in 1908, but it came close. In 1908 Charlie was big enough to carry two ten-quart buckets of water from the spring to the house. He made many trips.

In tolerable weather the spring was a good place to go. The water issued from a cleft in the ledgerock down near the creek. The place was always in deep shade. The spring itself and the little basin where the water collected had been enclosed with a rock wall and roof, and fitted with a door, to keep the livestock out. The water striders and the round-and-about bugs conducted their daily business in the pools downstream, and the shike-pokes came and fished. But for Charlie, in the drouth of 1908, it became a place of suffering. He would come down with his buckets, dip one full from the basin, and then wait a long time for the basin to fill again so that he could dip the second.

The drouth, the withering foliage, the heat, and the diminished flow of the spring filled Charlie with misery, and his misery was made worse by his longing for rain. Until it finally rained again, something fundamental seemed to have gone wrong with the world. In the secrecy of his thoughts, after the way of boys, he mourned and he was afraid.

Noticing his misery, his father gave him an instruction that Charlie always remembered when he needed to. "You think it's awful. And it is. But I'll tell you something. You can't believe it now, but times will come when this won't be on your mind. You won't think of it."

And that, Charlie said, was true. There had been times when he had not thought of it.

But hearing him tell about it put it on *my* mind. *I* thought about it. And so when the first drouth of my own experience and memory came to our part of the country during the war year of 1944, I already knew one thing about it: It was not the first.

In addition to the drouth and the war, and the absence of my uncle Virgil, my mother's brother, who had gone off to fight, the summer of 1944 was the summer of the death of my namesake and hero, Uncle Andrew, my father's brother. For me, it was a summer of need—of more need, probably, than I was capable of recognizing or feeling. That one may be grieved and in need and all the while living one's life, often enough with interest and even pleasure, was an ordinary oddity far beyond my years and understanding. Grief, great as it might be, did not consume all the world, but now, for me, it had taken its place among the world's other things.

I was staying that summer with my father's parents, Dorie and Marce Catlett. As the days without rain accumulated until the word "drouth" took its place in our daily vocabulary, I learned of two other drouths that were still new in the memory of my elders. One had come in 1930. Another, a worse one, had come in my own lifetime, in 1936 when I was two years old, though I did not remember it.

A drouth is an event of the atmosphere of the earth. It is also an event of the atmosphere of the human mind, which suffers a disturbance that affects everything. It affects the meanings of memory and history. It affects one's sense of the future. Everybody on the place old enough to remember the 1930s regarded our present drouth with a fearful respect that could be described as primeval: It had been felt by country people since the beginning of time. It was not qualified by youth or innocence. I felt it, I think, as fully as my elders, for I had quickly caught their memories and their awe.

Grandpa Catlett showed me a rewired place in the line fence where in 1936 a gap had been cut, allowing the neighbors to drive their cows to our spring that had kept flowing. He and his black hired hand Dick Watson remembered how they and others had hauled water to the livestock in barrels dipped full one bucket at a time. They told of people who drove their cattle miles through the heat to drink at the river, and the cattle would be as thirsty when they got home as they had been when they left. Who could not see the misery of that? And how, having seen it, could you keep it from filling your mind?

We looked at the parching ground and at the drying creek whose pools got smaller every day, we suffered the heat, and we watched the sky. We expected, or at least I did, the end of the world. I was much under the influence, in those days, of Grandma Catlett and Dick Watson's wife, Aunt Sarah Jane, to whom about equally the end of the world was a scheduled event, though nobody knew the schedule. The end of the world was not as exactly predictable but was just as expectable as Christmas or the Fourth of July. And of course they were right.

Grandpa, I think, did not give much thought to the end of the world. It was the continuance of the world that worried him. Of the theologies then available on the place, Grandpa's was probably the simplest: Old Marster is in charge, and we are not; Old Marster knows, and we don't. But Grandma had pondered a good deal about the end of the world. It was fearful to her, and in times of unusual weather she dwelt upon it. If, for instance, there would come a spell of cold weather in late spring, she would say to me, perhaps wishing not to, to spare me, but unable to contain her thought, "Oh, Andy, they speak of a time when we'll not know the summer from the winter but by the budding of the trees."

I would sit with her in a bay of one of the upstairs rooms whose windows looked out to the north. She would have her lap full of sewing or mending, we would talk, and we would watch the clouds that passed, stately and aloof, in their procession from west to east. According to her, they followed the great river to the north of us, leaving us dry. Around here, you still sometimes hear that thought—"The rain follows the river," meaning the Ohio—but with the support, I think, of little evidence.

In the minds of us humans, weather draws superstition as molasses draws flies. It draws also a sort of supernatural mystification that is a cut or two above superstition. Aunt Sarah Jane was full of the spaciousness, and the enchantment too, of mystery, and in the network of attractions that ruled me in those days I would be drawn down to listen to her in the two-room house where she and Dick lived at the corner of the woods. Like Grandma, Aunt Sarah Jane was thoughtful of the end of the world. But whereas Grandma regarded it with some deep disturbance of temporality and dread, Aunt Sarah Jane, who held it sufficiently in fear, also looked upon it with some approval as the time when justice would rain down at last. I think she anticipated with a certain pleasure the look on some people's faces when suddenly they would hear behind them the "great voice, as of a trumpet, Saying, I am Alpha and Omega, the first and the last."

So to Aunt Sarah Jane, the weather and all things of the realm of the sky were heavy with portent. From the sky, news of eternity irrupted into the daily world. To her, the events of the sky—rain, no-rain, clouds, rainbows, winds, the phases and attitudes of the moon —all were signs. The significance of the signs might not be discernable then or ever, but they were never merely what they appeared to be. They were signs.

Aunt Sarah Jane had a whole curriculum of fascinating subjects. She was precisely a spellbinder. I listened to her, as Grandpa would sometimes say, with all the ears I had. And yet her spells had their limits. Her unrelenting sense of the convergences of worlds, of the hereafter with the here, finally would so unsteady me that I would have to leave and walk the solid footpath back up to the barn.

For comfort in that season of my first knowledge of loss and cosmic dread, I spent as much time as I could with Dick Watson. If he loved me as I loved him, I was indeed blessed, but of course I will never know. He seemed ancient to me then, ancient perhaps in knowledge, though now I believe that he was younger than Grandma, and that by now I have outlived him in years.

In my hearing at least Dick did not pay much attention to the great mysteries and mystifications, nor was he much preoccupied with doubts. He did not dwell with regret upon the past. He looked forward to small pleasures and relished them when they came. He lived, he pleased himself as he was able, he endured. Small amusements lasted him a long time. He had a cheerful heart and a sympathetic one. I think he suffered the drouth as the plants and animals suffered it. He believed that it finally would rain, for finally it always had, but he did not know when.

With Dick too I watched the sky, watched the clouds pass over us one after another without shedding a single drop of rain, watched the signs. Dick's weather signs, unlike Aunt Sarah Jane's, were merely practical, and he observed them with appropriate humor. If the sun rose red in the morning, if it set behind clouds, if the chickens lay on their sides to sun their feet, if the raincrow called, all those were signs of rain. And all those signs were subject to a higher truth that even Dick spoke with a certain solemnity but also with a certain amusement: "All signs fail in a dry time." For the sun did rise hot and red in the morning, it set behind clouds, the chickens sunned their feet, the raincrow called, and it did not rain. Dick said, "All signs fail in a dry time, buddy," and he apparently felt some reassurance in the certainty of that.

There was work to be done every day. Sometimes I would walk to the back of the place to find my friend Fred Brightleaf, or he would come to find me, and we would slip away to the pond for a swim. But often I would be at work with Grandpa and Dick, hoping to find something manly that a boy could do, often failing, sometimes having to be tolerated as I blundered at men's work while shirking the boy's jobs that would actually have been useful, sometimes needing to be warned out of the way, but always glad to be at large in the great open world that, even dry, was better than the house and far, far better than school.

When quitting time came and we drove the mules to the barn, and Dick had unharnessed and watered and fed them, the three of us would sometimes rest for a while together, sitting on upturned five-gallon buckets in the big doorway of the barn, watching the evening changes in the sky. We watched it not rain. Sometimes we spoke hardly a word. Sometimes, the drouth weighing on his mind, Grandpa would speak of previous dry times, and Dick would confirm him, speaking his own memories. Dick would sit perfectly still, relishing his stillness as rest came upon him. Grandpa too sat still, gazing out under the brim of his straw hat, one hand on his cane, the fingers of the other worrying at the sore on his shin that would not heal.

He had fallen out of the barn loft several years before, and so had by his carelessness, Grandma said, made the wound. It would not heal perhaps because of his absent-minded prodding and picking, perhaps because otherwise he ignored it, forgetting or refusing to use the special soap and salve that Grandma had sent off for. He spoke of the hardships of other years, never exclaiming, never lamenting, allowing the remembered and uttered facts simply to stand on their own. Of all my elders, his sense of difficulty was probably the keenest. It called forth his memories and established the tone of his voice. To live from the farm and preserve it had been difficult. To stay solvent at the bank had been difficult. His experience was summed in a single sentence that he repeated often: "I know what a man can do in a day." At times this bore the sense of tragedy, for what a man can do in the little light of a day, with his little knowledge, with his little strength, is rarely enough. But sometimes he spoke it in exultation: What a good man, a good hand, could do in a good day could sometimes be a wonder.

But I was happiest, I think, when Dick and I would be out somewhere together, just us two. Maybe we would go on an errand to Port William or a neighboring farm, Dick riding Grandpa's saddle mare Rose and I on Beauty the pony, or we would go on foot to salt the steers or clean the spring. At such times we found much to talk about.

The great theme of our conversation, in that summer and others, was an event that Dick and his people called "The Big Day." When Dick and I talked about it, I too called it The Big Day. The Big Day came every year on a Saturday in August. It was attended by the black people in Hargrave and from the farms for miles around. For the ones who had moved to the northern cities, it was a homecoming. It was for its participants the greatest, grandest event of the year. On that day the black people of our part of the country were the absolute center of their own attention. The white people, if they wished, might observe the public display, but they were observers merely. They observed, moreover, from a polite distance.

The Big Day began with a parade through Hargrave, led by the only marching band to be heard there all year. The men of the lodge marched in white gloves, badges, and sashes, carrying a variety of medieval weapons. The women of the churches marched in white dresses, badges, and sashes. The parade ended at the tree-shaded lawn of a grand old farmhouse just beyond the outskirts of town, where for the rest of the day there would be eating and drinking and talking. There would be many excellent things to eat, and Dick recited again and again the list of them. There would be joyful greetings, mourning over the newly departed, many memories retold and renewed. And then that night, at the Lodge Hall, the marching band would transform itself into a dance band, and there would be dancing.

Dick Watson looked forward to The Big Day with all his mind and heart. He had to talk about it, and because I often was the only available listener he talked about it to me. Probably he could not have found a better listener, for I identified utterly with him in his anticipation. I fully shared his enthusiasm. I held excitedly to every word he said about it, and my ears were not filled with hearing. But this realizable reality of Dick's was for me only a vision, a sort of inward ritual of the intensest comradeship and love. Though we were living in the great tremor of the drouth and its betokening of the end of time, we also foresaw the coming of this merely local event that caused Dick's mind, and therefore my own, to tremble with a presentiment of joy. For a while I took part in these conversations about The Big Day as if I would be going to it myself, hand-in-hand with Dick, for as we tramped about together we often would be holding hands. And then as we approached the great event, we would arrive finally, inevitably, at the racial division. Dick would be going without me. He would be part of it, party to the joy of it, and I would not.

I still feel the disappointment and sorrow of that parting of ways, and I feel the strangeness of it. Thanks to Grandma Catlett and Aunt Sarah Jane, the end of the world was not strange to me. I did not greatly like the thought, but I knew then, as I know now, that some day will be the last. But categorical divisions among people still seem to me to be strange. I understand them, I believe, and I have felt their attraction. But it matters to me that as a small boy in Kentucky sixty-odd years ago I could have had a vision in which for a while the racial difference simply disappeared. I suppose— though I suppose I should say I may be wrong—that such divisions are best mended outdoors, unobserved by crowds, and in some mutuality of needs, if only those of speaker and listener. I have the feeling that all this means and matters more than I can understand. I do understand now, having learned well my ingrained distaste for great public events, that if I had been allowed to attend The Big Day I would have enjoyed it less in fact than I had supposed.

We talked also, Dick and I, of foxes and fox hounds, of horses and mules, and of the nature of things. I remember a day when, walking along the road, our attention was captured by the humming of the telephone wires. We stopped and stood still, the better to listen. The humming, we thought, was the sound of people's voices passing through the wires. To get through the wires, voices had to become hums, and then mysterious small machines inside the telephones had the power to change the hums back into voices. This may have been Dick's explanation, but I myself was a dauntless scientific theorist in those days. It seems lovely to me now that we could speak freely of mysteries of all kinds, not burdened in the least either by doubts or facts. We imagined the world as we were passing through it. We saw it all in pictures and visions.

I was with Dick, standing in the barn lot, watching and listening, when at last the rain came. Grandpa was sitting by himself on his bucket in the barn door, but Dick and I had got up because there was a change in the sky and a change in the air, and we could no longer sit still. All across the south and the west a great smooth-looking cloud was rising and darkening over the horizon of ridgelines and woodlands and open fields. Presently we could hear, far and faint, the thunder grumbling in the cloud, as though it was possessed and inhabited by some great living creature. And then we could see the lightning playing in it, and the thunder grew louder.

"It's raining at Goforth right now," Dick said.

We watched and listened again, and then a freshening wind reached us, smelling of rain.

"It's raining on Port William now," Dick said. "It's about to the grave-yard."

And then the Alpha and Omega of all the world seemed to break upon us from directly overhead. BLAM! Thunder and lightning came all at once—and we ran, scared and laughing, into the barn. It came again, that simultaneous lightning and thunder, and what appeared to be a large round ball of electrical fire burst in the lot, just outside the barn door. Beauty the pony, who had been standing tied in the driveway, made a violent lunge and snorted as if to expel something terrible from her nostrils.

"She *breathed* that lightning," Grandpa said.

I remember how solemnly he said that, and how inadequate it sounded. Also palpably inadequate were Dick's and my efforts, later, to discuss the ball of fire. For a minute there, reality had got way ahead of us. We couldn't even decide what color the fire had been. We thought maybe it had been all colors, all at the same time.

With that second thunderclap, anyhow, the rain was suddenly with us, falling in spouts and sheets as if it had never started and would never stop. None of us said another word. Dick and I had returned to our own buckets. We sat with Grandpa in a row there in the doorway and watched.

Before too long the rain slacked off. Dick went to get the milk buckets, and I got on the pony and went to bring in the cows. Soon enough we had done the night work, Grandpa and I had washed at the washstand on the back porch and come in to our places at the supper table. It was getting dark. We were then on what we would come to call "the old time," and night came two hours earlier than it does now.

The rain, the steady dizz-dozzle, had not stopped. It had set in for the night. The storm having deprived us of electricity, we ate by the light of an oil lamp and listened through the open door to the fall of the rain on the back porch roof. We said nothing. It was as though we were being told something that we had forever longed to hear.

Finally, raising his head to listen, Grandpa said, "This breaks the drouth."

It was the voice of a sufferer. I didn't know much, but I knew that. And in my mind or heart, or whatever the affected organ was, I felt the breaking of the drouths of 1936, 1930, 1908, and all the other drouths backward and forward to both ends of time.

Stand By Me (1921–1944)

When Jarrat married Lettie in 1921 and bought the little place across the draw from our home place and started to paying for it, in that time that was already hard, years before the Depression, he had a life ahead of him, it seemed like, that was a lot different from the life he in fact was going to live. Jarrat was my brother, four years older than me, and I reckon I knew him as well as anybody did, which is not to say that what I knew was equal to what I didn't know.

But as long as Lettie lived, Jarrat was a happy man. As far as I could see, not that I was trying to see or in those days cared much, he and Lettie made a good couple. They were a pretty couple, I'll say that, before this world and its trouble had marked them. And they laid into the work together, going early and late, scraping and saving and paying on their debt.

Tom was born the next year after they married, Nathan two years later. And it seemed that Tom hadn't hardly begun to walk about on his own until Nathan was coming along in his tracks, just a step or two behind. They had pretty much the run of the world, Lettie and Jarrat being too busy for much in the way of parental supervision, at least between meals.

The hollow that lays between the two places, that most people call Coulter Branch, before long was crisscrossed with boy-paths that went back and forth like shoestrings between the boys' house on one ridge and the old house on the other where I lived with Mam and Pap. The boys lived at both houses, you might as well say. They'd drop down through the pasture and into the woods on one side, and down through the woods to the branch, and then up through the woods and the pasture on the other side, and they'd be in another place with a different house and kitchen and something different to eat. They had maybe half a dozen paths they'd worn across there, and all of them had names: the Dead Tree Path, I remember, and the Spring Path and the Rock Fence Path.

And then, right in the midst of things going on the way they ought to have gone on forever, Lettie got sick and began to waste away. It was as serious as it could be, we could see that. And then instead of belonging just to Jarrat to pay attention to, she began to belong to all of us. Dr. Markman was doing all he could for her, and then Mam and the other women around were cooking things to take to her and helping with her housework, and us others were hoping or praying or whatever we did, trying to help her to live really just by wishing for her to. And then, without waiting for us to get ready, she died, and the boys all of a sudden, instead of belonging just to her and Jarrat, belonged to us all. Nathan was five years old, and Tom was seven.

And I was one of the ones that they belonged to. They belonged to me because I belonged to them. They thought so, and that made it so. The morning of their mother's funeral, to get them moved and out of the house before more sadness could take place, I put a team to the wagon and drove around the head of the hollow to get them. Mam had packed up their clothes and everything that was theirs. We loaded it all and them too onto the wagon, and I brought them home to the old house.

Jarrat wasn't going to be able to take care of them and farm too, and they didn't need to be over there in that loneliness with him. But Pap and Mam were getting on in years then. Pap, just by the nature of him, wasn't going to be a lot of help. And Mam, I could see, had her doubts.

Finally she just out with it. "Burley, I can be a grandmother, but I don't know if I can be a mother again or not. You're going to have to help me."

She had her doubts about that too. But it didn't prove too hard to bring about. I belonged to them because they needed me. From the time I brought them home with me, they stuck to me like burrs. A lot of the time we were a regular procession—me in front, and then Tom in my tracks just as close as he could get, and then Nathan in Tom's the same way. The year Lettie died I was thirty-four years old, still a young man in my thoughts and all, and I had places I needed to go by myself. But for a long time getting away from those boys was a job. I'd have to hide and slip away or bribe them to let me go or wait till they were asleep. When I wanted to hunt or fish the best way to be free of them was just to take them with me. By the time they got big enough to go on their own, we had traveled a many a mile together, day and night, after the hounds, and had spent a many an hour on the river.

The grass and weeds overgrew the paths across the hollow. The boys somehow knew better than to go over there where their mother was gone and their daddy was living by himself. It took them a while to go back there even with me.

Jarrat did a fair job of batching. He kept the house clean, and he didn't change anything. He sort of religiously kept everything the way Lettie had fixed it. But as time went on, things changed in spite of him. He got busy and forgot to water the potted plants, and they died. And then gradually the other little things that had made it a woman's house wore out or got lost or broke. Finally it took on the bare, accidental look of the house of a man who would rather be outdoors, and then only Jarrat's thoughts and memories were there to remind him of Lettie.

Or so I guess. As I say, there was a lot about Jarrat that nobody in this world was ever going to know. I was worrying about him, which I hadn't ever done before, and I was going to worry about him for the rest of his life. I began to feel a little guilty about him too. I had a lady friend, and by and by we began to come to an understanding. When I wanted company, I had friends. When I didn't want company, I had the woods and the creeks and the river. I had a good johnboat for fishing, and always a good hound or two or three.

Jarrat didn't have any of those things, not that he wanted them. In his dealings with other people he was strictly honest, I was always proud of him for that, and he was friendly enough. But he didn't deal with other people except when he had to. He was freer than you might have thought with acts of kindness when he knew somebody needed help. But he didn't want kindness for himself, though of course he needed it. He didn't want to be caught needing it.

After Lettie died, he wasn't the man he was before. He got like an old terrapin. He might come out of his shell now and again to say something beyond what the day's work required: "Hello," maybe, or he would compliment the weather. But if you got too close, he'd draw in again. Only sometimes, when he thought he was by himself, you'd catch him standing still, gazing nowhere.

What I know for sure he had in his life were sorrow, stubbornness, silence, and work. Work was his consolation, surely, just because it was always there to do and because he was so good at it. He had, I reckon, a gift for it. He loved the problems and the difficulties. He never hesitated about what to do. He never mislaid a lick. And half of his gift, if that was what it was, was endurance. He was swift and tough. When you tied in with him for a day's work, you had better have your ass in gear. Work was a fever with him. Anybody loved it as much as he did didn't need to fish.

So when Tom and Nathan needed him the most, their daddy didn't have much to offer. He wanted them around, he would watch over them when they were with us at work, he would correct and caution them when they needed it, but how could he console them when he couldn't console himself?

They were just little old boys. They needed their mother, was who they needed. But they didn't have her, and so they needed me. Sometimes I'd find one or the other of them off somewhere by himself, all sorrowful and little and lost, and there'd be nothing to do but try to *mother* him, just pick him up and hold him tight and carry him around a while. Their daddy couldn't do it, and it was up to me.

I would make them laugh. It usually wasn't too hard. Nathan thought I was the funniest thing on record anyhow, and sometimes he would laugh at me even when I was serious. But I would sing,

> Turkey in the straw settin' on a log
> All pooched out like a big bullfrog.
> Poked him in the ass with a number nine wire
> And down he went like an old flat tire.

I would sing,

> Stuck my toe in a woodpecker hole,
> In a woodpecker hole, in a woodpecker hole.
> Woodpecker he said, "Damn your soul,
> Take it out, take it out, take it out!"

I would sing one of them or some other one, and dance a few steps, rais-ing a dust, and Nathan would get so tickled he couldn't stand up. Tom would try to hold his dignity, like an older brother, but he would be ready to bust. All you had to do was poke him in the short ribs, and down he would go too.

What raising they got, they got mainly from their grandma and me. It was ours to do if anybody was going to do it, and somehow we got them raised.

To spare Grandma, and when they were out of school, we kept the boys at work with us. That way they learned to work. They played at it, and while they were playing at it they were doing it. And they were helping too. We generally had a use for them, and so from that time on they knew we needed them, and they were proud to be helping us to make a living.

Jarrat nor Pap wouldn't have paid them anything. Jarrat said they were working for themselves, if they worked. And Pap, poking them in the ribs to see if they would argue, and they did, said they ate more than they were worth. But I paid them ten cents a day, adjusted to the time they actually worked. Sometimes they'd get three cents, sometimes seven. I'd figure up and pay off every Saturday. One time when I paid him all in pennies, Nathan said, "Haven't you got any of them big white ones?"

They worked us too. They didn't have minds for nothing. Sometimes, if the notion hit them, they'd fartle around and pick at each other and get in the way until their daddy or grandpa would run them off. "*Get* the hell out of here! Go to the house!"

But they wouldn't go to the house. They'd slip away into the woods, or go to Port William or down to the river. And since they were careful to get back to the house by dinnertime or suppertime, nobody would ask where they'd been. Unless they got in trouble, which they sometimes did.

I worried about them. I'd say, "Boys, go to the river if you have to, but don't go *in* it." Or I'd say, "Stay *out* of that damned river, now. We ain't got time to go to your funeral."

But of course they did go in the river. They were swimming, I think, from frost to frost, just like I would have at their age. Just like I in fact *did* at their age.

Or they would wander over to Big Ellis and Annie May's, which was the one place they could be sure of being spoiled. Big would never be busy at any job he wouldn't be happy to quit if company came. Annie May always had cookies in a jar or a pie or cold biscuits and jam to feed them when they showed up, and so they showed up pretty often.

Annie May and Big weren't scared of much of anything except lightning. They could be careless and fearless when they ought to have been scared. They would drive to Hargrave in their old car, calm as dead people, while Big drove all over the road and looked in every direction but ahead. But let a thunderstorm come up and they'd quiver like gun-shy dogs. They'd get into the bed then, because they slept on a feather-tick and they believed lightning wouldn't strike a bird.

I went in over there one day just ahead of a big black storm, and there were Big and Annie May and Tom and Nathan all four piled up in the bed together, all four smoking cigarettes to calm their fear.

One day when we were in the woods we saw a big owl, and I pointed out how an owl can turn his head square around to look at you. I said if you came upon an owl sitting, for instance, on a tree stump, you could walk round and round him, and he would turn his head round and round to watch you, until finally he would twist his neck in two and his head would fall off. I said that was the way we killed owls all the time when I was a boy.

I told them just about any bird would let you catch him if you crept up and put a little salt on his tail.

"Why?"

"He just will."

"But why will he?"

"You'll have to ask somebody smarter than me."

I told them how when I was a boy, back in the olden times, you could hear the wangdoodles of a night, squalling and screeching and fighting way off in the woods.

"Do they still do that?"

"Naw, you don't hear 'em so much anymore."

At first they believed everything I said, and then they didn't believe anything I said, and then they believed some of the things I said. That was the best of their education right there, and they got it from me.

When they were little, you could always see right through Nathan. He didn't have any more false faces than a glass of water. Tom you couldn't always tell about. Maybe because Nathan was coming along so close behind him, Tom needed to keep some things to himself. It did him good to think he knew some things you didn't know. He wanted to call his life his own. He wasn't dishonest. If you could get him to look straight at you, then you had him.

As long as they were little, there would be times when they would be needing their mother, and who would be in the gap but only me? One or the other or both of them would be sitting close to me in the evening while it was getting dark, snuggled up like chickens to the old hen, and I would be doing all I could, and falling short. They changed me. Before, I was oftentimes just on the loose, carefree as a dog fox, head as empty as a gourd. Afterwards, it seemed like my heart was bigger inside than outside.

We got them grown up to where they weren't needy little boys anymore. They were still boys. They were going to be boys a while yet, but they were feeling their strength. They were beginning to find in their selves what before they had needed from us. Tom was maybe a little slower at it than he might have been, Nathan a little faster; Nathan was coming behind and was in a hurry.

It was a wonderful thing to watch that Tom grow up. For a while there, after he was getting to be really useful, he was still an awkward, kind of weedy, mind-wandery boy who needed some watching. To him, young as he was, it must have seemed he stayed that way a long time. But before long, as it seemed to me, he had gathered his forces together, body and mind. He got to be some account on his own. He could see what needed to be done, and go ahead and do it. He got graceful, and he was a good-looking boy too.

And then, the year he was sixteen, a little edge crept up between him and his daddy. It wasn't very much in the open at first, wasn't admitted really, but there it was. I thought, "Uh-oh," for I hated to see it, and I knew there wasn't much to be done about it. Tom was feeling his strength, he was coming in to his own, and Jarrat that year was forty-seven years old. When he looked at Tom he got the message—from where he was, the only way was down—and he didn't like it.

Well, one afternoon when we were well along in the tobacco cutting, Tom took it in his head he was going to try the old man. Jarrat was cutting in the lead, as he was used to doing, and Tom got into the next row and lit out after him. He stayed with him too, for a while. He put the pressure on. He made his dad quiet down and work for his keep.

But Tom had misestimated. The job was still above his breakfast. Jarrat wasn't young anymore, but he was hard and long-practiced. He kept his head and rattled Tom, and he beat him clean. And then he couldn't stop himself from drawing the fact to Tom's attention.

Tom went for him then, making fight. They were off a little way from the rest of us, and both of them thoroughly mad. Before we could get there and get them apart, Jarrat had just purely whipped the hell out of Tom. He ought to've quit before he did, but once he was mad he didn't have it in him to give an inch. It was awful. Ten minutes after it was over, even Jarrat knew it was awful, but then it was too late.

It was a day, one of several, I'm glad I won't have to live again. Tom was too much a boy yet to get in front where he wanted to be but too much a man to stay and be licked. He had to get out from under his daddy's feet and onto his own. And so he bundled his clothes and went away. Afterwards, because the old ones were so grieved, me too, Nathan too, the house was like a house where somebody had died.

Because he didn't need much and asked little, Tom found a place right away with an old couple by the name of Whitlow over on the other side of the county, far enough away to be separate from us. I knew he would do all right, and he did. He knew how to work; and the use of his head, that was already coming to him, came fast once he got out on his own. He began to make a name for himself: a good boy, a good hand.

When we had found out where he was, Nathan and I would catch a ride on a rainy day or a Sunday and go over to see him, or we'd see him occasionally in town. After he got his feet under him and was feeling sure of himself, he would come over on a Sunday afternoon now and again to see his grandma and grandpa. In all our minds, he had come into a life of his own that wasn't any longer part of ours. To the old ones, who had given up their ownership of him by then and their right to expect things from him, every one of those visits was a lovely gift, and they made over him and honored him as a guest.

He stayed at the Whitlows' through the crop year of 1940. Mr. Whitlow died that summer. After the place was sold and Mrs. Whitlow settled in town, Tom struck a deal with Ernest Russet from up about Sycamore. Ernest and Naomi Russet were good people, we had known them a long time, and they had a good farm. Going there was a step up in the world for Tom. He soon found favor with the Russets, which not everybody could have done, and before long, having no children of their own, they'd made practically a son of him.

After Tom had been with them a while, the Russets invited us to come for Sunday dinner. Jarrat wouldn't go, of course, but Nathan and I did. The Russets' preacher, Brother Milby, and his wife were there too, a spunky couple. I took a great liking to Mrs. Milby. It was a good dinner and we had a good time. Ernest Russet was the right man for Tom, no mistake about that. He was a fine farmer. The right young man could learn plenty from him.

By the time he went to the Russets, Tom was probably as near to the right young man as the country had in it. He had got his growth and filled out, and confidence had come into his eyes. He was a joy to look at.

One Sunday afternoon after the weather was warm and the spring work well started, he paid us a visit. Grandpa had died the summer before, so now it was just Grandma and Nathan and me still at home, and it was a sadder place. But we were glad to see Tom and to be together; we sat out on the porch and talked a long time.

Tom got up finally as if to start his hitchhike back to the Russets', and so I wasn't quite ready when he said he thought he'd go over to see his dad.

That fell into me with sort of a jolt. I hadn't been invited, but I said, "Well, I'll go with you."

So we went. We crossed the hollow, and clattered up onto the back porch, and Tom knocked on the kitchen door. Jarrat must have been in the kitchen, for it wasn't but seconds until there he was, his left hand still on the door knob and a surprised look on his face. Myself, I wasn't surprised yet, but I was expecting to be. I could feel my hair trying to rise up under my hat. I took a glance at Tom's face, and he was grinning at Jarrat. My hair relaxed and laid down peacefully again when Tom stuck out his hand. It was a big hand he stuck out, bigger than mine, bigger than Jarrat's. Jarrat looked down at that hand like it was an unusual thing to see on the end of a man's arm. He looked up at Tom again and grinned back. And then he reached out and took Tom's hand and shook it.

————

So they made it all right. And so when the war broke out and Tom was called to the army and had to go, he could come and say freely a proper good-bye to his dad.

It wasn't long after Tom got drafted until Nathan turned eighteen, and damned if he didn't go volunteer. I was surprised, but I ought not to've been. Nathan probably could have got deferred, since his brother was already gone and farmers were needed at home, and I reckon I was counting on that. But he had reasons to go, too, that were plain enough.

Nathan and Jarrat never came to an actual fight. Nathan, I think, had Tom's example in mind, and he didn't want to follow it. He was quieter turned than Tom, less apt to give offense. But Jarrat was hard for his boys to get along with. He just naturally took up too much of the room they needed to grow in. He was the man in the lead, the man going away while everybody else was still coming. His way was the right way, which in fact it pret' near always was, but he didn't have the patience of a henhawk.

"Let's go!" he'd say. If you were at it with him and you hesitated a minute: "Let's go! Let's go!"

When we were young and he would say that, I'd say back to him,

"Les Go's dead and his wife's a widder.

You be right good and you might get her."

But nobody was going to say that back to him anymore, not me, much less Nathan.

After Jarrat's fight with Tom, I would now and again try to put in a word for Nathan. "Why don't you let him alone? Give him a little head room. Give him time to be ready."

And Jarrat would say, "Be ready, hell! Let him be started."

It didn't take much of that, I knew, to be a plenty. When Nathan came back from the war his own man, Jarrat did get out of his way, and they could work together, but for the time being Nathan needed to be gone. Of course he got a bellyful of bossing in the army, but it at least didn't come from his dad. He also had a brotherly feeling that he ought to go where Tom had gone. Grandma was dead by then. There was nothing holding him. So I reckon he went because he thought he had to, but I didn't want him to. For one thing, it would leave us short-handed. For another, I would miss him. For another, I was afraid.

As it turned out, Nathan never saw Tom again. They kept Nathan on this side till nearly the end of the war, but they gave Tom some training and taught him to drive a bulldozer and shipped him straight on across the waters into the fight. He was killed the next year. I know a few little details of how it happened, but they don't matter.

It came about, anyhow, that in just a couple of years the old house was emptied of everybody but me. It took me a while to get used to being there by myself. When I would go in to fix my dinner or at night, there wouldn't be a sound. I could *hear* the quiet. And however quiet I tried to be, it seemed to me I rattled. I didn't like the quiet, for it made me sad, and so did the little noises I made in it. For a while I couldn't hardly bring myself to trap the mice, I so needed to have something stirring there besides me. All my life I've hunted and fished alone, even worked alone. I never minded being by myself outdoors. But to be alone in the house, a place you might say is used to talk and the sounds of somebody stirring about in it all day, that was lonesome. As I reckon Jarrat must have found out a long time ago and, like himself, just left himself alone to get used to it. I've been, all in all, a lucky man, for the time would be again when the old house would be full of people, but that was long a-coming. For a while there it was just Jarrat and me living alone together, he in his house on one side of the hollow, me in mine on the other. I could see his house from my house, and he could see mine from his. But we didn't meet in either house, his or mine. We met in a barn or a field, wherever the day's work was going to start. When quitting time came we went our ways separately home. Of course by living apart we were keeping two houses more or less alive, and maybe there was some good in that.

The difference between us was that I wasn't at home all the time. When the work would let up, or on Saturday evenings and Sundays, for I just flat refused to work late on Saturday or much at all on Sunday, I'd be off to what passed with me for social life or to the woods or the river. But Jarrat was at home every day. *Every* day. He never went as far as Port William except to buy something he needed.

If you work about every day with somebody you've worked with all your life, you'd be surprised how little you need to talk. Oh, we swapped work with various ones—Big Ellis, the Rowanberrys, and others—and that made for some sociable times along, and there would be good talk then. But when it was just Jarrat and me, we would sometimes work without talking a whole day, or maybe two together. And so when he got the government's letter about Tom, he didn't say but two words. We were working here at my place. After dinner, when he walked into the barn, carrying the letter in his hand, he said, "Sit down."

I sat down. He handed me the letter, and it felt heavy in my hands as a stone. After I read it—"killed in action"—and handed it back, the whole damned English language just flew away in the air like a flock of black-birds.

For a long time neither one of us moved. The daily sounds of the world went on, sparrows in the barn lot, somebody's bull way off, the wind in the eaves, but around us was this awful, awful silence that didn't have one word in it.

I looked at Jarrat finally. He was standing there blind as a statue. He had Tom's life all inside him now, as once it had been all inside Lettie. Now it was complete. Now it was finished.

And then, for the first and last time I said it to him, I said, "Let's go." The day's work was only half finished. Having nothing else we could do, we finished it.

*   *   *

What gets you is the knowledge, and it sometimes can fall on you in a clap, that the dead are gone absolutely from this world. As has been said around here over and over again, you are not going to see them here anymore, ever. Whatever was done or said before is done or said for good. Any questions you think of that you ought to've asked while you had a chance are never going to be answered. The dead know, and you don't.

And yet their absence puts them with you in a way they never were before. You even maybe know them better than you did before. They stay with you, and in a way you go with them. They don't live on *in* your heart, but your heart knows them. As your heart gets bigger on the inside, the world gets bigger on the outside. If the dead had been alive only in this world, you would forget them, looks like, as soon as they die. But you remember them, because they always were living in the other, bigger world while they lived in this little one, and this one and the other one are the same. You can't see this with your eyes looking straight ahead. It's with your side vision, so to speak, that you see it. The longer I live, and the better acquainted I am among the dead, the better I see it. I am telling what I know.

It's our separatedness and our grief that break the world in two. Back when Tom got killed and the word came, I had never thought of such things. That time would have been hard enough, even if I had thought of them. Because I hadn't, it was harder.

That night after supper I lit the lantern and walked over to Jarrat's and sat with him in the kitchen until bedtime. I wasn't invited. I was a volunteer, I reckon, like Nathan. If it had been just me and I needed company, which I did, I could have walked to town and sat with the talkers in the pool room or the barber shop. But except that I would go to sit with him, Jarrat would have sat there in his sorrow entirely by himself and stared at the wall or the floor. I anyhow denied him that.

I went back every night for a long time. There was nothing else to do. There wasn't a body to be spoken over and buried to bring people together, and to give Tom's life a proper conclusion in Port William. His body was never going to be in Port William again. It was buried in some passed-over battlefield in Italy, somewhere none of us had ever been and would never go. The word was passed around, of course. People were sorry, and they told us. The neighbor women brought food, as they do. But mainly there was just the grieving, and mainly nobody here to do it but Jarrat and me.

There was a woman lived here, just out the road, a good many years ago. She married a man quite a bit older—well, he was an old man, you just as well say—and things went along and they had a little boy. In four or five years the old man died. After that, you can imagine, the little boy was all in all to his mother. He was her little man of the house, as she called him, and in fact he was the world to her. And then, when he wasn't but nine or ten years old, the boy took awfully sick one winter, and he died, and we buried him out there on the hill at Port William beside his old daddy.

We knew that the woman was grieved to death, as we say, and everybody did for her as they could. What we didn't know was that she really was grieving herself to death. It's maybe a little hard to believe that people can die of grief, but they do.

After she died, the place had to be sold. I went out there with Big Ellis and several others to set the place to rights and get the tools and the household stuff set out for the auction. When we got to the room that had been the little boy's, it was like opening a grave. It had been kept just the way it was when he died, except she had gathered up and put there everything she'd found that reminded her of him: all his play pretties, every broom handle he rode for a stick horse, every rock or feather or string she knew he had played with. I still remember the dread we felt just going into that room, let alone moving the things, or throwing them away. Some of them we had to throw away.

I understood her then. I understood her better after Tom was dead. When a young man your heart knows and loves is all of a sudden gone, never to come back, the whole place reminds you of him everywhere you look. You dread to touch anything for fear of changing it. You fear the time you know is bound to come, when the look of the place will be changed entirely, and if the dead came back they would hardly know it, or not recognize it at all.

Even so, this place is not a keepsake just to look at and remember. You can't stop just because you're carrying a load of grief and would like to stop, or don't care if you go on or not. Jarrat nor I either didn't stop. This world was still asking things of us that we had to give.

It was maybe the animals most of all that kept us going, the good animals we depended on, that depended on us: our work mules, the cattle, the sheep, the hogs, even the chickens. They were a help to us because they didn't know our grief but just quietly lived on, suffering what they suffered, enjoying what they enjoyed, day by day. We took care of them, we did what had to be done, we went on.

Not a Tear (1945)

Dick Watson was my grandfather Catlett's farm hand, and he was my friend. When he died, I did not go to his funeral. I was in school. It occurred to nobody that I should have gone, but I should have. I wish I had.

My father and Grandpa Catlett did go to the funeral and so I know about it. Maybe other white people were there too, about that I don't know. But it is important to know that at least two were there. This would have been the fall of 1945, and so everybody there belonged to the old division of the races we came to call "segregation." They had been born in it, had lived in it, partly at least had been made as they were by it. And yet that formal and legal division, applied after all to people who were neighbors, made within itself exceptions to itself. And so they came together, the white with the black, in duty to Dick Watson, at one in loss and in sorrow.

"Well, sir, it was perfect, Andy. It was just right," my father said to comfort me, for he knew I was grieving. "That preacher was splendid."

From time to time he recited parts of the sermon to me as he remembered it, for he could not forget, and I have not forgot. I will try to line it out as the preacher sounded it. "It was not a speech," my father said. "It was a song."

Standing above the open coffin in which Dick's body lay in his Sunday clothes in its stillness and Aunt Sarah Jane who sat in the black dress of her sorrow nearby, the preacher gestured broadly with his opened hands, all the while looking at the people, as if to see if they knew already what he was going to say. He said:

This ain't him.
He ain't here.
This ain't no more our brother,
our beloved. For he
ain't here. Where he is
all is well.
All is well with Dick Watson.
All is well.
He has come to a door
to a mansion
didn't have to knock
to get in. He had heard
that voice.
He has heard, O Lord,
thy voice.
"Brother Watson, come in.
Well done.
Well done, thou good
and faithful servant.
Well done. Enter
into the joy of thy Lord."

"*Something* like that," my father said. "For one man can't do it by himself. He has got to have help. He has got to have inspiration, and help too from the other people."

The sermon took a while. The people took up the preacher's phrases and sang them back to him. They called out to him to encourage him:

"Amen!"

"Yes!"

"Amen!"

They shouted to him to go ahead, to preach it, for he had it right.

At first some of the people were crying, and Grandpa cried with them. And then, as the voice of the preacher called them, a sense of triumph grew among them, and the tone shifted. Heaven and earth drew together. The preacher said:

Blessèd!
Blessèd are the poor
in spirit, for theirs
is the kingdom of heaven.
Blessèd!
Blessèd are they that mourn,
for they shall be comforted.
Children,
don't cry no more.
Sister Sarah Jane,
don't cry no more.
Our brother,
where he is,
he don't hear no crying.
For his burden is lifted.
For freedom
has come to him
and rest.
For where he is
ain't no crying there.
Not a sigh.
Not a tear.

The preacher stood then with his hands again opened. A beautiful voice sang back from among the people: "Nooo, not a tear." The other agreeing voices quieted and fell away. While the preacher regarded the people with his hands still lifted, my father said, an immense quiet came upon them, and the freedom of Dick Watson in that moment was present to them all.

They sang a hymn, they said a prayer, and then they let him go.

The Dark Country (1948)

Burley Coulter is bone-tired, thirsty, hungry, lost, and entirely happy. He has his worries and his griefs, but for the time being they are not on his mind, nor is his workaday life. All that is eight or ten hours behind him, a long time yet ahead of him, and a world away.

He is somewhere, he believes, way up in the headwaters of Willow Run, far out of his home territory. Since his hounds last treed, at a branchy white oak where an upland pasture dropped off to a wooded bluff, he has been walking along a seldom-used farm road on the crest of a long ridge. The road has so far led him past a cornfield and a tobacco patch, both sowed in barley, and a big field of grass and clover, mowed early for hay, then pastured, now deserted. That is as much as he knows of where he is.

Except for the ambient glow of the coal oil lantern he carries in his hand, the night is perfectly dark. It is too late, or too early, for a house light to show, and the sky is thickly clouded. Beside him his shadow stretches on the ground, disappearing before it is complete into the greater darkness. Two hounds walk with him, and he is alert to keep them close; he does not want them to start hunting again.

He, his brother, Jarrat, and Jarrat's son, Nathan—mostly just the three of them—had stood at the stripping room benches from early winter until a few days ago, already February of 1948, preparing the previous summer's tobacco crop for market. The work had been steady, consoling in a way, for it was always there, but it was confining too, and finally they were weary of it, happy to be done. They had gone, the day before, to the warehouse in Hargrave to see the last of it sold.

When he got home, having for a change nothing else to do, Burley did his chores early, putting out hay for his cattle and his mules, and corn for his hogs. The old house, once he was back in it, felt too empty. As often, now that he was living in it alone, it did not satisfy. After a bright cold spell, the weather had turned cloudy with a warming wind. The snowless frozen ground had thawed on top and grown slick. He did not even bother to build up the fires.

He took off the fairly new work clothes he had worn to the warehouse and put on older ones. He strapped on his long-barreled .22 pistol in its shoulder holster and dropped a few extra cartridges into his pants pocket. He took his everyday felt hat and the hunting coat he wore as a work jacket from their nail by the back door and put them on. Into one pocket of the coat he put a flashlight, and into another, in a paper sack, six cold biscuits made by himself just the way they had been made by his mother and her mother and her mother, except maybe with less shortening so they'd be a little more durable. He felt his pants pockets to make sure he had matches and his knife. The knife was a heavy one with the handle worn smooth and pale; it had two blades that were razor sharp and a dull blade that he used for scraping and digging. The knife as much belonged to his sense of himself as either of his thumbs. He shook the lantern beside his ear to make sure it was full of oil. At the edge of the porch he sat down and pulled on and buckled his overshoes. He stood again, picked up the lantern, called the dogs, and headed down into the woods along Katy's Branch.

Behind him now was not just the old weatherboarded log house that he had thought of as empty since the death of his mother, who all his life before had been its presiding genius; the old crop year too was at last behind him. It had been a good enough year. The crop had been, he would say, better than the year, and had sold well, thanks to their nearly perfect work, which Burley does not credit to himself. It was owing, as he knows and will readily say, to his brother and nephew, to their love of the work, their sense of the beauty of it, their passion. Burley's own submission to work was characterized, not by reluctance, let us say, but by a division of mind; he would have settled for less perfection. And yet, in the background of his present eagerness, there was satisfaction with the completed year, the crop beautifully cultivated and beautifully handled.

In this completion he began to feel the opening of what he recognized as freedom, unobstructing by the least taint of guilt or regret his wish to do exactly what he was doing. He went down through the pasture toward the hollow they called Stepstone, which descended steeply to Katy's Branch. When he reached the woods, the old house and its outbuildings on the ridgetop, and the open slope also, were out of sight. The woods enclosed him, quieted the light, and changed the way he felt. It was as if an old world had passed away and another, forever new, had risen up around him. The air bore the smells of the woods, of leaf mold stirred by his footsteps, of the thawing ground. The new, warmer air was playing its way into the spaces around him as if excited by its own arrival. He seemed to breathe into himself the presence of his country.

Burley was a man always aware of the neighborhood of the people and the creatures—in his thoughts he calls it "the membership" — and of his own living and moving in it. Always when he was outdoors, where he had been in most of his waking hours all his life, and especially when he was in the woods, he was aware that he was more seen than seeing. In the woods he kept company with the original life of the place, a life intricately knowing of itself, even of him, but never to be fully known by him.

Soon after he entered the woods he began checking a line of traps that he kept set and watched over through the winter. He was a man of two worlds: the world that produced crops and animals by his work, and the world that by his knowledge merely, and to his pleasure, gave him pelts, wild meat, fish, wild fruits and nuts, herbs, and good places to be.

He approached the traps only near enough to see that they had caught nothing and were still set. Not until he came to the small pool in Katy's Branch just at the outfall of the Stepstone hollow did he find a trap gone from its place and a mink caught and drowned in the pool. He reset the trap, quickly skinned the mink, turned the pelt furside out, and flung the water from it before putting it into the game pocket of his coat. He washed his hands in the pool, wiping them dry first on the grass and then his sleeves. That done, he remained kneeling where he was, listening.

The thaw was a little new yet, the ground yet a little cold, for the best tracking. And it was still too early for the night creatures to be stirring. But down the branch crisscrossing between the slopes on either side, he could hear his hounds. They were indulging their daytime hobby of hunting rabbits. As they well knew, he did not approve, and he thought they sounded embarrassed.

He listened a while, telling himself where the dogs were, what they were doing, how they were moving, seeing them precisely in his mind's eye. They were a large bluetick, a he-dog, with a deep resonant voice, who had a nickname but not a name. From the first bawl out of him when he first opened on a track, Burley had been calling him Frog, wishing at the same time for a name with more dignity, but finding none. By now old Frog had begun looking like a dog whose name was Frog. The other was a black bitch, Jet, sweet-mouthed but of uncertain breeding. Perhaps he had thought, when she was offered to him as a pup, that he himself had no standing from which to disdain off-the-record breeding. He remained on his knees by the little pool. He slowly turned his head to the distances all around. He looked, he listened, he let the quiet come to him.

Down the branch the dogs were speaking from time to time, one here, one there, never together, and there was no excitement in their voices, or even much interest.

Burley got up and brushed off his knees. He set off slowly down the branch. The dogs had gone that way, it was downhill, and one direction was as good as another. He took his time, listening and looking about, breathing and savoring the rich air. Because he was in no hurry, because any direction was as good as another, because it was a good place without a wrong turn anywhere, every breath brought smells that he sorted and recognized, that brought the country into him.

Before too long he met Jet coming down through the trees on the slope to his right, not in much of a hurry. She stopped and looked at him to see what he would have to say.

He said, "Come on," without changing his pace or direction, and Jet fell in behind him—glad, he thought, of an excuse to quit pretending to hunt.

Raising his voice a little, he said, "Come on, Frog," and soon the bluetick was walking behind him too.

"You all are out of business," he said. "It'll be a while yet, I expect."

He spoke to the dogs casually, not looking back at them, as if they perhaps were other humans. And they listened, following, glancing up at him, as if he perhaps were another dog. They all three seemed to have concluded to their satisfaction that there was as yet no reason to hurry.

Burley said no more. They took their time, going on down the hollow, finding the least obstructed way. From time to time Burley walked in the creek itself, stepping from stone to stone. Presently they came to a cleared strip of bottomland and beside it a tobacco barn built when Burley was hardly more than a boy. He lingered there, looking carefully about, and then went on.

As they came near the house of Gideon and Ida Crop, to keep from rousing their dogs, Burley turned away from the branch in a slow swerve that finally headed him back upstream along the side of the hollow opposite to his own place. Allowing the dogs to range ahead again and more or less following them, he took a long upward slant through what they would still call for a while the old Merchant place, though Roger Merchant, the last of that line, was dead. When dark had about completely fallen, he lit his lantern.

Not long after that, and hardly bothering to comment, the dogs treed a possum in a little cedar. Burley set down the lantern and took out the flashlight. He walked around the tree, saw what he was looking for, and then, shining the light beam over the sights of his pistol and onto the possum, precisely made the shot. Shortly, working in the light of the lantern, he emptied the possum out of its hide and stuffed that hide also into his coat, adding in his mind the small worth of the possum to the several dollars he would get for the mink. He liked the money he got by his hunting and trapping. He thought of it as "free money," for one thing, but it seemed to him also to be more real than the money he earned from farming. He would know exactly where every cent of it came from—from what animal and what spot of the country.

Frog and Jet, having in their youth outgrown any great excitement over possums, were long gone. Like the dogs, Burley was not greatly excited by possums, but, also like the dogs, he was hunting now. Everything was changed. The dark was full of possible directions. He was intently listening. He stood, again brushing the leaf litter off his knees, and continued his slanting climb up the slope in the direction he supposed the dogs had gone.

He heard from them presently, but they were on a cold track, of historical interest only. He let them worry at it, glad to be notified from time to time of their whereabouts.

When he had overtaken them a little, he called them to him, this time to make a wide circuit around the Merchant house, which since Roger's death has been, as Jarrat says, "infested with half the damned tribe of Berlews and a pack of half-wild, half-starved damned Berlew dogs."

For a while as he made his circuit, dropping back toward Katy's Branch and crossing the Port William road, he could hear the Berlews' dogs barking at the Lord knew what threat to Berlew peace and tranquility. Jet and Frog heard them too, and Frog started a low grumble that was ready to become a full-voiced challenge.

"You *hush*," Burley said. He remembered one day driving with Jarrat past the old Merchant house, and there were Berlews at every window just like Christmas candles. "What the Hell are they looking for?" Jarrat said. "The end of the world?"

After they no longer heard any commotion from the Berlews, and still a while after that, Burley said, "Go on."

The dogs left him, and he too went on, walking generally on the level now along the wooded bluff. It grew quiet all around. Listening, he could hear only the sounds of his own steps, just as he could see only within the slowly advancing room of light from the lantern. And yet he knew precisely where he was, for in the dark he was moving also in his mind's map of the country and his own passages over it. He even had a notion of where his dogs were, but he did not know that exactly, and so the whole darkness and all the silence were of interest to him.

And then, making one place out in the distance exact and paramount, Frog bellowed as though stung, and Burley heard him as with every vein and nerve.

He thought, "Now he knows what he's talking about. Now he believes what he's saying."

Jet agreed. There was a brisk race then, a way through the dark as clear to the dogs as if lighted. Burley stood still to listen. For a while then he was empty of himself, his mind gone out into the dark with the dogs, knowing where they were and how it was with them. He did not move again until their voices told him, "Treed!"

He went to them, their cries growing in excitement as he came up. It was a coon this time, a young one with a nice pelt. Burley added it to those of the mink and the possum, and soon was on his way again.

Burley Coulter is, by nature perhaps, a sympathetic man. He has lived much under the influence of sympathy, and it has taught him much—though, as he has often said, he has never learned anything until he had to. It is possible to feel a certain sorrow for the life of an animal taken by hunting or trapping, just as for the life of a slaughtered hog or chicken. Burley feels this always. He would just as soon not feel it, but it always comes with the same stab of consciousness: This creature loved its life, just as a man loves his. At the same time, from his earliest childhood as from the earliest childhood of humankind, there has been knowledge and acceptance: No life lives but at the cost of other lives.

Invariably the moment of consciousness comes, and the stroke of regret, and then it passes and is replaced by happiness, we could call it thanks, for the acquired good. And the love for what he takes freely from the woods and waters is his particularly and strongly. Some don't have it. Jarrat, for one, doesn't have it. He might go along with Burley now and again, for company, but not long after dark he'll be wanting to be in bed. Nathan is pretty much the same way, though he followed Burley through the woods many a night when he was a boy—until finally he got girls on his mind, and that about ended Nathan's nighttime walking in the woods.

For a while, in fact for a long time, it would more than likely be women that kept Burley himself out late at night. Come a Saturday night, women would be scattered about out there in the dark, and he would be hunting them, smelling them out, just like a hunting dog. The smells of women, when you got close enough, were almost as good as the look and feel of them. He can remember the smells of certain ones, certain girls, going all the way back maybe to when he started to school. Amongst the smells of paper and paste and ink and pencil shavings and air from the windows or smoke from the stove would drift the smells of girls, fragrant, secret, and warm.

And then it was *a* woman who was keeping him away from home at night. Kate Helen Branch. After that got started, the woman hunting wasn't quite what it had been. It wasn't sport anymore, unless you would call it that when two people are hunting for what they both know they will find. What it was was love, and Kate Helen made him say so.

"Do you love me, Burley Coulter?"

"Why, hell yes! Course I do!"

"Then why don't you tell me so?"

"Well, Kate Helen, I love you, how does that suit you?"

"*Just fine.*"

In fact it suited even him just fine. To have found somebody, a woman you loved, who loved you back—oh my! —that was fine. And too it might be that a man with *a* woman was a good bit freer in the woods at night than a man looking for women. This, he supposed, was what might be called settling down.

Though they were quiet now, the dogs would be ranging ahead of him, and he too went ahead. They had treed on the bluff at the back of what he knew as the Proudfoot place, where big old Tol Proudfoot, hero of many a good story, and his little wife, Miss Minnie, had passed their years together. Tol, who was a good farmer, had been dead five years, and his "ninety-eight acres more or less" had begun to run down, as farms are inclined to do when devoted care no longer is living on them. And just last summer Miss Minnie too had passed on from this world, leaving the place and her much-loved small house with its steep gingerbreaded gables to a fate not yet settled. Tol and Miss Minnie never had children. Their heirs were mostly strangers, great-nieces and great-nephews they had never seen.

When Burley came up to the feed barn he found the rusty can that Tol had left hanging on the wall of the barn next to the well, and he pumped himself a drink. The water was as fresh and good as he remembered it. He drank his fill, hung the can back in its place, and then, the dogs remaining quiet, he sat down on the well top. He rolled a cigarette, and then turned down the lantern flame to save oil.

The Proudfoot farm adjoined the Merchant land at the back. On the other three sides it was bounded by Katy's Branch, the Goforth Hill road and the Cotman Ridge road. The house and barn and other buildings stood on top of the ridge in the angle between the two roads. Where Burley sat, the barn was at his back and he was facing the back of the house, which faced the Cotman Ridge road. He could not see beyond the few feet dimly lit by the lantern, but he saw clearly in his mind the layout of the place and the country around. He knew the pattern of Tol's fields, the barn lots and the garden, the buildings, the driveway turning in off the county road and coming back past the house to the barn, Miss Minnie's flower patch by the cellar wall.

He said half aloud, "Miss Minnie," to summon the thought of her into his mind.

Miss Minnie had been his teacher in all the eight grades of his schooling. In that old long time he and Miss Minnie had been, we might say, philosophically opposed. Miss Minnie believed that learning was desirable; she thought that students should *love* to learn. Burley, on the contrary, believed in not learning a speck of anything until he absolutely had to. She taught him his numbers and letters, she taught him about syllables, she taught him to read words one by one and then whole pages of them, and she taught him to add and subtract and multiply and divide any numbers you might mention. He did not learn any of those things because he wanted to. He learned them because she taught them to him over and over and over again until he realized that, whether he had wanted to learn them or not, he knew them. And that was the way it went for eight long years, in which it seemed to him he experienced eight good days: the last day of school in every one of those years.

By her persistence and her undiscourageable belief in the possibility of "human improvement" and the "goodness in every human heart," she taught him a great deal that he was unwilling to learn. He still remembers all she taught him, and now, as she often prophesied, he is grateful. After their long struggle was over, she had the grace, to his surprise, to remain interested in him and to be nice to him, and he finally found the grace in himself, also to his surprise, to respect her and to look for ways to be kind to her. When it popped into his mind one day that she had the full approval of her husband, Tol Proudfoot, that was a revelation, and it helped.

Sitting on the well top, he felt the presence out there in the dark of the dark and empty house, and he felt Miss Minnie's forever absence from it so recently begun.

The farm would be sold. That much Burley knew for sure. As soon as the various heirs, scattered about in their various other places, could agree on the conditions of the sale, it would be sold. And who would buy it? Would somebody buy it, and come to live in the little house, and give light to it in the evenings and the early mornings, and give the place such love and care as Tol and Miss Minnie gave it? He thought of the Merchant place, gone to the Devil by the indifference of Roger, the last of the Merchants, then bought as an "investment" by somebody who will never live on it, or maybe even see it for years at a time, and the house filled with Berlews who will use it up just by battering around in it. He thought of the good, still fixable and livable stone house under its big white oak on the Riley Harford place, empty now for years. He thought of the young men who hadn't come back after the war, some like Jarrat's boy Tom, bless his heart, like Virgil Feltner, bless his, the young gone with the old, gone forever, and others gone to city jobs and the bright lights. Burley looked through the dark and thought, and he shivered.

He had to get up, he told himself, if he was ever going to, for there was no point in just sitting there, getting stiff. Burley is fifty-two years old. Soon enough he will be fifty-three. He still has full use of himself, can still do a proper day's work, can still stay at it with younger men, daylight to dark, but he doesn't get up or down anymore without thinking about it. He is, in his mind, still a young man, sometimes still a boy, repeatedly surprised to find himself with the knowledge and the aches of a man going on fifty-three. He turned up the lantern flame and stood, grunting aloud for the luxury of doing so where nobody could hear. He walked out the driveway past the house to the road, and crossed the road and the tumbling rock fence beyond. From time to time one or the other of the dogs had mouthed, their pronouncements conjectural and far apart, but allowing him to walk now with a sense of direction.

He crossed the broad, open fields of Cotman Ridge, and before long he was in the woods again, on the near side of the Willow Run valley. And some time after that, after crossing a tributary hollow or two, he no longer had a very sure idea of where he was. He wasn't lost, maybe, but then at night you *could* get lost in that country. At night, as far as that went, you could get lost right at home. Given a little mist, say, or a little mistake at the top of the hill as you were starting for the bottom, talking to somebody maybe or hurrying to the dogs, and you could get lost right in the middle of your own farm.

He told himself the story of getting lost on the Rowanberry place one night, hunting with the Rowanberry brothers and Elton Penn. Art and Mart Rowanberry were in an argument about where they were. It was getting late, the hunt seemed to be over, and everybody was feeling a little bit concerned.

And then Elton said, *"I* know where we are."

"Where?"

"Where?"

"Right *here.*"

Burley laughed out loud, as he always does when he tells himself that story.

Wherever he was, he was pleased and oddly comforted by the weight of the pelts in his coat. At home in his barn he had a number of thin poplar boards of various sizes, square at one end, tapered and rounded at the other, and on these he would stretch and clean the hides and hang them up to dry. Burley did a good job with the hides, and he would be proud of them when the time came to sell them.

He got reminded then of the fellow who had an extra smart little hunting dog. Whenever this fellow wanted a pelt, he would show a stretching board of whatever size to the little dog. The little dog would look at the board, tear out for the woods, and pretty soon come back with a possum or coon whose hide would just fit that board. Everything went fine with this fellow, he was the envy of everybody, until the day he made the mistake of letting the little dog into the kitchen where he caught sight of the wife's ironing board. The little dog took a careful look, tore out for the woods, and nobody ever saw hide nor hair of him again.

Burley used to tell that story to Jarrat's boys, and then to his own boy, his and Kate Helen's boy, Danny, until they got too old to believe it. But Burley still thinks it's a pretty good story, and now and again he tells it to himself.

Well, he was in fact lost, he decided, and that was fine. It was a big country now. The more lost you are in it, the bigger the country is. The bigger the country, the more he rejoiced in the size of it.

He was on a hillside of fairly sizeable trees that, like most hillsides of the country he knew, had once been cleared and cropped, maybe more than once. He was just loafing along, waiting to hear from the dogs, looking around at what he could see by lantern light. The night was still thawing, but it was far from warm, and the chill had begun to creep through his clothes. Here and there on the slope were piles of rocks that had been carried and heaped up when the ground was prepared for planting in some springtime a long time ago.

That kind of work belonged to the past now. It had about ended with the Depression, with the beginning of the war, and it seemed unlikely ever to be done again. Burley hoped it would never be done again. He had done it himself in his time, and he knew how hard it was, how damaging, and how poorly paid.

"Wasn't a thing automatic into it," he said to himself.

But he sought out one of the rock piles, one of the taller ones that would give some shelter from the flow of cold air that was moving down the slope. He found one that suited. He set the lantern on top of the pile and searched about for dead wood. Soon he had gathered and broken into proper lengths a good supply of fallen branches, big and little, and a rootless chunk of a stump for a backlog. Against the backlog he built over heaped-up dry leaves a lean-to of little sticks and then bigger ones. He struck a match and presently had a brisk small fire going about its work of light and warmth. He leveled a good, broad, flat rock to sit on, gathered more fuel to where he could reach it without getting up, extinguished the lantern, and sat down.

He made himself at home. He had built the fire for warmth, but now he saw that he had needed it also for company. It made a cheerfulness all around, lighting the near sides of the trees and bushes and the branches overhead and throwing their shadows in tangles out into the dark. Burley loved a fire as he loved a good-working mule and a johnboat—good, useful, wondrous things—and he let the living light and warmth come to him and fill his mind. He had sat many nights beside such fires, sometimes by himself, sometimes with other fellows, maybe a little whiskey passing around, and the talk sometimes so good you half hoped the hounds wouldn't call you away.

And there had been times when the company he had wasn't fellows at all, and no dogs either to interrupt. It had been just him and Kate Helen

and a little fire and maybe a little something to cook over it. That Kate
Helen would come along with him at night that way, and be just as much
there, wherever they were, as he was, that was another one of his rev-
elations. Maybe he hadn't taken any women seriously before. Maybe he
hadn't intended to take her seriously, but it turned out that he did. Kate
Helen reached into him. She found his heart and wrung it so that he would
never again cease to feel her hold on it.

He knew a certain big old hollow sycamore. The tree is still standing in
fact, on the lower end of the old Cuthbert place: a grand, great old tree,
hard to tell how old, with a hollow in it big as a room, big enough for a
man and a woman to lie down in, with an opening, as if intended for a
doorway, toward the creek, a little fire outside the opening, a fine spring
night with half a moon, the sound of the creek running, and a man and a
woman together that way, *happy* that way, happy to sleep close and wake
up still together, still happy, the fire gone out and the moon low, quiet,
quiet, and a man such as he was, old enough to know better, maybe, and
yet still plenty young, head entirely emptied out and filled entirely up again
with happiness and closeness and generosity and welcome, Kate Helen
there with him at the end of the one true known way of his life.

He thought, "Oh my! Old Marster come up with something good as
that, maybe what they say about Him is right. Not all of it, maybe. A lot
of it. Whoo! Who knows? But something so good." He said aloud, "Mnh!"
And then, "Mnh-mnh-mnh!"

Their boy, Danny Branch, you might say came out of that old hollow tree.
Danny is sixteen now. To the amusement of Burley, and some others,
Danny still calls him "Uncle Burley," as Nathan still does. Danny is a good
boy, has a girl, Lyda, and is in what he is determined will be his last year
of school. He is already raising his own crop, and he has at Burley's place
his own team of mules. He wants to get out in the world on his own and
farm. Burley and Kate Helen, in their various ways, living apart in their
unofficial marriage, have brought the boy up, teaching him and requiring
of him as they have known to do. And he—too much like Burley, as Burley
fears—has cared far more for what they have taught him than what he has
learned in school. He wants to live free. He seems to know, better than

Burley or anybody else, and maybe without exactly having been taught, what to do about this modern world they're in, with its machines coming everywhere and the people going. He pays it little mind, and no respect.

"What do you reckon? Could the place where a boy was got have something to do with the way he is? A boy that comes out of a hollow tree is maybe going to be different from one that comes out of a house in town or the back seat of an automobile, or even out of a proper bed in a farmhouse."

It has seemed to Burley that a man with a sixteen-year-old boy ought to be worried, but he has never been able to settle on a way of worrying about Danny. Maybe he ought to worry about him quitting school as soon as the law allows, but Danny already has more school than Burley and is better at books too than Burley ever was. And the boy has a way of stepping up to the mark before anybody can expect him to. It even looks like maybe he has settled on this girl Lyda, a good-looking girl too, with blue eyes that look straight at you until you blink.

The boys Burley had really worried about had been Tom and Nathan when they were in the war. He had worried about Tom until Tom was killed, which is a bad way to stop worrying about somebody. He had worried about Nathan until the war ended and Nathan got home, and then he kept worrying about him. Nathan came home and went to work, went right back into it with Jarrat and Burley as if there had been no interruption. But when he wasn't at work, it appeared like he couldn't come to rest, couldn't find a place to stop. And he was god-awful quiet about whatever had happened to him. He was like his daddy and had never had a big amount to say, but you couldn't get a peep out of him about the war.

"I reckon it got pretty bad over yonder."

"Yep."

But maybe things have started to get better for Nathan. Burley is afraid to say even to himself what he thinks Nathan now has on his mind, but now maybe he has started circling a place he wants to light.

Burley said aloud, "Well, bless him!"

And then he said, "Bless 'em *all!*"

For a tremor of love for the three boys, the dead and the living, had passed through him and shaken him.

Propped as he was on the pile of cold rocks, he could hardly have been surrounded by warmth. But it was a good fire, and its warmth had penetrated deeply into him. Having become still and warm after his long walk, late in the night as it was, he drowsed in his thoughts.

He slept, and he dreamed he was where he was, wherever that was. It was such a dream as he had never dreamed within walls, under a roof. He dreamed that the trees stood around him in the firelight, reaching above the light into the darkness, in their own long winter dream. He dreamed that the fire was the light of all the knowledge he was dreaming. In his dream the fire dwindled and cooled, and the darkness drew in. And then Jet called into his dream to awaken him, her voice urgent and a long way off. She cried again, and Frog sang a long bass note in agreement. "Yes!" Frog sang. "She's right!"

For some time Burley did not know whether he slept or woke. And then he was for sure awake, knowing where he was, wherever that was, sitting up on his flat rock, yawning, smacking his mouth, looking around in the dwindled firelight for his lantern. Using a little twig, he transferred fire to the lantern and adjusted the wick, and then he set off on his long walk to reach the dogs.

It was an old boar coon this time. He knew his business, and he made a long race of it. Twice he "marked" a tree, going up the trunk, out to the end of a long branch, dropping off, running again, and thus he delayed the hounds until Frog, who had his own cunning, made a wide circle and picked up the scent again.

Now as they walk the backbone of that slowly widening, long ridge, wherever it is, in the tiny geography of the lantern light, both man and dogs are weary. After the final tree, the dogs maybe would have run on, but Burley has kept them close, and they have by now accepted his sense that the hunting is over.

From the lay of the land, as they have felt it, walking over it, from the wear of the road as paths have gathered to it, Burley guesses that eventually they will come to a barn.

Eventually they do. Burley has half-expected to hear house dogs barking. If he had, he would have turned aside. As a courtesy to sleepers and to his pleasure, he avoids houses when he can. But now the silence remains complete. They go through a gate into what will turn out to be a barn lot, and then they have the hulk of a barn ahead of them, a greater darkness more felt than seen. Burley again takes out the flashlight and carefully shines it around, moving so as to see clearly past the barn.

There is no house in sight. The barn stands by itself on the ridge that extends on farther than the light can reach. Burley hasn't formed his thoughts into words for a long time, not since he woke by the remains of the fire, and he does not do so now. But now that he is sure of his isolation, need comes upon him. He needs to drink, eat, and sleep.

Within the barn lot, close beside the barn, there is a second lot, only a few feet square, planked off to enclose a cistern with a chain pump. Beyond the fence there is a half-barrel used for a drinking trough, now emptied and turned on its side. Burley goes through the little gate in the plank fence. He looks around for a can or something to drink from, but finds none. He cups his left hand under the spout of the pump, and cranking with his right hand, bends and drinks. Drinking big swallows of the clean-tasting, teeth-aching water, he floods his innards, he gratifies himself. He drinks until he can hold no more, and then straightens and wipes his mouth on his sleeve.

The two hounds have sat politely and watched him drink. Now they continue to watch him, as with forbearance, not moving.

"You all thirsty?" he says. "Well, I reckon so."

He is wearing what was once a good felt hat, now misshapen by use, but still a pretty good one. He takes it off, punches in the crown, pumps water into the concavity, and offers it. The dogs drink, Frog first, then Jet. Burley flings away the surplus water, restores his hat by punching out the crown, and puts it on again.

He then sits down on the concrete top of the cistern, leans back against the pump, and feels into the pocket where he put the biscuits. They're still there in their paper sack, to his relief, for he hasn't thought of them since he left home. He imagines that the dogs have lunched on fresh meat in the lags after treeing, but he doesn't think it right to eat in front of them without offering them something. Having seen no sign that dogs can count, he gives them a biscuit apiece and keeps the other four for himself.

He eats the biscuits slowly, with relish, for they taste good and, as his friend Art Rowanberry often says, there is a world of strength in a biscuit.

He is not thinking in words, but only knowing as he knows. The sky is still overcast. It is dark as dark can be. He has no way of knowing the time, except for the instinct that tells him it is now well on the morning side of midnight. He is not going to make it home for his morning chores.

There was a time maybe that would have been a worry, if at that time he had been much inclined to worry. That was when Burley and Jarrat had not quite seen eye to eye, when Jarrat, knowing that Burley hadn't made it in, would say, "If it suits him to let it go to the Devil, let it go to the Devil." But that time is gone. Jarrat, in his mostly silence, still carries his old griefs, his loneliness, his rage for work. But they get along now. They grieve some of the same griefs now. And now Burley is dependable mostly and, when not dependable, predictable. In the morning, guessing that Burley probably will have disappeared, Jarrat will walk across the hollow and do his chores for him, and won't feel righteous enough even to mention it.

When he has eaten all the biscuits and again pumped himself a drink, he goes into the barn, taking great care with the lantern. It is a feed barn, an old one well kept up, with a hayloft, a small corn crib, four horse stalls, and a large pen for feeding cattle. The cattle have been sold, or moved nearer home where maybe, so far into the winter, there is more hay. Everywhere are the signs and traces of a good farmer, somebody who knows what he is doing and likes doing it.

Along one wall of the cattle pen there is a manger with two-by-four stanchions. It still has hay in it, fairly fresh, still fragrant. The dogs, knowing Burley, lie down under the manger and curl up. Burley extinguishes the lantern. He stands to let the dark complete itself, and then, feeling his way, he climbs between two stanchions into the manger. Before he has completed the deep nest he has in his mind, he is already sleeping.

A New Day (1949)

For Mary and Stan Flitner

Elton Penn thought Sunday was a good idea, not that he was apt to be found in church. Like many farmers, he knew he lived in the presence of mystery and of wonders, and he responded with his version of reverence, but he was not a churchman. He liked the idea of Sunday because six days of work, the way he went at it, were about enough for anybody. He was glad of a good excuse to rest on the seventh day. There were Sundays when, as they said around Port William, "the ox was in the ditch," and Elton would have to work, but that could put thirteen hard days in a row. It pleased him to be able to stop on Sunday. "Six days *ought* to be enough," I often heard him say, "and they *are* enough."

His problem was that he couldn't rest at home. When he tried to sit and be still—or, worse, attempted just to wander around—at home, pretty soon he would see some job that needed to be done, and first thing he knew he would be doing it. Elton had a weakness, you might say, for work. Unlike some people born and brought up to the work of farming, Elton loved it. When he saw work that needed doing, he wanted to be the one who did it. With him there was never much time between thinking of it and starting in to do it.

To rest he needed to go someplace else. There were various places he would go. Sometimes he would even go to Port William to sit with the loafers, and that way he learned many things of interest. But loafing in town, maybe because some of the loafers loafed faithfully every day, would begin to seem to him less restful than merely idle, and he would become dissatisfied. The resting place that most suited him was Arthur and Martin Rowanberry's place down at the lower end of the Sand Ripple valley below Port William.

Not so long after the war had ended and Art had made it home, both of the elder Rowanberrys had died. In the early spring of 1946, Mr. Early Rowanberry died in the night, having worked all day the day before. A little more than a year later, Miss Stella, to whom nothing had seemed quite right after Mr. Early's departure, followed him out of this world. With the parents gone, Art and Mart had stayed on in the old house, sharing the housework and batching it out together tolerably well.

And now it was 1949, and the bachelors' household down at the Rowanberry place had become an established thing, taken for granted in Port William. Mart, the younger brother by five years, enjoyed going places, and he had a longtime girlfriend, Oma Settle from down by Hargrave, but nobody expected him to get married.

His brother was in some ways his opposite. Art Rowanberry was born in 1905. He had been an old soldier, an "old man" among the boys with whom he had fought the war. When he had at last got out of Bastogne, his travels, as far as he was concerned, were over. He traveled on, under orders, to the wound that took him out of the war and nearly out of the world. When he was strong enough again, he traveled home. And that pretty much was that. He had seen by then as much of the world as he wanted to see, except for the stretch of country between Bird's Branch and Katy's Branch, and from Port William and Goforth to the river, which was home to him far more than the great nation he had fought for. After he came back from the war and the government was finished with him except for taxes, he would go to Port William or Hargrave if he had to, but for pleasure he stayed home.

What the two brothers had in common was the boundary of land—arable ridges and creek bottom, wooded slopes and hollows—that Columbus Festus Rowanberry, their grandfather's grandfather, had received for his service in the War of Independence. They had the place, and the ways of it, that they were born to. They had the farming of it, which they thought of as work. And they had the free hunting and gathering from it and the fishing from the river, about as strenuous as work but which they thought of as rest.

They were good men, the Rowanberrys, work-hardened from earliest boyhood, good at their work, and well-furnished with knowledge of their place and neighborhood. Like Elton, they honored Sundays by their rest, which included various pleasures. Their rest had about it always the sense of having been earned, and so it was in their rest that Elton too could rest. With them he loved to sit and talk, inside by the stove in cold weather, out on the porch overlooking the creek valley if the weather was fine, allowing the time to go by without wishing it would go faster or slower, or even thinking of it.

On many a Sunday morning, I sat with the three of them and some-times with Jayber Crow too on that porch, watching the light change over the little valley and listening to their talk. Because I was by far the youngest, I mostly listened. Though I was not present for the events I am going to tell about, I know about them from listening, lately and long ago.

As the winter was ending in that year of 1949, early on a rainy Sunday morning, Elton left the old Beechum place on the Bird's Branch road, where he was then living as a tenant, and headed down to the Rowanberry place. For weeks he had been kept close to home, seeing his ewes through lambing. Now it was March, and he had entered a sort of between-times. The last of his tobacco crop of the year before had been sold. The last of the lambs had been born. As soon as the weather permitted, the plow-ing and the other work of the new crop year would have to begin. It had not begun yet, but he had ahead of him the drying ground, the coming warmth, the growing light, and the relentless prompting of several things needing to be done at once. After the work was started, the various jobs fallen more or less into order, he would feel better. The thought of all of it awaiting him, unbegun, had set his teeth on edge. Or so he put it to himself. And so, leaving their old car for his wife, Mary, to drive to church, he got into his even older truck and drove out the lane.

He drove slowly, deliberately slowly, as if by doing so he could force himself to think slowly. It helped a little. He drove out the Bird's Branch road to the blacktop, went through Port William, and just beyond the town turned down the Sand Ripple road. The lane into the Rowanberry place forded the creek a couple of hundred yards from the house, but backwater from the rising river was standing deep over the ford. The creek was now crossable only by a swinging footbridge: two steel cables with split-locust joists wired between them, a narrow row of planks nailed to the joists, two number-nine wires for banisters. Elton pulled the truck out of the lane, killed the engine, and got out into the big silence and the chill of the morning. He crossed the creek on the lurching footbridge, walked up the slope to the house and around to the back. He stepped into the small enclosed back porch with its stack of firewood, a variety of outdoor clothing on a row of hooks, a lantern hanging from a nail, and a two-gallon coal oil can with a spout. He knocked twice on the kitchen door.

"Hang on," Art Rowanberry called from inside.

"It's just me," Elton said, letting himself in to keep Art from having to get up. He shut the door carefully behind him. "Morning," he said.

"Come in, come in!" Art said. "Take a chair. Good to see you back down on the creek."

Art was sitting tilted back in a straight chair by one of the kitchen windows with the Sears, Roebuck catalog opened across his lap. There was a fire in the stove, and the room was dry and warm.

"You about to make an order?"

"Well," Art said, "I was reading up on the price of socks. I've just got started on mine when the heels and toes are gone. But I'm down to some now ain't nothing but tops."

Elton unbuttoned his jacket and stood by the stove with his hands over it a moment, soaking up the warmth.

"It's a fine morning out, if you like a rainy morning," Art said.

"I don't mind a rainy morning," Elton said. "But a week of dry weather wouldn't hurt a thing."

"No. It wouldn't hurt," Art said.

Elton pulled a chair away from the table and sat down.

Art said, "I allowed you'd be playing basketball."

"No, I reckon not," Elton said, puzzled but passing it off. "Where's Mart?"

"Playing basketball."

"Basketball!" Elton said. He was grinning now at the thought of Mart playing basketball. "What's he doing playing basketball?"

"Oh, a bunch of 'em been getting together Sunday mornings and playing basketball in Hackett Dunham's barn loft. Hackett and his boys, Spence Gidwell and Tomtit, Pascal, Burley—a bunch of 'em, I don't know who all. Some of 'em play, and some of 'em watch."

"And Mart plays?" To Elton's knowledge, neither of the Rowanberry brothers had ever played basketball, at least not until now. And now Mart was thirty-nine years old. It was a late start.

"Oh, I reckon Mart's took back to running with the boys."

Of the two brothers, Elton liked best to work with Mart. He knew what to expect of Mart, they were tuned up pretty much alike. But Art interested him the most. Art did not say everything he thought, and he did a lot of thinking. He had been through a lot and had a lot to think about.

Elton said, "How come you're not down there playing with them?"

"Well, everybody needs something he don't have to do. It appears like basketball has got along well enough so far without me."

Elton passed a little more time with Art to hear how things were going with him and Mart and their dogs and other animals. And then he got up and rebuttoned his jacket. "Maybe I'll go see what they're up to." He had in fact grown intensely curious about the events in Hackett Dunham's barn.

"Oh, I imagine they'll be needing you down there," Art said. "Come back when you can stay longer." He said this in perfect good humor, but all the same, as Elton well knew, he loved the quiet and would be happy for the morning to continue as he had started it.

Hackett Dunham's farm lay below the mouth of Bird's Branch, in the angle between the creek and the river. It was a sizeable place, lying on both sides of the river road, containing some good high bottomland that never flooded, and rising up the valley side across the grassed lower slopes to the wooded bluffs along the rim. Hackett was a trader in livestock, which gave him a peculiar status in the community. People liked him. He was an affable, humorous man, never at a loss for a comeback. And yet people's liking for him shaded off into uneasiness and sometimes into a low-grade fear. It was understood that in any trade he was likely to know more than the man he was trading with. They had to assume that he was trading in his own interest and to his own advantage, which was fair enough—why else would he be trading? —but it was a little intimidating too, a little scary. He was there to be traded with, he performed a needed service, so far as could be figured out he was not dishonest. And yet a trade with him was apt to leave an aftertaste of self-doubt.

There was, for instance, a famous conversation between Burley Coulter and Big Ellis:

"Where'd you get them cows, Big?"

"Hackett Dunham."

"Well, did you get 'em worth the money?"

"Well, I don't *think* I got as good a deal as I *believe* I did."

To cap off his standing in the Port William neighborhood, Hackett Dunham was a serious and successful participant in horse-pulling contests, in Kentucky and neighboring states. A part of his trade, a very lucrative part of it too, was in horses suitable, by strength and character, for the contests. It was known locally that his reputation was wide and better than moderately high. Along with their wariness of him, people around were proud of him. He had won championships.

Though Hackett was older than Elton by four or five years, by then, in Elton's twenty-ninth year, the two of them were long past the sort of worry that Hackett so often caused. They were cousins. Their mothers were sisters, and in the maternal line back at least to the granddam there had been a quick practical intelligence that Hackett and Elton knew in themselves and recognized in each other. Neither of them, certainly, found the other in any way to be feared.

When he got to the Dunham place, Elton turned into the lane that went back past the house to Hackett's big feed barn that was partitioned into box stalls and tie stalls for horses and gated pens for other animals. There were several vehicles parked in the barn lot, one of them being Mart Rowanberry's old car. Another, of about the same prewar vintage but worse used, Elton recognized as Big Ellis's. And so Big's neighbor, Burley Coulter, was probably in attendance also.

Elton switched the engine off, and then, sure enough, he could hear a ball bouncing, loud voices, and a rush of many feet, sounds that could be coming from nowhere but the loft of the barn.

He sat, listening, a moment. And then he got out of his truck, went into the barn through the wide-open front doorway, and stepped into a tackroom full of harness and other equipment. From there he went up a set of stairs into the loft.

There was a bunch of them up there, just as Art had said, some playing, some watching. By that time of the year the loft was maybe two-thirds empty of hay. At its front end, the end away from the hay rick, was a netless iron hoop and a backboard, well made and well braced. By the look of it, Elton thought, it was a product of the blacksmith shop up at town. Hackett no doubt had had it made for his boys, June and Billy, and for Tomtit, son of Spence Gidwell who lived on the place, sharecropping and working by the day. The Dunham and Gidwell boys, and probably J. L. Safely's boys too, had been playing ball up there. And that, Elton guessed, was the way the Sunday games had started. The watchers were sitting on bales of hay along the sides of the loft.

Among them, sitting alone near the opening in the floor that Elton had come up through, was old Mr. Milt Wright, by far the unlikeliest presence in that time and place. Mr. Wright was one of the last of the generation that grew up after the Civil War. He was Hackett's wife's grandfather—"an old remnant man," he called himself—who had come to shelter with her and Hackett in his final days. He sat with his cane leaning back against his breast, his hands resting as idly on the crook of it as a pair of gloves on a clothesline. He wore what would prove to be the last thing he would ever buy: a too-large, misbuttoned army surplus overcoat that he now wore almost all year round, for his blood had got thin and he was cold all the time. The coat, Hackett would say in a mood compounded of affection and amusement, "looked like the whole damned war had been fought in it." He wore a felt hat with a punched-up crown that, before its decrepitude, might have belonged to Hackett. A stain of ambeer descended from one corner of his mouth. Hackett had known him a long time, could remember when he was strong and capable, when you could imagine him young, one of the better horsemen of his own day whose experience and judgment, as Hackett knew, were still useful. Now he had grown too old to notice himself. "He's the daddy of us all," Hackett would say in a mood part indulgence, part respect, and part mockery too sometimes of the old man's habit of speaking as a ghost: "Ay God, I've done outlived my time. Ain't nar' a man living I knowed when I was a boy."

Elton leaned to offer his hand to the old man, whom he liked and enjoyed listening to. But if Mr. Wright was looking at the players he was not seeing them. He was not seeing anything until Elton laid a hand on his shoulder and was recognized.

"Ab Penn's boy! Ay God, how are you, son?"

They shook hands. Elton greeted with a wave and a nod the several others in the row of watchers, and sat down between Burley Coulter and Big Ellis who, pleased to see him, scooted apart to make him room.

It seemed that everybody who wanted to play was playing, a full dozen by Elton's count. But it took him a while to determine who was on which side, since there was only the one goal and the players all were in work clothes. The only readily visible difference among the players was that on both teams the boys were wearing the rubber-soled shoes that they called "tennis shoes," though none of them had ever so much as seen a game of tennis, but the men all were wearing their work shoes. A considerable part of the interest of the game was the men's efforts to start and stop and stay upright in those shoes on boards that had been polished by the hay shoved across them for fifty years. Also the boys, who had been playing basketball at school all winter, were in practice, young and agile and comparatively fast, whereas the men were out of practice or had never played before, and were comparatively slow and awkward in addition to being poorly shod.

Among the players, sure enough, were Mart Rowanberry and his brother-in-law Pascal Sowers, whose wife was Sudie, the lone sister of the Rowanberry brothers. Pascal who, like Mart, had been innocent of basketball until the past two or three Sundays, was playing clumsily and hard, and in the process finding, as usual, much to say. Mart, who had once been truly capable at baseball, was playing earnestly, alert and careful, going at play about as he went at work. But when he dribbled he bounced the ball as high as his waist, watching it to keep it from getting away, so that invariably it was stolen by one of the boys. And so when he got the ball Mart got rid of it again as soon as he could.

Elton had been there only a little while, watching and talking with Burley and Big Ellis, when somebody threw a wild pass. The ball came flying straight to Elton, he caught it, stood up, shot at the goal, and, for a wonder, made the shot.

A little later I am going to tell of something Elton did that was truly wonderful and altogether to his credit. But the goal he made, his first and last that Sunday morning, was a pure piece of luck, as Elton himself knew, though he claimed full credit for it. It was a fine accident, and it stopped the game.

Hackett caught the ball as it dropped through the hoop, and he held it. "Wait a minute. Whose side are *you* on, Elton?"

"Why, hell, he's on *my* side," Pascal said. "Can't you see he is?"

But Elton was the thirteenth man, a problem that much arguing and rearranging failed to solve, until Cocky Jones said he had had enough basketball for one day and gave his place to Elton.

And so Elton was in the game. Like some of the others, he had played basketball, or at least had played *with* a basketball in the course of his eight grades of education. The teacher in the Goforth school of one room, needing to keep the bigger boys as tired as possible, had bought with her own small store of money a proper basketball. For a goal, the boys fastened a succession of barrel hoops to a tree. For their play they knew some rules and made up the rest. Such as their game was, Elton became good at it. He was naturally athletic, and on that Sunday morning in Hackett Dunham's barn loft he played pretty well, though he did not make another goal.

Some while after the game resumed, Pascal Sowers dashed furiously after the ball, tried suddenly to stop, skidded, and then disappeared through a long hole in the floor. The hole was used for feeding hay down into the manger below. The week of feeding since the last game had left the hole wide open. It was so far from the area where they mostly played that nobody until then had given it a thought.

After Pascal fell through the hole, everybody thought of it. They all, players and watchers alike, gathered around it, staring down through it at Pascal who lay in the manger, staring back up at them. By another piece of pure luck, the morning's second fine accident, there had been enough hay left in the manger to break his fall. The bunch of heifers penned down there had not yet finished their breakfast. Onto the piled hay Pascal had lighted more or less feet first and flopped backwards. In the first seconds afterward, those in the loft could hear the trampling and colliding of the panic-stricken heifers.

When enough staring back and forth had convinced him that Pascal was conscious and in no pain, Hackett called down to him, "Well, I reckon you're thanking me for being a generous feeder."

At that, Pascal returned fully to life as himself. "Thanking you, hell! If your damned old hay was fit to eat, Sudie would be burying me. And I hope she'd be suing you for the two dollars you don't already owe somebody." They all laughed. Pascal climbed out of the manger and returned to the loft. The others discovered various ways to congratulate him on his survival. Hackett, Pascal's neighbor, and his friend too though neither would have admitted it, said, "I thought, 'Pore old Pascal. If he's dead, it sholy will stop him from lying.'"

It was one of the best moments of the sporting life of the Port William neighborhood. Fifty years later you could still find people who hadn't been there who could tell you all about it.

The interruption of the game continued while they stacked up a barrier of hay bales alongside the hole. But by then it was too late to continue playing. Pretty soon the wives and mothers of some of them would be getting home from church. The boys started idly shooting goals. The men stood around retelling the story of Pascal's fall and laughing. If any of them knew which side had won the game or what the score was, the subject was never raised. Maybe the boys knew.

After that, when they played basketball on Sunday mornings Elton was with them. The game went on for a few more Sundays, and then there came a bright warm Sunday morning early in April when basketball was no longer a thinkable thought. They came to Hackett's place as before, but they stayed in the sun. They merely accumulated in front of the barn, sitting on the fenders of their vehicles or on upturned buckets or standing propped against the wall, pleased with the bright day and the warmth, joking back and forth, talking without urgency about the weather, the condition of the ground, the work to come.

Elton Penn was the last to turn into the lane that morning. When he came to the open stretch between the house and the barn, the bunch of ex-ballplayers and ex-fans saw him slow down and then stop altogether. He was looking, they supposed and they turned out to be right, at several draft horses, twelve or fifteen of them, standing in a small grove of beech trees in the pasture adjoining the barn lot. He took his time looking, and then he came on into the lot, stopped the truck, and got out.

"Hackett," he said, "I'll pick a team out of that bunch and beat you pulling."

Hackett didn't say a word. He pushed himself off the fender he had been sitting on, went into the barn, into the tackroom, and came out again, carrying two halters and two lead ropes, which he handed to Elton, who took them and started out into the pasture where the horses were.

In a show of indifference typical of him—typical, the others would have said, of the trader in him—Hackett resumed his seat on the fender. The others remained much as they had been, only now they were not talking. The morning, having excluded basketball, had wanted a purpose, and now it had one. Or maybe it now had just a center of attention, and the center of attention was a mystery.

Had Elton intended for events to go as far as they already had? His challenge had been brash, but that did not surprise them any more than Hackett's calm response. Elton was brash and Hackett was calm, according to knowledge well-established. But what was next, how far would it go, and how would it end?

Elton had had an unusually hard time leaving home that morning. It was a day he could have worked, had it not been Sunday. The weather was fine, the ground drying, the new season at hand. His teeth were worse on edge than before.

But had he been running his mouth just for want of something to say, or had he meant what he said? The others knew at least that he had never driven a team in a pulling contest in his life, and they knew that Hackett was long-experienced and a proven master. And yet every one of them knew that Elton had to be taken seriously. He was a good horseman, a good teamster, and had been since he was hardly more than a boy. Horsemanship was second nature to him. Partly, it may have been his first nature. Albert Penn, Elton's father, dead now for twenty years, had been in his day an uncanny teamster, who could control his horses, it was said, by his voice alone. It was said, and always in the same words, with the same awe, "He could hook a team to a sawlog and make one stand and one pull, and never touch a line." And so maybe Elton had what his daddy had: a gift, a sleight, that most others did not have.

As Elton knew it in himself, it was indeed a gift, one that might well have come to him from his father. It was a feel beyond word or thought for the beings of the creaturely world that he hunted or nurtured or used.

By then experience had told him that sometimes he knew things he did not know he knew, until he dared them, so to speak, to reveal themselves. *How* he knew those things, he knew he would never know.

Elton was starting out into the pasture, carrying the halters and the lead ropes, and Hackett paid him no attention at all, never looked in his direction. Perhaps in deference to Hackett, perhaps from politeness, as they had come as guests, for a time nobody else moved either except for Mr. Wright, who without respect to manners had hobbled three-leggedly after Elton as far as the gate. Nobody said anything. But their own curiosity was working on them now. It came on them like an itch needing more and more urgently to be scratched. And presently, one by one, they stood up or pushed free of the wall where they had been leaning and walked over to the lot fence where they could watch Elton, Hackett coming along with them, for of course he too was curious.

They lined up along the fence, most of them having discarded their jackets, but still wearing the corduroy caps or the old felt hats that they had worn through the winter. They were of a kind now extinct in this part of the country, and no doubt also in the rest of it. They had lived by hard and exacting work all their lives from childhood. They had known the work of horses and mules all their lives. But by then, except for Mr. Wright of course and Burley Coulter and maybe another holdout or two, every man there had bought a tractor. Elton himself had bought his first tractor three years before.

Of the gathering at Hackett Dunham's that day, all the men are dead now, and the boys, the ones still living, are old. I am more or less the same age as the boys. I knew all the people in this story, the boys and the men. Some of them I knew as well as I have known anybody, as well as I knew the place and the community we all belonged to.

I have known the history of the basketball game from about the time it happened. I heard versions of it, then and later, from Elton and Mart Rowanberry and Pascal Sowers. But the part of the story I am telling now, the story as it continued from the game to the contest of the two horsemen, I did not hear until nearly sixty years after it happened. That I didn't hear it from Elton himself is strange. We were friends for the last thirty years of his life, and we worked together many days. Perhaps he simply let it go out of his mind along with the time it belonged to. For this is a story, really, of two stories. It is about several people, including me, who lived through a great change, for we were born in the last years of one story and lived into the beginning of another.

Two years ago, Lisby Knole, the last of my mother's generation in Port William, one of her dear friends from childhood, died at the age of a hundred and one. When I went to the funeral home for her visitation I got into a long talk with Spencer Gidwell Jr., who once had been Tomtit. The various remindings of our conversation brought us to the name of Elton Penn, and then Spencer told me the story that now I am telling. After the funeral the next day, when Billy Dunham and I had served as pall bearers, I mentioned the story that Spencer had told me, and then Billy told it, his version agreeing with Spencer's in every significant detail.

"Andy," Billy said, "you ought to been there. That was a day!"

And so I have this story in the nick of time, and as a gift. But it is a living gift, having a place among the brightest things I know. In my mind's eye those ex-players of the basketball game in the barn loft and the ex-watchers of the game are as present to me as if I *had* been there. I see them too with the tragic vision of hindsight, as they could not have seen themselves. Except for old Mr. Wright and Burley Coulter, all of the men for a good many years had been owners of automobiles. The history of speed and shortening distances, those exhilarations, but also breakdowns, wrecks, and highway deaths had become familiar to them, though it was a history still fairly new. And now nearly all of them were owners of tractors, and in the Port William neighborhood that history had hardly more than begun. Though they had opened the way for the machines to intrude between themselves and the ground they worked and lived on and for a while would continue to live from, the men lined up along Hackett Dunham's lot fence, watching Elton Penn walk toward the beech grove where the horses stood, the men and the boys too, even the most inept of them, were still contained within the culture of horsemanship that they were born into. The old language of the collaboration of men with horses and mules was still lively in their minds, still unthinkingly speakable.

By the effort and willingness of living creatures that labored, suffered, and grew old like themselves, they had joined themselves to the living world in which nothing is machine-like. But by their acceptance and excitement, and against the resistance of a few of them, the machines came. As I look back at those men across sixty years, I see that they had already come past a difference that most of them would not live to recognize. Their kind as it had been through centuries mostly forgotten was already being replaced by a kind that no farmers, and in fact no humans, had ever been before.

Though they stood in the shadow of a great and portentous story still ongoing sixty years later and so far without an imaginable end, they were nonetheless perfectly competent witnesses to the story of that day. They all belonged to the old story, the story of Port William before it was domi-nated by machines, the ancient story of people and animals moving over the earth. They watched and knew and judged the events of that day by the sort of mind-work that is so practiced and habitual as hardly to be conscious. What they were acutely conscious of was a number of things they did *not* know. In any transaction between humans and horses there would be mysteries, unknowns that would remain unknown. But there were also questions as yet unanswered that were going to be answered.

Carrying the halters and lead ropes looped over his shoulder, Elton walked out to the beech grove and in among the horses. They were a mixed lot, varying in color and conformation and somewhat in size, though none was small. They were a bunch of culls, horses maybe with something to be said in their favor that Hackett had picked up cheap, brought home, tried out, and found wanting. They were to be loaded the next day, Billy Dunham told me, and trucked off to a sale. Most of them, no doubt, would go to the kill. All over the country the work teams were being replaced by trac-tors, and the horse market was off.

Elton was with the horses a longish time. He reached out his hand to every one of them. Some accepted it and some shied away. The ones who did not move he made move. The men watching from the lot fence could have told you then, as I can tell you now, something of what he was looking for.

He would have been looking for harness marks, for this would be no time to break a horse. He would have been mindful of questions of size, strength, conformation, soundness—qualities sufficiently clear and explainable. But just as important to him would have been subtler ques-tions of bearing, demeanor, the look in the eyes. He would have wanted to know how each horse felt about himself. But he would not have been articulating those questions as I have written them here. Though he would have been aware of all that I have said, and more, he would not have been thinking in the manner of speaking to himself. If he had been putting his thoughts into words at all, he would have been saying something like "This one? Or this one? Not that one."

Elton took his time, but soon enough he had picked his horses, haltered them, and was leading them toward the lot gate. He had chosen two geldings, a buckskin and a paint.

As he brought them through the gate, J. L. Safely said, "Well, Elton, they ain't exactly a dead match."

Everybody laughed, for Elton's pair were odd-colored individually, for draft horses, and they were colored as unlike each other as they possibly could have been. But the laughter was as free as it was because, except in color, the two horses went together well enough. They were not significantly different in size or gait or bearing, and they were, to the eye, plenty good.

The watchers knew this, and so did Elton, but he said, "Oh, I reckon they'll have to do. They're the ones I could catch." He spoke out of the habit of his humor, and the others laughed again, but it was clear that he had not spoken his mind. He had flung his joke at them, so to speak, over the top of his seriousness. He was completely serious, more concerned than he wanted them to see, but they saw.

Hackett Dunham was the only one who had not laughed. He said quietly to Elton, "Take 'em on in the barn. We'll find 'em some harness." He too was serious.

Elton led the horses into the driveway of the barn. He had no more than got them tied than Hackett, who had gone into the harness room, was handing out collar pads and collars to be tried for a fit. Immediately too many of the others were hastening to help. Elton dealt with this by addressing his questions to Mart Rowanberry and Burley Coulter, with whom he had worked and hunted and whose judgment he trusted.

"How about that, Burley? A little too tight?"

"I'd say a little tight."

"Now, Mart. How about this one?"

"I'd call that a fit."

When the right pads and collars had been found and the horses were wearing them, Hackett handed out harnesses, first for one horse and then the other. He was standing in the harness room door, alertly watching to see what was needed.

Until it is on the horse, a set of harness is a perfect blather of straps. But Elton and his friends knew the form within the tangle. They laid the harness over the horse's back. As they fastened buckles and snaps, the use of each part declared itself. When Elton lengthened or shortened straps on one side, adjusting to a fit, Burley or Mart made the same adjustment on the other side. They fitted the harness according to their understanding of its use, but also, by sympathy, they fitted it as they would have dressed themselves. They wanted the harness snug enough, neat enough, unslovenly, but nowhere binding, so that the horse wore it comfortably and moved freely in it. With the same care they adjusted and fitted a pair of bridles.

And then they untied the horses and stood them side by side, the buckskin on the left or "lead" side, the paint on the "off." Hackett handed out a set of lines, which were threaded through the hame rings and snapped to the bits. Burley stood at the horses' heads, holding them and speaking to them, for they were showing some nervousness, while Mart straightened the lines over their backs.

When Elton had looked again at everything and was satisfied, he came to his place. Mart, with just a hint of ceremony, handed him the lines.

And so the horses were joined to each other, to their driver, and their driver to them.

Elton tightened the lines a little to get the horses' attention, to tell them he was there. He said, "Come up!" and drove them out of the barn.

Almost at once it was clear that something was wrong. The horses responded to Elton's voice and to the pressure on their bits, but still they were nervous. They seemed uncertain and somehow distressed. Though they were held together by the lines, they were not consenting to be a team. And their confusion excluded Elton. The three of them needed to be at one, but they remained, separately, three.

Finally Elton, who had started and stopped them several times, again said, "Whoa!"

He looked at Burley. "Reckon we ought to switch sides?"

Burley shook his head once, but he said, "I'd try it."

Since they had nothing else to try, Burley again stood at the horses' heads, holding them, while Elton and Mart unsnapped and removed the lines. They then turned the pair "inside out," as Mart put it, placing the paint on the left side, in the lead, and the buckskin on the right.

By the time the lines were in Elton's hands again, there was already a difference. The horses were quieter, as if a while ago they had not known where they were, but now they knew, though it was impossible to say which horse had thought he was on the wrong side, or if both of them had thought so. When Elton asked them this time to come up, they moved off more quietly and almost together. They weren't a team yet, but maybe they were going to be.

"Maybe they'll work it out," Mart said.

And Burley, who was intently watching, said, "Maybe."

Elton, as Mart and Burley understood, was caught between two mysteries. What was going to happen he did not know, of course. But he was dealing also with an unknown past. He and those nameless horses were strangers to one another. Even so, it was early in the year. Hackett's horses were not yet work-hardened. They had not yet been shod, as Elton's had not. The contest would be as fair probably as it could be.

Presently Hackett, whose boys had given him the help he needed, had his team standing harnessed in the doorway of the barn. And then, with the slack of the lines coiled in his hands, he was driving them out into the sunlight.

Hackett's horses were closely matched. They were red sorrels with blazed faces. They had wintered well, and their coats shone back at the sun. They were alike in conformation and in size. But more than that, as a team they were "put together," as Burley said in open commendation. There was no "maybe" attached to them. They knew each other. They knew Hackett, and he knew them. They were joined by history, by mutual knowledge and experience, as much as by the leather lines and the snaps and buckles. They were put together by an understanding beyond anything visible, and yet those with eyes to see, who knew what they were seeing, could see it.

Hackett looked back as if to say something, but his boys, who knew what was wanted, were already coming with a set of heavy doubletrees for each team. The horses were hitched then, and Hackett's two boys and Mart and Burley lifted the doubletrees clear of the ground as Hackett and Elton drove. Spence Gidwell trotted ahead to open the gate at the back of the barn, and the teamsters, Hackett first and then Elton, drove their teams out of the lot, followed by the straggle of watchers.

Far enough behind the barn to be fairly out of the way, a low sled that some might have called a stoneboat sat at the end of the bare strip it had worn as summer after summer Hackett had used it to condition his pulling horses. It had been idle so far that spring and weeds were sprouting from the scoured ground. The sled was loaded with concrete blocks weighing about thirty pounds apiece.

When he saw how well-settled the ground of the pulling strip was, maybe dry enough to plow, Elton fell into a moment of distraction, of disorientation and near-panic, such as he would sometimes feel on his Sundays of principled rest when he might have worked. The voice of self-judgment sprang in his mind like a trap cunningly set: "What in the hell am I doing?"

But that passed. It passed because the pair of lines joining him to his team was alive in his hands with a nervous and urging life. He was joined to the two horses by a connection as immediately living as his flesh and theirs. It drew him from any possible thought of elsewhere into a time older than memory and now again present, in which the bone and blood, muscle and weight, and the elation also, of a pair of strong horses became the felt thought of a man, so that while their common effort lasted he would not, he could not, distinguish between himself and them.

"Whoa!" Hackett said. And Elton also stopped his team.

"Lighten it up, boys," Hackett said. He watched as the boys and younger men began hurriedly to unload the blocks and set them aside. "Take 'em all off," he said. And then he turned to Elton. "Elton, you might want to practice your horses just on the sled before we start. These of mine are all right, I think."

Hackett had the double role of competitor and host. He was being fair.

Elton drove his team into position and backed them to the sled. Mart and Burley hooked them, stepped out of the way, and Elton spoke to his team. He drove them the length of the course, stopping them and starting them again.

Elton was not always a patient man, but that day he was being patient. He had to be. He was paying attention too, but he was always good at that. He wasn't requiring much of his horses, only that they should start and stop when asked. He was requiring them to know that he meant what he told them, either speaking or by pressure on their bits. He did not blunder. He gave them no false signals. And they began to give him their respect. They began to trust him. His coherence and determination in himself extended to them. They began to work together and to work for him. They had begun to be a team.

When they got to the far end of the course, Mart and Burley unhooked them. Elton drove them around the sled, to be hooked again to its other end, and he worked them back the opposite way.

Hackett had set no limit to this time of practice, but of course there had to be a limit. Time was passing. Hackett was waiting. Everybody was waiting. Elton himself, though he had not relaxed his attention to his horses, had begun to feel the pressure of waiting, everybody else's and his own. And so when he had worked his way back to where he had started, he stopped his team and turned to Hackett. "We're as ready as we're going to get."

"Good enough," Hackett said. "You make the first pull." He turned to his boys. "Lay on about three hundred pounds. We'll load 'em up easy." He was again being the good host.

Three hundred pounds was not much of a load. Burley and Mart helped Elton to hook again to the opposite end of the sled, and his team quietly pulled it the requisite twenty-seven and a half feet.

Hackett's team, unlike Elton's, knew exactly the business they were in. So did Hackett's boys, who hooked them virtually without requiring them to stop, and they snatched the front end of the sled clean off the ground. Hackett laughed, exhilarated by their readiness. And so the contest had begun.

As the load was increased, three hundred pounds at a time, the sense of purpose increased in drivers and horses alike, and so did the sense of contending in the minds of the watchers. The contest, as was increasingly evident, was not just between two teamsters and two teams, but between two ways of working, of moving the load. As they had been schooled to do, Hackett's horses started the load into motion by snatching it, flinging their whole weight against it, thus gaining an immediate momentum for the rest of the pull. Elton could not have risked exciting his horses to such a pitch. Though by the rules he could not have struck them even with the end of a line, as they warmed to their work and learned to expect greater weight at each pull he might have roused them, as Hackett's were aroused, by his voice alone. But could he have controlled them then? He didn't know, and he had no safe way of finding out.

And so, never raising his voice, he asked them each time to pull from a standing start as if they were drawing a wagon loaded with hay. He was discarding deliberately the advantage of lunging, and asking his team to make up the difference by sheer willingness and strength. Rather than exciting them in response to himself, he was perforce leaving them free to become excited in response to the effort he was asking of them—if they had it in them to do that. Whether or not they had it in them to do that was one of the questions Elton had been asking when he had picked them out of the bunch of Hackett's rejects. And now, pull by pull, they were answering. So far, yes, they did have it in them to do that.

After four pulls, with the burden increased to twelve hundred pounds, the two teams were seriously at work. When the load increased, after four more pulls, to twenty-four hundred pounds, they began to be tested. They began to sweat. Especially Elton and his team were being tested. Hackett's team, starting each pull with that calculated lunge, still were making it look easy. But Elton's team were increasingly required, and against apparently increasing odds, to pull steadily, to take on the difficulty without flinching from it or anticipating it with too much excitement. Elton's voice, when he spoke to them now, asked them to exert themselves, but only just enough. And they continued to give him, each time, the just enough that he asked for.

Hackett's mind was beginning to be oddly divided. Both teams belonged to him, and so in a sense he could not lose. But it was becoming plain to everybody that, even more than Elton, Hackett had put his judgment on the line, and of the two of them he most needed to win. As Elton's team completed their pulls, at twenty-seven hundred and three thousand and thirty-three hundred pounds, Hackett's worry increased. But he felt also, he could not *not* feel, a growing admiration as Elton and that wildly mis-colored pair of horses revealed, pull after pull, yet more ability.

By the rules, each team would have three tries at each increase of weight. So far, both had gone the full twenty-seven and a half feet on the first pull. But when the load went to thirty-three hundred pounds, both teams began to suffer noticeably the disadvantage of being unshod. As the friction between sled and ground increased, the horses' hooves found less purchase. On his first pull at thirty-six hundred, Elton's buckskin lost his footing. Before the horse's knees had touched the ground, Elton had called, "Whoa!" and the paint had stopped. The buckskin was instantly on his feet again, but the pull had failed, and the mishap had upset the horses. When they were unhooked Elton handed the lines to Burley. While Hackett's team made the pull successfully, Elton went to his horses' heads, laid his hands on their faces and spoke to them. "Be easy, boys. Be easy." In response to his touch and the sound of his voice, they grew quiet.

When they were hooked again, he said, "Easy now. Easy." And this time as they tightened against their collars they struck their toes into the ground, they stayed on their feet, they kept going, and they made the pull.

A murmur of surprise and admiration ran among the watchers. They, like Elton, had passed into the old moment of union and communion between man and team, reduced now to a Sunday morning's pleasure, only a pastime, but while it lasted, it held them out of time. Like Elton, they were in the old time, and while it lasted it kept them. The weight of the load was raised to thirty-nine hundred pounds. The three hundred pound increment, which at first had been negligible, had now become critical. Everybody knew it. Both teams, barefooted and at that time of the year not hardened to the work, were coming to their limit.

Elton's two tries to Hackett's one at thirty-six hundred pounds had dis-rupted the order of the contest. If they were to keep to the original order, Elton's team would have had to go from one hard pull directly to another. Again Hackett did the gracious thing. "My turn," he said.

Now Hackett's horses, expecting the heavier load and champing at their bits, hurled themselves into their collars, but then the force of their effort appeared to swing them out leftward, and the sled stopped. They had moved it six feet and five inches. So near their limit, the horses' all-out lunge into their collars did start the load, but at the same time it threw them off their footing. To go further, they would have to start again.

In his turn, Elton again said, "Easy, boys," and a fraction of a second before they would have quit on their own he said, "Whoa!" They had gone ten feet and seven inches.

They each had, by the rules, two tries remaining. On his second try, Hackett's team threw themselves forward with the same willingness as before, but they were wearing out. The force with which they bore against the load seemed at once to fling them backward. The traces slackened, and the sled had moved a fraction of an inch less than three feet.

Elton's team also was weary. It was clear that he would make the second try only to honor the rules. Again his horses moved the sled, and again, knowing maybe sooner than they did that they had done all they could do, Elton stopped them before they could quit. They had gone this time five feet and three inches.

When the watchers turned to Hackett, he shook his head and lifted an opened hand. He would not waste his horses on a useless try. "That's all, boys. We had a question. Now we've got the answer."

In his triumph, instead of the elation he might reasonably have felt, Elton felt himself suddenly stranded in a kind of embarrassment. A charge passed through him, as if he had wakened from a dream. He had made a dare, and had fulfilled it so far in excess of what he might have expected, and so much further in excess of what the others had expected, that he did not know where to look or what to say. He was now the exceptional man. He had become, strangely, new to himself and to them all.

And then old Mr. Wright, who was standing closer to Elton's lead horse than the others would have allowed him to do if they had been watching him, said for all to hear, his voice trembling, "As good a ones as 'ar a man drawed a line over!" Utterly oblivious of the others standing behind him, he was leaning on the cane held in his right hand. With the flat of his left hand he stroked once the horse's black-and-white rump, and then he turned to Elton. "And ay *God*, son! You're a *teamster!*"

Mike (1939–1950)

After my parents were married in 1933, they lived for three years with my father's parents, Marce and Dorie Catlett, on the Catlett home place near Port William. My mother and my grandmother Catlett did not fit well into the same house. Because of that, and I suppose for the sake of convenience, my parents in 1936 moved themselves, my younger brother, Henry, and me to a small rental house in Hargrave, the county seat, where my father had his law practice.

And then in 1939, when I was five years old, my father bought us a house of our own. It was a stuccoed brick bungalow that had previously served as a "funeral home." It stood near the center of town and next door to a large garage. After we had moved in—there being six of us now, since the births of my two sisters—my parents improved the house by the addition of a basement to accommodate a furnace, and by the installation of radiators and modern bathroom and kitchen appliances.

My brother and I were thus provided with spectacles of work that fascinated us, and also with a long-term supply of large boxes and shipping crates. The crate that had contained the bathtub I remember as especially teeming with visions of what it might be reconstructed into. These visions evidently occasioned some strife between Henry and me. The man who installed our bathroom assured me many years later that he had seen me hit Henry on the head with a ball-peen hammer.

One day, while Henry and I were engaged in our unrealizable dream of making something orderly and real out of the clutter in our back yard, a man suddenly came around the corner of the house carrying a dog. The dog was a nearly grown pup, an English setter, white with black ears and eye patches and a large black spot in front of his tail. The man, as we would later learn, was Mike Brightleaf.

Mr. Brightleaf said, "Andy and Henry, you boys look a here. This is a pup for your daddy."

He set the big pup carefully down and gave him a pat. And then, with a fine self-assurance or a fine confidence in the pup or both, he said, "Call him Mike."

We called, "Here, Mike!" and Mike came to us and the man left.

Mike, as we must have known even as young as we were, came from the greater world beyond Hargrave, the world of fields and woods that our father had never ceased to belong to and would belong to devotedly all his life. Mike was doomed like our father to town life, but was also like our father never to be reconciled to the town.

Along one side of our property our father built a long, narrow pen that we called "the dog lot," and he supplied it with a nice, white-painted dog house. The fence was made of forty-seven inch woven wire with two barbed wires at the top. These advantages did not impress Mike in the least. He did not wish to live in the nice dog house, and he would not do so unless chained to it. As for the tall fence, he would go up it as one would climb a ladder, gather himself at the top, and leap to freedom. Our father stretched a third strand of barbed wire inside the posts, making what would have been for a man a considerable obstacle, and Mike paid it no mind.

As a result, since our father apparently was reluctant to keep him tied, Mike had the run of the town. For want of anything better to do, he dedicated himself to being where we children were and going where we went. I have found two photographs of him, taken by our mother. In both, characteristically, he is with some of us children, accepting of hugs and pats, submissive, it seems, to his own kindness and our thoughtless affection, but with the look also of a creature dedicated to a higher purpose, aware of his lowly servitude.

One day our father found Henry and me trying to fit Mike with a harness we had contrived of an old mule bridle. We were going to hitch him to our wagon.

Our father said, "Don't do that, boys. You'll cow him."

I had never heard the word "cow" used in that way before, and it affected me strongly. The word still denotes, to me, Mike's meek submission to indignity and my father's evident conviction that *nothing* should be cowed.

Mike intended to go everywhere we went and he usually did, but he understood his limits when he met them. One Sunday morning we children and our mother had started our walk to church. Mike was trailing quietly behind, hoping to be unnoticed, but our mother looked back and saw him. She said sympathetically, "Mike, go home." And Mike turned sadly around and went home.

He was well-known in our town, for he was a good-looking dog and he moved with the style of his breeding and calling. But his most remarkable public performance was his singing to the fire whistle. Every day, back then, the fire whistle blew precisely at noon. The fire whistle was actually a siren whose sound built to an almost intolerable whoop and then diminished in a long wail. When that happened, Mike always threw up his head and howled, whether in pain or appreciation it was impossible to tell. One day he followed us to school, and then at noon into the little cafeteria beneath the gymnasium. I don't believe I knew he was there until the fire whistle let go and he began to howl. The sound, in that small and supposedly civil enclosure, was utterly barbarous and shocking. I felt some pressure to be embarrassed but I was also deeply pleased. Who else belonged to so rare an animal?

But Mike knew well that his deliverer was my father. He might spend a lot of time idling about in town or playing with children, but he was a dog with a high vocation, and he knew what it was. He knew too that my father fully shared it. Mike loved us all in the honorable and admirable way of a dog, but his love for my father was too dedicated to be adequately described as doglike. He regarded his partnership with my father as the business of his life, as it was also his overtopping joy.

My father was a man of passions. I don't think he did much of anything except passionately. When he was removed from his passions, as in some public or social situations, he would be quiet, remote, uncomfortable, and unhappy. I think he was sometimes constrained by a sense of the disproportion between the force of his thoughts and the demands of polite conversation. He loved serious talk and the sort of conversation that is incited by pleasure. He loved hilarity. But he had little to offer in the way of small talk, and he always seemed to me to be uncomfortable or embarrassed when it was required of him.

He was passionate about the law. He loved its argumentative logic, its principles and methods, its discriminating language. He was capable of working at it ardently for long hours. His sentences, written or spoken, whatever the circumstances, were concise, exact, grammatically correct, and powerful in their syntax. He did not speak without thinking, and he meant what he said.

He used such sentences when instructing and reprimanding us children. We were not always on his mind, I am sure, but when we were he applied himself to fatherhood as he did to everything else. When we were sick or troubled he could be as tender and sympathetic as our mother. At other times, disgruntled or fearing for us as his knowledge of the world prompted him to do, he could be peremptory, demanding, impatient, and in various ways intimidating. I was always trying to keep some secret from him, and he had an uncanny way of knowing your secrets. He had a way of knowing your thoughts, and this came from sympathy. It could only have come from sympathy, but it took me a long time to know that.

I have always been a slow thinker, and he was fast. He could add, subtract, and figure averages in his head with remarkable speed. He would count a flock of sheep like this: one, five, seven, twelve, sixteen, nineteen, twenty-four . . . One day when he had done this and arrived promptly at the correct number, a hundred and fifty or so, he turned and looked at me for my number. I was still counting. "Honey," he said with instant exasperation, "are you counting by *twos*?" That was exactly what I was doing, and in my slowness I had started over two or three times.

He was as passionate about farming as about the law. He could not voluntarily have quit farming any more than he could voluntarily have quit breathing. He spent great love and excitement in buying rundown farms, stopping the washes, restoring the pastures, renewing the fences, buildings, and other improvements. He performed this process of regeneration seven times in his life, eventually selling six of the farms, but he kept one, and in addition he kept and improved over many years the home place where he was born and raised. He hired out most of the work, of course, but he worked himself too, and he watched and instructed indefatigably. He would drive out to see to things in the morning before he went to the office, and again after he left the office in the afternoon. He took days off to devote to farming. He would be out looking at things, salting his cattle and sheep, walking or driving his car through the fields, every Sunday afternoon. In the days before tractors he would be on hand to take the lines when there were young mules to break. He did the dehorning, castrating, and other veterinary jobs. All the time he could spare from his law practice he gave to the farms. Because of his work for an agricultural cooperative, he would frequently have to make a trip to Washington or some other distant place. Sometimes, returning from one of those trips in the middle of the night, he would go to the home place or one of the other farms and drive through the fields before going home to bed.

Of farming, he told me, "It's like a woman. It'll keep you awake at night." He loved everything about it. He loved the look and feel and smell of the land and the shape of it underfoot. He loved the light on it and the weather over it. He loved the economics of it. As characteristic of him as anything else were pages of yellow legal pads covered with columns of numbers written in ink in his swift hand, where he figured the outgoes and the incomes of his farming, or drew the designs of farm buildings to be built or rebuilt.

When he went to the farms, he would often take Mike with him. He would hurry home from the office, change his clothes, and hurry out again. Going to his car, he would raise the trunk lid. "Here, Mike! Get in!" And Mike would leap into the trunk and lie down. My father would close the trunk, leaving the latch unengaged so Mike would have air.

If there were farm jobs to be done, Mike would just go along, running free in the open country, hunting on his own. If it was hunting season, my father might bring along his shotgun in its tattered canvas case. The gun was a pump-action Remington twenty-gauge, for in those days my father had excellent eyes and he was a good shot.

In those days too the tall coarse grass known as fescue had not yet been introduced here. That grass and the coming of rotary mowing machines have made the good old bobwhite a rare bird in this country now. The improved pastures in Mike's time were in bluegrass, and a lot of fields would be weedy in the fall. There was plenty of good bird cover and as a result plenty of birds. My father would know where the coveys were, and he and Mike would go to seek them out.

And here they came into their glory, and here I need to imagine them and see them again in my mind's eye, now that I am getting old and have come to understand my father far better than I did when I was young. For right at the heart of his passions for his family, for the law, and for farming, all consequential passions with practical aims and ends, was this other passion for bird hunting with a good dog, which had no practical end but was the enactment of his great love of country, of life, of his own life, for their own sake.

When he stepped out in his eager long strides, with Mike let loose in front of him, he was walking free on the undivided and priceless world itself. And Mike went out from him in a motion fluid and swift and strong, less running than flying, and he would find the birds.

Once he had learned his trade, I think Mike was a nearly perfect dog, giving a satisfaction that was nearly complete. I never heard my father complain of him. He understood that little pump gun in my father's hands as if it were a book of instructions, and he did what he was supposed to do.

He was remarkable in another way. He would retrieve, and to reward him my father started feeding him the heads of the birds when he brought them back. Before long, Mike got the idea. From then on, he ate the head of the downed bird where he found it and brought back the headless carcass.

From time to time during my father's life as a bird hunter, which had its summit during Mike's life, he would go somewhere down south on a hunting trip, usually with one other hunter. I know about these trips only from a handful of stories, all of which had to do in one way or another with the prowess of my father's great dog.

In Hargrave we lived across the street from Dr. Gib Holston who was the town's only professed atheist. He had the further distinctions of a glass eye and a reputation for violence. Once, in the days of his youth, a man had insulted him, and Dr. Holston had killed the offender by shooting him from a train window. Most of our fellow citizens who used profanity might properly have been said to cuss, for they used it thoughtlessly as a sort of rhetoric of emphasis, but Dr. Holston *cursed*, with blasphemy aforethought and with the intention of offending anyone inclined to be offended. He was a small man, not much above five feet tall, but strongly built and without fat to the end of his days. He thought of himself as outrageous, and so of course he was, and he enjoyed his bad reputation. He was a strange neighbor for my good mother, a woman of vigilant faith, who obliged him by finding him on all points as outrageous as he wished to be. She, with conscientious good manners, and my father, with a ceremoniousness always slightly tainted with satire, called him "Dr. Holston." The rest of us called him "Doc" or, when we wished to distinguish him from other doctors, "Dr. Gib."

Doc, then, was one of my father's clients, which sometimes required them to make a little business trip together, and at least once they went together on a hunting trip. Why my father would have put up with him to that extent I am not sure. Perhaps, as a man of my grandparents' generation, Doc knew and remembered things that my father was interested in hearing; he always liked his older clients and enjoyed listening to them. But mostly, I believe, he put up with Doc because Doc amused him. It amused him that when they went somewhere together, Doc insisted on sitting by himself in the back seat of the car. It amused him to see in the rearview mirror that when Doc dozed off, sitting back there bolt upright by himself, his glass eye stayed open. Once, when my father advised him that a neighbor of ours, an aristocratic and haughty old lady, Mrs. J. Robert La Vere, had been "dropped" in a certain town that they visited, Doc said, "God damn her, I wish she had dropped on through!" That amused my father as if it had been the gift of divine charity itself and he was therefore *obliged* to be fully amused. The one story that came of their hunting together is about my father's amusement.

They had come to their hunting place, uncased and loaded their guns, and turned Mike loose. The place was rich in birds and Mike soon began finding them, working beautifully in cooperation with my father, as he always did, and my father was shooting well as *he* always did. But this story begins with my father's growing awareness and worry that Doc was not shooting well.

There is a good possibility, in my opinion, that Doc by then was not capable of shooting well. His one eye could not have been very clear. I have been on hunts with him myself, and I never saw him hit anything. He had bought a twelve-gauge Browning automatic, which he pointed hither and yon without regard to the company. You had to watch him. I think he bought that gun because he couldn't see well enough to shoot well. It was an expensive gun, which counted with him, and that it was automatic impressed him inordinately. He had the primitive technological faith that such a weapon simply could not help compensating for his deficiency. He had paid a lot of money for this marvelous gun that would enact his mere wish to hit the birds as they rose. If you can't shoot well, you must shoot a lot. And so when he heard the birds rise, he merely pointed the gun in their direction and emptied it: Boomboomboom! And of course he was missing.

And of course he was eventually furious. He vented his fury by stomping about and cursing roundly everything in sight. He called upon God, in whom he did not believe, to damn the innocent birds who were flying too fast and scattering too widely to be easily shot, and his expensive shotgun that was guilty only of missing what it had not been aimed at, and the cover that was too brushy, and the landscape that was too ridgy and broken, and the day that was too cloudy. My father, who instantly appreciated the absurdity of Doc's cosmic wrath, took the liberty of laughing. He then, being a reasonable man, recognized the tactlessness of his laughter, which doubled his amusement, and he laughed more. Doc thereupon included my father in his condemnation, and then, to perfect his vengeance, he included Mike who, off in the distance, was again beautifully quartering the ground. This so fulfilled my father with amusement that he was no longer able to stand. As we used to say here, his tickle-box had turned completely over. He subsided onto the ground and lay there on his back among the weeds, laughing, in danger, he said, of wetting his pants. He was pretty certain too that Doc was going to shoot him and he was duly afraid, which somehow amused him even more, and he could not stop laughing.

How they leveled that situation out and recovered from it, I don't know. But they did, and my father, to his further great amusement, survived.

*   *   *

In the general course of my father's life, I suppose Doc was a digression, an indulgence perhaps, certainly a fascination of a sort, and a source of stories. His friendship with Billy Finn was another matter. Between the two of them was a deep affection that lasted all their lives. On my father's side, I know, this affection was weighted by an abiding compassion. Billy Finn was a sweet man who sometimes drank to excess, and perhaps for sufficient reason. He had suffered much in his marriage to an unappeasable woman, "Mizriz Fannie Frankle Finn" as my father enjoyed calling her behind her back. To the unhappy marriage of Mr. and Mrs. Finn had been added the death in battle, early in World War II, of their son, their only child. The shadow of shared grief, cast over the marriage, had made it maybe even more permanent than its vows. Mr. Finn was bound to Mrs. Finn by his pity for her suffering, so like his own, he suffering in addition, as she made sure, his inability to pity her enough. Life for Mr. Finn, especially after the death of his son, was pretty much an uphill trudge. I think his friendship with my father was a necessary solace to him to the end of his life, near which he said to a member of the clergy visiting him in the nursing home: "Hell, preacher? You can't tell me nothing about Hell. I've lived with a damned Frankle for *forty-nine years!*"

When my father would go away on one of his bird-hunting trips, his companion almost invariably would be Mr. Finn. Mr. Finn loved bird dogs, and he always had one or two. The dogs always were guaranteed to be good ones, and nearly always they disappointed him. He was not a good hand with a dog, perhaps because he had experienced too much frustration and disappointment in other things. He was impatient with his dogs, fussed at them too much, frightened them, confused them, and hollered at them. He was a noisy hunter, his utterances tending to be both excessive and obsessive, and this added substantially to my father's fund of amusement and of stories, but also to his fund of sorrow, for Billy Finn was a sad man, and my father was never forgetful of that.

On one of their hunting trips down south, as a companion to Mike, Mr. Finn took a lovely pointer bitch he called Gladys, a dog on the smallish side, delicately made, extremely sensitive and shy—precisely the wrong kind of dog for him.

When the dogs were released, Mike sniffed the wind and sprang into his work. Gladys, more aware of the strangeness of the new terrain than of its promise, hung back.

"Go on, Gladys!" Mr. Finn said. But instead of ranging ahead with Mike, Gladys followed Mr. Finn, intimidated still by the new country, embarrassed by her timidity, knowing what was expected of her, and already fearful of Mr. Finn's judgment.

"Gladys!" he said. "Go on!"

And then, raising his voice and pointing forward, he said, "Damn you, Gladys, go on! *Go on!*"

That of course ended any possibility that Gladys was going to hunt, for after that she needed to be forgiven. She stuck even closer to Mr. Finn, fawning whenever he looked at her, hoping for forgiveness. And of course, in his humiliation, it never occurred to him to forgive her.

They hunted through the morning, Mr. Finn alternately apologizing for Gladys and berating her. His embarrassment about his dog eventually caused my father to become embarrassed about *his* dog. For in spite of Mr. Finn's relentless fuming and muttering, they were having a fairly successful hunt. Mike was soaring through the cover in grand style and coming to point with rigorous exactitude. And the better it was, the worse it was. The better Mike performed, the more disgrace piled upon poor Gladys, the more embarrassed Mr. Finn became, and the more he fumed and muttered, the more my father was punished by the excellence of Mike.

"Oh, Lord, it was awful," my father would say later, laughing at the memory of his anguished amusement and his failure to think of anything at all to say.

And it got worse.

Sometime early in the afternoon Mr. Finn's suffering grew greater than he could bear. He turned upon Gladys, who was still following him, and said half crying, "Gladys, damn you to Hell! I raised you from a pup, I've sheltered you, I've fed you, I've loved you like a child, and now you've let me down, you thankless bitch!" He then aimed a murderous kick at her, which she easily evaded and fled from him until she was out of sight.

My father would gladly have ended the day there and then if he could have thought of a painless or even a polite way to do it. But he could think of no way. They hunted on.

But now Mr. Finn was the one who needed forgiveness, and Gladys did not return to forgive him. He began to suffer the torments of the guilty and unforgiven, of shame for himself and fear for his dog. He began to imagine all the bad things that might happen to her, unprotected as she was and in a strange country. She might remain lost forever. She might get caught in somebody's steel trap. Some lousy bastard might find her wandering and steal her. She would be hungry and cold.

My father, being guilty of nothing except the good work of his own dog, was somewhat calmer. He thought Gladys would not go far and would be all right, and he sought to reassure his friend. But Mr. Finn could not be comforted. From his earlier mutterings of imprecation he changed now to mutterings of self-reproach and worry.

As evening came on, they completed their long circle back to the car, and Gladys still was nowhere in sight. Mr. Finn had been calling her for the last mile or so. For a long time they waited while Mr. Finn called and called, his voice sounding more pleading, anxious, and forlorn as the day darkened. They were tired and they were getting cold.

Nearby, there was a culvert that let a small stream pass under the road. The culvert was dry at that time of year, and it would be a shelter.

"Billy," my father said, "lay your coat in that culvert. It's not going to rain. She'll find it and sleep there. We'll come back in the morning and get her."

The only available comfort was in that advice, and Mr. Finn took it. He emptied his hunting coat, folded it to make a bed, and laid it in the culvert. They went back to their hotel to their suppers, their beds, and an unhappy night for Mr. Finn.

The next day was Sunday. On their hunting trips, my father and Mr. Finn scrupulously attended church on Sunday. That morning they shaved, put on their church-going clothes, ate breakfast, and then hurried out into the country where they had lost Gladys and Mr. Finn had left his coat.

Aside from ordering his breakfast, Mr. Finn had said not a word. But now as they drove through the bright morning that still was dark to him, he uttered a sort of prayer: "Lord, I hope she made it back."

My father, who was driving, reached across and patted him on the shoulder. "She'll be there," he said.

She was there. When they climbed the fence to look, she was lying in the culvert on Mr. Finn's coat, a picture of repentance and faithfulness that stabbed him to the heart. He knelt on the concrete beside her. He petted her, praised her, thanked her, and called her his good and beautiful Gladys, for she was at that moment all the world to him. And then he gathered her up in his arms, went to the fence, and started to climb over. It was a tall fence, fairly new with a barbed wire at the top, a considerable challenge to any man climbing it in a suit, let alone a man climbing it in a suit and carrying a dog. He got one leg over and was bringing the other when he lost his balance and fell, one cuff of his pants catching on a barb. And so he hung, upside down, with Gladys frantic and struggling in his arms.

My father would tell that story suffering with laughter, and then he would look down and shake his head. It was sadder than it was funny, but it was certainly funny, and what was a mere man to do?

I loved to hear my father tell those stories and others like them, and I can still see the visions they made me see when I was a boy. But now I love better to try to imagine the days, for which there are no stories, when Mike and my father hunted by themselves at home. On those days they passed beyond the margins of my father's working life and his many worries. Though they might have been hunting on a farm that my father owned, they passed beyond the confines even of farming. They entered into a kind of freedom and a kind of perfection. I am thinking now with wonder of the convergence, like two birds crossing as they rise, of a passionate man and a gifted, elated, hard-hunting dog, and this in a country deeply loved and known, from many of the heights of which the man could see on its hill in the distance the house where he was born. And it would be in the brisk, fine weather of the year's decline when every creature is glad to be alive.

My father would have been in his early forties then, young still in all his energy and ability, his body light with thought and implicit motion even when he stood at rest. He and Mike would pass through a whole afternoon or a whole day in the same excitement, the same eagerness for the hidden birds and for the country that lay ahead.

Thinking of him in those days, I can't help wishing that I had known him then as a contemporary and friend, rather than as his son. As his son, I was to see him clearly only in looking back. He was obscured to me by his anxious parenthood, his fears for me, and by my own uneasy responses.

And yet I remember standing with him one day, when I was maybe eight or nine years old, on the top of a ridge in a weedy field. We were on the back of the farm we called the Crayton place. Beyond us, Mike was working with the beautiful motion that came of speed and grace together. My father held his gun in the crook of his left arm, at ease. He was in the mood that made him most comfortable to be with, enjoying himself completely, and with his entire intention allowing me to see what he saw.

Mike came to point, a forefoot lifted, his body tense from the end of his nose to the tip of his tail with a transfiguring alertness. Without looking at me, without looking away from the dog, my father allowed his right hand to reach down and find my shoulder and lie there.

"It comes over him like a sickness," he said.

Like lovesickness, I think he meant, and even then I somehow understood. He was talking about a love, paramount if not transcendent, by which Mike was altogether moved, which he felt in his bones and could not resist.

And now of course I know that he was speaking from sympathy. He was talking also about himself, about his love, not only for the birds yet hidden and still somewhere beyond the end of Mike's nose, but for the country itself, his life in it, and the great beauty that sustained it then and always.

It was lovesickness, recognized in the dog because he knew it more fully in himself, that held him still, his hand on my shoulder, in that moment before we started forward to wake up the birds.

Mike, I think, was my father's one superlative dog, and his noontime just happened to coincide with my father's. It did not last long. After Mike, there were other dogs, but my father did not exult in them as he had in Mike. And he had less time for them. Griefs and responsibilities came upon him. His life as a hunter gradually subsided, and in his later years I don't think he much wished for it or often remembered it.

It may be that those summit years made the measure of the later ones, revealing them as anticlimactic and more than a little sad. The years with Mike may have established a zenith of performance and companionship that he could not hope, and even did not wish, to see equaled.

Mike lived long enough to become Old Mike to us all. And then the day arrived when we came down to breakfast and our mother told us, "I wouldn't go out there if I were you. Your daddy's burying his dog." And we could see him with a spade down in the far end of the garden, digging the grave.

That was all I knew about the burial of Mike until one day, near the end of his own life, when my father told me a little more: "I had almost covered him up, when it occurred to me that I hadn't said anything. I needed to say something. And so I uncovered his head. I said, 'Blessings on you, Mike. We'll hunt the birds of Paradise.'"

Who Dreamt This Dream? (1966)

Grover Gibbs had a way, at odd times, of lying for pleasure. And he was good at it. He had a gift for it. Sometimes he would tell you something utterly preposterous, giving you all the time as straight and honest a look as if he was reciting the list of states and their capitals that he had learned in school, which he also would do from time to time. Sometimes he would tell you something utterly plausible and you would believe it, and he would walk out of the shop, serious-faced, leaving you to find out for yourself that it was a stretcher.

Later, when I accused him, he would say, "Wait a minute, Jayber. Wait a minute, Mr. Crow. Maybe I dreamt that. Or maybe you did."

One day I was the only one in the place when he came in. I was sitting in the barber chair reading the paper. I lowered the paper to see who it was. Knowing Grover didn't need a haircut, I raised the paper up again.

"Have a seat, Grover," I said. "Tell me a big one."

He ignored that. I finished the paragraph I was reading, folded the paper, and laid it down. Grover sat down. We each had an item of news or two and a comment or two, and we chatted a while.

The talk went on as some others came in and I got busy. The customers went out, and it was just Grover and me again.

After a while more, Grover got up and settled his hat on his head. He looked very sober.

"Well, I reckon I better go out and see if there ain't something I can do for Danny and Lyda and them."

I said, "*What?*"

"Oh. Burley Coulter died last night. I thought you knowed."

"*What!*"

"Yep," he said, meaning, "It's one of them things. It finally comes to us all." He gave his head a solemn little shake and stepped on out the door.

And there I stood with a chill passing over me as if I was standing in a window and somebody was drawing down the shade.

I went to the front door and turned around my paper clock that always said "Back at 6:30," and ran outside. I borrowed a car from the first friendly face I saw, which happened to be Mart Rowanberry's.

When I drove in out at the old Coulter place where Burley lived with Danny and Lyda Branch, who were his son and daughter-in-law, there Burley was, sitting on a bucket in the barn door, sharpening his knife.

I barely got the car stopped. I sort of fell back against the seat and for a while just looked at him, and he looked, wondering, back at me.

"Well," he finally said, "are you traveling or just going somewheres?"

"I heard you were dead!"

"Aw," he said. "Aw. Well, *I* heard that. Did *you* believe it?"

The Requirement (1970)

Well, you get older and you begin to lose people, kinfolks and friends. Or it *seems* to start when you're getting older. You wonder who was looking after such things when you were young. The people who died when I was young were about all old. Their deaths didn't interrupt me much, even when I missed them. Then it got to be people younger than me and people my own age that were leaving this world, and then it was different. I began to feel it changing me.

When people who mattered to me died I began to feel that something was required of me. Sometimes something would be required that I could do, and I did it. Sometimes when I didn't know what was required, I still felt the requirement. Whatever I did never felt like enough. Something I knew was large and great would have happened. I would be aware of the great world that is always nearby, ever at hand, even within you, as the good book says. It's something you would maybe just as soon not know about, but finally you learn about it because you have to.

That was the way it was when Big Ellis took sick in the fall of 1970. He was getting old and dwindling as everybody does, as I was myself. But then all of a sudden he wasn't dwindling anymore, but going down. First thing you know, he was staying mostly in bed. And then he had to have help to get out of bed.

Heart, the doctor said, and I suppose it was. But it wasn't just that, in my opinion. I think pretty well all of Big's working parts were giving out. He was seventy-six years old.

I'd walk over there through the fields every day, early or late, depending on the weather and the work. I was feeling that requirement, you see.

I would say, "Big, is there anything you need? Is there anything you want me to do?" hoping there would be something.

And he would say, "Burley, there ain't one thing I need in this world. But thank you."

But he didn't mean yet that he was giving up on this world. I would sit by the bed, and he would bring up things we would do when he got well, and we would talk about them and make plans. And in fact he really didn't need anything. Annie May, who loved him better than some people thought he deserved, was still healthy then. As far as I could tell, she was taking perfect care of him.

We called Big "Big" of course because he was big. He was stout too. His strength sometimes would surprise you, even as big as he was. He sort of made a rule of not putting out more effort than the least he could get away with. He wouldn't pull his britches up until they were absolutely falling off. But if he thought he needed to, or ought to, he could pick up a two-bushel sack of wheat and toss it onto a load like it wasn't more than a basketball. Once I saw him pick up an anvil by its horn with one hand and carry it to where he needed it and set it down gently as you would set down an egg.

Big was a year or so older than me, and for a while that made a difference and I had to give him the lead. But as we got older we got closer to the same age, and we ran together as equal partners. We didn't settle down when we were supposed to, we were having too good a time. For a long time we stayed unattached, unworried, and unweary. We shined up to the ladies together, and fished and hunted together, and were about as free as varmints ourselves. We ran a many a Saturday night right on into Sunday morning. I expect we set records around here for some of our achievements, which I don't enjoy talking about now as much as I once did. But some of the stories about Big himself I will always love to tell.

One time we heard about a dance they were giving at the schoolhouse in a little place named Shagbark over on the far side of the river. We went to it in one of Big's old cars that never got anywhere except by luck. But we did get there, after a stop in Hargrave to get a lady to sell us some liquor. It was good stuff, Canadian whiskey, the real article.

It was a good dance too, good musicianers. They had this fellow playing the piano. He had twelve fingers and he was making music with every one of them. I never saw such a thing before. I haven't since. And they had a better than average number of good-looking girls. We got to where we were just letting it happen, we didn't mind what. We didn't know a soul over there and nobody knew us. We didn't have a thing to worry about, and we were cutting up like a new pair of scissors. And then all at once it went kaflooey.

Big was wearing his suit. We'd had to buy our whiskey in half-pints, it was all the lady had, and he had stuck one of those into the inside pocket of his jacket. He got to dancing with this girl, a good-looking girl, a big girl, a fair match for him. She must have set a record for bracelets and things. She was wearing enough metal to draw lightning. She was jingling like a two-year-old mule in a chain harness. Big got to feeling fond of her, and he pulled her up close to him, to where she could feel that bottle. And that was what changed things. Maybe she wasn't too smart, maybe she was a little bit looney, as some girls are, but she thought that bottle was a handgun.

Well, John Dillinger was on the loose at that time, and nobody knew for sure where he was. That gave this event a sort of framework, you see. First thing you know, everybody was glancing toward us and whispering. We got the story later. That big girl hadn't much more than told what she thought Big had in his pocket before they figured out that he was John Dillinger and I was his driver.

Everybody began to leave. They weren't long about it. They made use of both doors and every window, all of them being wide open, for it was a hot night. It wasn't long until Big and I were the only ones left. We were puzzled until, as I say, we heard the story. And then we enjoyed it. Especially Big enjoyed it. For a good while after that if you wanted to make him giggle all you had to do was call him "John."

To know how funny it was you have to picture Big the way he looked that night, all rumpled up in his suit and sweating, hot too on the track of that big girl, smiling like sugar wouldn't melt in his mouth, his feet stepping and prancing all on their own for he had forgotten about them, and if you'd asked him to tell you right quick where he was, he wouldn't have known.

He was a wonderfully humored man. Things that would make most people mad just slid off of him. He would forgive anything at all that he could get the least bit of amusement out of. And any amusement he got he paid back with interest. He was full of things to say that didn't have anything to do with anything else. You'd be talking to him maybe about getting his hay up or fixing a fence, and he would say, "You know, I wish I'd a been born rich in place of pretty."

One time when we were hardly more than grown boys, I got sent word of a dance they were giving on Saturday night down at Goforth. Well, it was a girl who sent the word, and I sent word back I couldn't come. The reason was I didn't have any good shoes, though I didn't tell her. I didn't have shoes nor money either. It was a time when money was scarce.

But the day of the dance I happened to go by Big's house and there his good shoes were, shined, sitting out on the well top. Wasn't anybody around, so I just borrowed the shoes and went my way and wore them to the dance that night. They were too big of course, and sometimes I had to dance a while to get all the way into the toes. I must say I danced the shine off of them too and nicked them up here and there. I left them on the well top at Big's house just before daylight.

Since he hadn't had any shoes to wear to the dance, Big got a full night's sleep. Next morning he left the house with the milk bucket on his way to the barn just after daylight, and there his shoes were, right where he'd left them the day before, but now they were all scuffed up.

"Well, shoes!" Big said. "I don't know where you been, but looks like you had a good time."

One evening after supper I walked over to his place. I'd heard about a litter of hound pups, pretty nice it was said. If Big was interested, I thought we might go together and see them for ourselves. I was ready for a young dog, and I thought Big might be.

Nobody was home, and Big's car was gone. I imagined he'd taken his folks off to visit somebody. On my way to the house I'd looked in the barn and seen his work harness lying in two pretty much heaps on the barn floor. I couldn't think why, and the matter got my attention. Big's daddy, I knew, would never ever have left his harness in any such a mess. But old Mr. Ellis was sick by then, and the place was coming under the influence of Big and his way of doing, which I didn't yet know as much about as I was going to.

When I saw nobody was at home, I stopped again at the barn, thinking to do Big a favor while I had it on my mind. I picked up his harness and straightened it out and hung it up on the pegs where I knew it belonged and went my way.

After breakfast the next morning, still wanting to talk about the pups, I went back again and found Big in the barn. He had one of the harnesses half on a mule and half on himself, his clothes in about as bad a shape as the harness. He was tramping and grabbling among the chains and straps, blowing at the sweat dripping off his nose, with the look of despair and anguish all over his face. Things he'd left in a heap made better sense to him than things put straight by me.

I could have laughed, but I didn't. I said, "Well, old bud, do you reckon you're going to make it?"

Before then he hadn't known I was there. He gave me a purely threatening look. He said, "I wish I had ahold of the son of a bitch that hung my harness up."

However mad he was, I knew he wouldn't stay mad more than a few minutes. He *couldn't* was why.

I helped him harness his mules. I told him about the pups, and we agreed to go look at them that evening. I never laughed, nor as much as smiled. And not one word did I ever say about that harness.

You almost couldn't make him mad. But if you didn't watch yourself he could make you mad, just by being so much himself he couldn't imagine that anybody could be different. He didn't go in much for second opinions. He stayed single until his mother and daddy both were dead, and then he married Annie May pretty soon, which maybe was predictable. He liked company. He didn't like to be by himself.

Being married to Big, after the long head start he'd had, was not dependably an uplifting experience. Though Annie May was a good deal younger than he was, she was made pretty much on his pattern, ample and cheerful.

But she could be fittified. I've seen her mad enough at Big, it looked like, to kill him, and maybe he'd be off on another subject entirely and not even notice, which didn't help her patience. One time when she got mad and threw an apple at him—it would have hurt, she had a good arm—he just caught it and ate it. I didn't see that. It was told.

But she never stayed mad long. One time when I went over there she was just furious at him, mainly because he wouldn't bother to argue with her over whatever she was upset about in the first place. She was crying and hollering, "I'm a-leaving you, Big! You've played hell this time! I'm a-leaving here just as soon as I get this kitchen cleaned up!" That was like her. You wouldn't have minded eating dinner off of her kitchen floor. And of course by the time she got the kitchen cleaned up she had forgiven him. I think she loved him *because* he was the way he was. They never had any children, and he was her boy.

Maybe because they didn't have children Big and Annie May let their little farm sag around them as they got older, the way a lot of such couples do. Big's daddy had the place in fair shape when he died, but he died early in the Depression, and so Big couldn't have made a fast start even if he had wanted to. He and Annie May lived well enough, but that was mainly Annie May's doing. She made a wonderful big garden every year, and kept a flock of chickens and some turkeys. They always had three or four milk cows, milked mainly by Annie May, and they sold the extra cream and fed the extra milk to their meat hogs. So they always had plenty to eat. Annie May was as fine a cook as ever I ate after. When they had company or a bunch of us were there working, she would put on a mighty feed. Both of them loved to eat, and they loved to see other people eat.

But Big never tried for much or did much for his place. He wasn't, to tell the truth, much of a farmer. When he went to help his neighbors he'd work as hard as anybody, but put him by himself on his own place, and getting by was good enough. He was a great one then for "a lick and a promise" or "good enough for who it's for."

I don't know that he ever owned a new piece of equipment, except for a little red tractor that he bought after the war just to be shed of the bother of a team of mules. When he got the tractor he stubbed off the tongues of his old horse-drawn equipment and went puttering about even more slipshod than before. My brother, Jarrat, and I swapped work with him all our lives, you might as well say, but when we went to his place we always took our own equipment. Jarrat's main idea was to get work done, and he didn't have enough patience to enjoy Big the way I did. "If he gets in my way with one of them cobbled-up rigs of his, damned if I won't run over him." That was Jarrat's limit on Big, and Big did keep out of his way.

His final sickness was pretty much like the rest of his life. He didn't seem to be in a hurry to get well, or to die either. He didn't make much of it. The doctor had said a while back that he had a bad heart and gave him some pills. Big more or less believed the doctor, but he also let himself believe he would sooner or later get well. I don't think he felt like doing much of anything.

Annie May said, "Big, for goodness sake, let's take you to a heart doctor or *something*. You can't just lie there. We can't just do nothing."

"I ain't going anywhere," he said. "I'm just feeling a little dauncy is all."

She knew better than to push him. Easy-going as he was, when he took a stand you couldn't shake him. He *could* just lie there. They *could* just do nothing.

If he had been suffering, if something had hurt him or he had been uncomfortable, maybe he would have done something. Maybe he would be living yet. But the only thing the matter was he was getting weaker. His strength was just slowly leaking out of him. He didn't have much appetite, and he was losing flesh. But he was comfortable enough. He wasn't complaining.

So nothing was what they did. That was the way Big had solved most of his problems. He would work hard to help his neighbors, because he liked them and liked to be with them and wanted them to get their problems solved. He would wear people out talking to them and fishing for their opinions on anything whatsoever. He would go to no limit of trouble to have a good time, and he'd had a lot of good times. But when it came to doing some actual work for himself, he often simplified it by not doing anything.

That was why, when Big took sick, the old Ellis place, as some of us still call it, was pretty well run down. There wasn't a chicken or a hog or a cow. Another neighbor, a young fellow, was growing the crop and making a little hay on the shares, but that was all. Social Security, I reckon, was taking up the slack.

I got used to making some time every day to go to see how Big was doing and to sit with him a while. What was harder to get used to was the place. The fences all gone down. The barns and other outbuildings all paintless, and the roofs leaking. The lots grown up in weeds and bushes so you couldn't open the doors that were shut, or shut the doors that had been left open. And every building was fairly stuffed with old farm tools, most of them going back to Big's daddy's time or before, for Big always figured they might come in handy.

What they did, it turned out, was come to be antiques. When the farm was sold to a Louisville businessman after Big died, and the tools and a lot of the household plunder were auctioned off, about everything was bought at a good price by antique collectors. After she was too old to use it, or even want it, Annie May had more money than she ever imagined.

Walking across the fields, the way I usually went when I went to see Big, I would have to appraise every time what had become of the place, a good little farm dwindled down almost to nothing. Nobody going out to milk anymore. Nobody going out to feed the chickens or the hogs. You really couldn't see that anybody still lived there until you got to the yard. The yard was still Annie May's territory—her last stand, you might say—and it was kept neat. The house itself, the cellar and smokehouse out back, they still showed care. And well off to the side, out of the way, the rusty dinner bell that hadn't been rung in years was still perched on its leaning pole. A man on a tractor couldn't hear it. The bell was going to turn out to be an antique too. At the sale two ladies bid for it until you'd have thought it was made out of gold.

The day that was going to be the day Big died I went over there first thing in the morning, as soon as we finished up at the barn and ate breakfast. It was a fine morning, cold and bright, the sky blue and endless right down to the horizon, and everything below shining with frost. We had finished with the hog-killing the day before, and I was bringing some fresh spareribs and tenderloin, thinking they might tempt Big to eat. Until then Big and Annie May both were talking like he was going to get well.

But that morning things had changed. I could feel it as soon as I stepped in through the kitchen door. Annie May was busy setting the kitchen to rights. She didn't try to keep me from seeing that she was crying. Two of her friends, neighbor women, had come to be with her and help her, as the women do when there's trouble. What had happened was they had figured out—Big first, I think, and then Annie May—that Big wasn't going to get well. The whole feeling of the house had changed. My old granny would have said the Angel of Death had passed over and marked the house. Call it superstition if you want to, but that was what it felt like.

"I brought some meat," I said. "Lyda thought maybe Big would like something fresh."

"Well, God love her heart!" Annie May said, taking the packages from me, as if she was mourning over them.

And then she said, "Go on in, Burley. He's awake."

I went in. Big was lying in the clean bed in the clean room, looking no different really, but that feeling of being in a marked house was there too. The counterpane was white as snow, and white as it was his hands lying on it looked pale. They looked useless. When I came in, he raised a hand to me and gave me a grin as usual. But now he seemed to be grinning to apologize for the feeling that was in the room. He would always get uneasy when things got serious, let alone solemn. He disliked by nature the feeling that was there, but he didn't refuse it either.

He said, "Well, Burley, it come over me that I ain't going to come out of this."

I went over to the bed and gave his hand a shake. I took my jacket off and sat down by him. His hand and his voice were weak, but they weren't noticeably weaker than the day before.

He said, "I'm about to be long gone from here."

"Oh, sho'ly not," I said.

"It's so," he said.

I said, "If it's so, old bud, it'll make a mighty difference around here. We'll look for you and we'll miss you."

He had been stronger than me all his life, and now he was weak. And I was sitting there by his bed, still strong. What could you do? What could you do that would be anyways near enough? I could feel the greatness of life and death; and the great world endless as the sky swelling out beyond this little one. And I began again to hear from that requirement that seems to come from the larger world. The requirement was telling me, "*Do* something for him. Do more than you've ever done. Do more than you *can* do."

As if he had read my mind, he said, "I appreciate you coming, Burley. You've stuck by me. I imagine I'll remember it as long as I live." And then he giggled, for in fact it was a fine joke.

"Well, I wish I could do more. Ain't there anything at all you want?"

"Not a thing. Not a thing in this world."

We talked then, or mostly I did, for a while, about things that were going on round about. And finally I had to leave. They were busy at home, and they'd be looking for me. Big had said he wasn't long for this world, but he looked about the same as yesterday. For all I knew, he might live a long time yet. When somebody tells you he's going to die, you can't say, "Well, go ahead. I'll just sit here till you do." I was going to be surprised when I got word that afternoon that old Big had sure enough left us.

"Well," I said, "I got to be getting on home." And I stood up.

He raised his hand to stop me. "Wait, Burley. There *is* something I want you to do."

"Sure," I said. "Name it."

"Go yonder to the press"—he used the old word—"and open the door."

I went to the closet and opened the door. It was where they kept their good clothes, Annie May's Sunday dresses, not many, and Big's suit, all put away there together.

"Ain't my pistol there, just inside?"

The pistol was in its shoulder holster, hanging on a nail in the door jamb. It was a .22 revolver, heavy-built and uncommonly accurate for a pistol. It was the only really good thing Big had ever owned, and he had taken care of it like a king's crown. He bought it new when times were good back there in the forties, and the bluing was still perfect except for a spot or two where the holster had worn it. I had always thought highly of it, and he knew I had.

"It's right here," I said.

"I want you to take it. I'd like to know where it'll be after I'm gone."

It flew into me then just how far toward the edge of things we'd come, two old men who'd been neighbors and friends since they were boys, and if I'd thought of anything to say I couldn't have said it. For a while I couldn't even turn around.

"Put it on," Big said. "Button your jacket over it. I don't want Annie May to see it when you leave."

I did as he told me. I said, "Thanks, Big."

"Sure," he said.

"Well," I said, "I'll be seeing you."

He said, "Yeah. See you later."

So I had come to do something for Big, if I could, and instead Big had done something for me, and I was more in debt to the requirement than ever.

I went out through the kitchen, speaking a few pleasantries with the women, and let myself out. I sat down on the porch step to put my overshoes back on, and started home. And all the time the requirement was staying with me. "Can't you, for God's sake, think of *something* to do?" When I got to about the middle of the barn lot, I just stopped. I stood there and looked all around.

Oh, it was a splendid morning, still frozen, not much changed at all. The ground was still shining white under the blue sky. I thought of a rhyme that Elton Penn was always saying in such weather: "Clear as a bell, cold as hell, and smells like old cheese." Maybe that was what put me in mind to do what I did.

When I looked back towards the house, the only thing between me and the sky was that old dinner bell leaning on its post like it was about to fall.

Big's pistol, when I pulled it out, felt heavy and familiar, comfortable. It was still warm from the house. There were five cartridges in the cylinder, leaving an empty chamber to rest the hammer on. I cocked it and used my left hand to steady my right. What I wanted was a grazing hit that would send the bullet flying out free into the air.

Even as the bullet glanced and whined away, the old bell summed up all the dongs it had ever rung. It filled the day and the whole sky and brought the worlds together, the little and the great. I knew that, lying in his bed in the house, Big heard it and was pleased. Standing in the lot, I heard it and I was pleased. It wasn't enough, but it was something. It was a grand sound. It was a good shot.

An Empy Jacket (1974)

Marcie Catlett was usually wakened in the morning by his father's voice calling up the stairs, according to his mood, "Marcie! Betty! Time to get up!" or, singing badly, "Dear ones, Harford Fork again awaits the sunrise!" or, beating on a pan, "Wake up and pee! The world's on fire!"

But this morning the telephone rang into Marcie's sleep in the dark before the house had stirred. Or maybe it was a pressure of calamity that woke him before the phone rang, as if the whole dark countryside were already disturbed by the knowledge that Elton Penn was dead.

And so Marcie lay under the covers, alert and still, through the long time until the fourth ring and then his father's voice answering. Marcie would never forget the sounds that followed.

"Hello?" And after a pause: "*Aw!*" And then after a long pause, and interrupted by further pauses: "What time? . . . Oh. . . . Oh. . . . Where are you now? . . . Well, I'm sorry, Henry. . . . I know you are. . . . All right. We'll be there."

Marcie heard his father hang up the telephone. He heard him say, his voice breaking on the last word, "Flora, Elton's dead."

Those words, his father's voice saying them, seemed fixed and continuing in the air. They seemed suspended as though they might fall, though they had not fallen.

He heard his mother: "Oh, Andy, I'm so sorry!"

And then the house began to sound like itself again. Marcie heard his father go out the back door to the barn. He heard his mother fixing breakfast. Presently he began to smell breakfast. It might have been any morning, except for the three words, "Flora, Elton's dead," that continued still, aloof from him, suspended in the air—and except that he and his sister had not been called, though ordinarily they would have been. Their father maybe was doing their morning chores in addition to his own. And so it was a different day.

Marcie and Elton had been friends. It was a family friendship. Marcie had inherited it, so to speak, from his father who, with his brother, Henry, had inherited it from their father. Marcie's father and Elton often worked together, and when they did, if he was not in school, Marcie would be with them. That had been a regular part of his life from before he could remember. Sometimes, now that he was nearly ten and getting bigger, he would be at work with Elton by himself, and Elton would let him help or give him jobs to do on his own. When Marcie had actually helped and been necessary, Elton would reach into his pocket for money to pay him, or he would write him a check.

To tell the truth, Marcie did not like working with his father as much as he liked working with Elton. This embarrassed him a little, and he tried to keep his father from knowing. But he belonged to his father, so his father clearly thought, and that was sometimes too tight a fit. His father had expectations that sometimes Marcie felt closing in on him, so that he could not to save his life work willingly or keep in a good humor. He and Elton, though, were nothing but friends. With Elton, he felt free, even when Elton was being hard on him, which Elton sometimes was and didn't mind being.

Marcie could be careless. Sometimes, even with Elton, he could not keep his mind on his business. He left a gate open and next thing he knew three sows were in the garden, and Elton was in what Marcie's father and his uncle Henry called a limited good humor. If Marcie had been older, as he well knew, it would not have been even limited good humor. Elton said, with limited amusement and even kindly but also sternly, "You're sorry, Marcie, but sorry don't shut the gate when you were supposed to shut it, and it don't keep the hogs out of the garden, and it don't undo the damage."

So he had to stand and take it, for Elton was neither more nor less than Elton. If you wanted to be with Elton, which Marcie did, you had to be with him as he was. To displease him was a way of finding out how much you wanted to please him.

Marcie had begun to imagine a time when he would be grown up and would work as an equal with Elton and his father and the Rowanberrys and the others, when even Elton would recognize him as a man good at work, capable of putting his hand to a job and doing it right.

But now, though this was far yet from Marcie's imagination, it was not going to be Elton who would recognize him as a hand and a man. The one who would grant him that formality, in another eight years, was going to be Mart and Art Rowanberry's not easily pleased brother-in-law Pascal Sowers who, when he came with the rest to harvest the first crop of Marcie's own that he grew entirely by his own work and knowledge, would nod his head in most serious commendation and pronounce, "Well, you *are* worth a shit!"

Their mother called them to get up.

When they dressed and came down, she met them at the foot of the steps to tell them, as Marcie understood, so that their father would not have to do it, "Elton's dead. He died last night. I'm sorry, kids. I'm sorry to have to tell you."

Marcie's big sister, Betty, cried and let herself be held and comforted by their mother. But when their mother looked at Marcie, he only looked back at her, waiting, for her words had not reached him. And then he went past her into the kitchen.

They were going to the Penns', they were going to Elton and Mary Penn's house, as soon as breakfast was over, and breakfast did not keep them long. They did not even clear the table. Marcie expected to be told to put on better clothes, but nobody mentioned clothes. Just as they were, nobody finding anything to say, they got into the car and went out the lane to the road. They went to Port William and on through it. They turned onto the Bird's Branch road, and passed the Catlett home place where Henry lived. They followed the road down into the Bird's Branch hollow and turned into the lane that went back along the old rock fence to the farmstead and the house that belonged to Elton and Mary.

Marcie had made this trip hundreds of times. Traveling the lane that

led to the Penns' house was as familiar to him as traveling the lane along
Harford Fork that led to his own house. This was the country he belonged
to, a permanent country, so far as he knew it, landmarked by people who
apparently always had been there, as firmly and finally planted as the
stones in the graveyard on the hill at Port William: his parents, his Catlett
grandparents, Penns, Rowanberrys, Coulters, Branches. So far as he had
known it, it was subject only to the changes of weather, of seedtime and
harvest, summer and winter, day and night.

But now a change of another kind had come upon it, a great change
that he could feel in his parents' silence and his sister's and his own. None
of them had said a word. It was a silence weighted with dread at coming
to this place now that it was changed. It was altogether changed, though
it looked the same as it always had, and this made the change by far the
worst he had ever known.

In the driveway beside the house, he saw his uncle Henry's car, new-
looking and clean, and behind it his grandfather's car that was black and
dust-covered and covered with scratches. There was a third car that he
knew belonged to Elton and Mary's daughter Martha and her husband,
who lived in Cincinnati. That, for the time being, was all.

Marcie followed his parents and his sister around the house to the back
porch and into the kitchen. Sitting in chairs drawn back from the table
were Marcie's grandfather and his uncle Henry. Also there were Elton and
Mary's son Jack, just home from the army, and Arch Hall, their son-in-law.
They were quiet. The whole house was quiet. Marcie could hear the quiet
in every room of it. Henry and Jack and Arch, who usually would have
said something to tease him a little, were quiet. His father went from one
to another, shaking hands and exchanging with each a word or two, and
then he sat down, and the quiet resumed.

And so Marcie would know from then on that baffled silence, the
silence of finding nothing adequate, and therefore nothing, to say.

Marcie's mother and his sister had passed through the kitchen to the
living room to sit with the other women, who had come to sit with Mary
and Martha in their grief. Marcie stood just inside the door where he had
stopped. He would have liked to be not there, but he did not know, now
that he was there, how to leave. And he had not thought of a place to go.

His grandfather was sitting nearest the door. When they had come in he had been staring down at the backs of his hands lying open on his lap. Now, sensing Marcie's discomfort, he reached for him, drew him over, and put his arm around him. Marcie submitted to this, saying nothing. He did take a certain comfort in his grandfather's presence, and for a while he was glad to stand close to him. His grandfather's hands were proprietary and unrefusable but there was a certain relenting in them too, on that day as on others. There was the feeling of his grandfather's own kind of tenderness.

For a while his grandfather's arm around him was a shelter. But the news of Elton's death was making its way through the community. Others came, and they kept coming, requiring the men at the table to stand and speak and shake hands, shifting about to make room for more chairs. Finally attention was withdrawn from Marcie and a way opened between him and the door. He slipped out, leaving the door a little ajar so as to make no noise.

He came to the cars clustered along the driveway, some he had never seen there before. He went through them without looking back. There had been frost in the night. There was still a sharpness in the air, but this was the outside air and he welcomed the feel of it. Just by breathing it he could tell how big and free it was.

With the assembly of cars behind him, he was again in the world as he knew it, though change was upon it. It was a day unchangeably changed. It would be forever what it now was. Though nobody had said it, the word "forever," along with the other words, began to be suspended in the air above Marcie's head. He himself had said no word at all. He had not made a sound.

He let himself through the gate in the lot fence that joined the fronts of the two barns, the implement shed, and the corn crib. He stopped and stood. It was as though he had come into the inside of Elton's mind. All around him were the things that were Elton's thoughts and the order that Elton had made. And yet everything was changed. It was unearthly quiet and still on a weekday morning when something ought to have been stirring. So early in his life Marcie had come to the confusion that would obsess his grandfather Catlett in his terrible forgetfulness at the end of his life: Though everything clearly had changed, everything looked exactly the same.

Various implements were in their places in the open-fronted shed, put away clean and in good repair, as Elton would always have them, ready to go to work again. Near the top of the ridge, two fences away, Elton's cows were grazing, some with young calves at their sides. The several shoats in the hog lot had eaten their fill and were lying along the fence, apparently asleep. As Marcie stood watching, Peg the Border collie, always in need of a job, drove a banty rooster between two boards of the board fence, herded him deftly through the open door of the feed barn, and lay down in the doorway to keep him from coming out again. Peg was a clever dog, one of the creatures of the place who could always make Elton stop and watch. On another day, Marcie would have called her to come to him and be patted, for her friendship was something of an honor. But the morning was too quiet. The quiet in the lot had too much the quality of having been there unusually long. It was a quiet he did not want to hear himself speaking into.

Instead, he walked quietly, not wanting to hear his footsteps either, past Peg and into the doorway of the barn. And from that threshold for a time he went no farther, for Elton clearly had been at work there, probably just yesterday. The dirt floor of the driveway had been raked and swept clean as a pin. A shovel, a rake, and a heavy push broom stood leaning against the wall. And near them, hanging from a nail, was Elton's work jacket. It hung still, still. It had not the shape of Elton's shoulders and back and arms, but the shape only of any garment dangling from a nail.

And now a strange freedom came upon Marcie. Now he could walk freely into the barn. Now he could touch the handles of the tools. Now he could touch the jacket. And all the while he heard himself crying, for he had recognized finally the changed world. The name of the change was absence. It was loss. And the changed world was the world he knew. It was the world known to his father and mother, to his uncle Henry and his grandfather, in which a man might grow warm at his work, take off his jacket and hang it on a nail, and forever not come back to put it on again.

At Home (1981)

And so, past the heavy gunnery, the bombs, the blood and fire of Bastogne and beyond, there was this: the creek valley opening below him as he rose step by step up the two-track road. Since the days and nights of combat, before the wound that set him free of the army and free very nearly of this world, he had borne in the back of his mind for going on forty years, as a sort of comment on everything else, the clamor of the big gun he had served, of the guns that accompanied his, of the guns that answered. Against that immense sounding, so long ago, so little receded, the small valley holds its plea, frail as a flower, and as undeniable.

The valley had widened below him now so that when he stopped and looked back the whole legend of it had come clear: the house backed against the near slope, the cellar and smokehouse, the barns on the near and far sides of the creek, the creek itself, Sand Ripple, twisting and shining between parallel rows of still-leafless trees on its way to the river, the inverted arc of the footbridge swung across at the edge of the woods upstream. The valley revealed itself now as a bowl, in the greatness of the country less than a cup, as familiar to him as the palm of his hand.

It was a small place, humble enough in all its aspects, except for an ordinary splendor that would possess it from time to time in every season. And it was, as some would have thought it, remote, tucked away in one of the folds of the much-folded landscape surrounding the town, also small and humble, of Port William. A stranger driving along the river road would not have suspected the existence of such a place, would have noticed no doubt the stand of trees that hovered about the creek mouth, but probably not at all the narrow opening, near the Sand Ripple bridge, of the lane that followed the creek upstream through the woods to the abrupt fall of light onto the opened valley.

He was Arthur Rowanberry, known as Art, whose family, ever intent on taking its living from the place, which the place, mostly hillside, yielded to them reluctantly, had forgot the number of their generations on it.

He was walking up the hill road to the Orchard Ridge, as they still called it, though the last of its apple trees was long gone from living memory, where he would count the calving cows and put out their daily ration of hay. His brother Martin, Mart for short, had gone up in the early morning to see about them, driving the tractor while the ground was frozen so that the heavy machine would do no harm to the road. Otherwise, Mart too would have walked. Unlike their eventual successors, four different owners in twenty-five years, who would wear the road to a raw wound by driving on it in all weather, no Rowanberry ever drove a wheeled vehicle up the hill when the ground was soft.

By the calendar it was almost spring. The days were lengthening, a tinge of green was showing in the pastures, and the buds were fattening on the water maples. But on that day the season was halted by a cold spell. A steady, bitter wind was blowing from the north, hard against his back as he came up into it and turned the sharp bend in the road. He warmed his hands by shifting them, first one and then the other, from his stick to a pocket.

But he liked weather, anyhow most weather. He liked its freedom from walls, its way of overcoming all obstructions and filling the world. And he liked walking, which was another kind of freedom: no preparation, no expense, just get up onto your legs and go. What he had liked best in the army was the marching, the passing through country, with the others, nearly all younger than he, stepping in the same cadence all around. But a greater pleasure was in walking by himself. There was pleasure also in the company of old Preacher, the gray-muzzled hound who was walking for the time being at Art's heels. Preacher knew the way, even the errand, as well as Art did, and like Art he was too old for needless haste.

With Mart away, at Port William or Hargrave or somewhere, doing whatever it was he did on Saturday afternoon, Art began his walk plenty early, giving himself time. It was not that he needed time, so early in the day, for anything in particular. He needed time only to take his time, to have time for the day and the weather, to walk in his own time, unhurried, with no reason not to stop and look around, or to take a "long cut" off the knapped stone of the road and into the woods. In his own time, time asked nothing of him except to live in it and to keep alert, to watch, to see what he could see, the day and its light coming to him unburdened.

He had never minded company. He had always liked to be in the field, in the barn, at a wood sawing or hog killing, with a crew of friends and kin. Even then, at the age of seventy-six, he would hurry to get in on a lift, to do his part. "Many hands make light work," he liked to say, for he knew it was true. But to be alone was a different happiness. At times it was almost a merriment, when he liked his thoughts.

Some thoughts that had gathered to him in his time gave him no pleasure. There was always something that had to be subtracted from pleasure, "always something," as he would say now and again, "to take the joy out of life." But he had acquired also many thoughts that gave him joy.

His thoughts were placed and peopled, and they seemed to come to him on their own, without any effort of his to call them up. He would think of the present day and place, as now, as the prospect widened below him and he felt in his flesh and in the breadth of the country the full, free stroke of the wind across the ridges.

"We'll have to face it, coming down," he said to Preacher. And then he stopped and looked about. As if to console the dog he said, "Well, maybe it'll fair up tomorrow."

Or it would happen that another time would open to him, sometimes from long ago, and he would see his grandmaw and grandpaw Rowanberry at the log house back on the ridge, and the old life they had lived there when he was a boy. He would see their going among the fields and along the roads, mostly afoot even when they went to town, and the network of paths that connected house and barn and corn crib and hog lot, well and cellar and smokehouse. The life they lived there he recognized, even in his childhood, as old beyond memory, little changed in so much time beyond their marking of the ground. Some of the marks they left were wounds in the steeper land, slow to heal, for hard times and the family's unrelenting will to endure had driven them to crop the slopes, and the rains had imposed their verdict. Art knew the stern requirement that his elders, remembered and forgotten, should survive if they could, as he knew the inexorable judgment of weather and time. He saw the fault, knew the wrong, yet placed no blame. They had paid to live as resignedly as they had expected to die. In his thoughts they went from day to day to day in their steady work, eating their large and frugal meals, going to bed precisely at darkfall, rising to work again long before daylight even in summer. Of the things they needed they grew and made much, purchased little.

Art had been the first grandchild, and the elder Rowanberrys, his father's parents, made much of him. As his younger brothers and sisters came along, and at the rare times when he could escape the chores that were assigned to him almost as soon as he could walk, then oftener as his grandparents grew older and had need of him, he liked to leave the house down in the creek valley and go up to stay days and nights at a time at the old house on the ridge.

It was a house of two tall rooms broadly square with a wide hallway between, a long upstairs room under the pitch of the roof, two rock chimneys at either end with wide fireplaces, and at the back a large lean-to kitchen, weatherboarded. The house was finely made, the logs hewed straight and square, the corners so perfectly mitered that you could not insert a knife blade into the joints. The rafters were straight poles, saplings, notched and pegged together at the peak with the same artistry as elsewhere. When he had stayed overnight, Art slept upstairs in the drafty, unceiled attic room illuminated in the daytime only by the light that leaked under the eaves. The wind too came under them. He had waked some mornings when blown-in snow had whitened the covers of the bed.

Of the old house in the time of its human life, before its abandonment after the deaths of his grandparents, he remembered everything. Of his grandparents, their life, and all they remembered and told him, he remembered much. Whether or not he thought their thoughts, he thought at least the thoughts that belonged to such a house and such a life.

And so when he went into the army in 1942, he passed from a world as old and elemental nearly as it had ever been into a world as ruthlessly new as by then it had managed to become.

He was the oldest child, the eldest son. It was his duty, as it appeared to him, to go first to the war, and by doing so to save his younger brothers from the draft—though at this he was not entirely successful. Early in the new year following the attack on Pearl Harbor, he volunteered. He was thirty-seven that year, old for a common soldier, which the younger men, the boys, he served with never let him forget. Soon enough the younger ones were calling him "Pappy," which he accepted, amused to know that he was old enough in fact to have been father to most of them, and recognizing with at least tolerance that to some of them the name alluded to his rural speech and demeanor, his origin, as they put it, "at the end of nowhere."

But they knew him soon enough as a man by a measure that few of them had met or would meet. The rigor of basic training he took in stride, finding it no harder and sometimes easier than the work he was accustomed to at home. He did not have to be taught to fire a rifle, or to fire it accurately. Nobody had to urge him to keep to the pace of a long march. Sleeping on the ground, he rested well. He never complained of the weather. When they were called upon to use an axe or a mattock or a spade, he was the exemplary man. Boys who had never so much as seen an axe would be astonished, watching him work. "You can tell a chopper by his chips," he said to them, and they stood around to admire him as he made the big chips fly. He might, as one of his officers told him, have been promoted as high as sergeant, but he submitted to authority without envying or desiring it.

When he got home from the war, still recovering from his wound, he knew his life was a gift, not so probable as he had once thought, and yet unquestionable as that of any tree, not to be hoarded or clutched at, not to be undervalued or too much prized, for there were many days now lost back in time when he could have died as easily and unremarkably as a fly. It was a life now simply to be lived, accepting hardships and pleasures, joys and griefs equally as they came.

*   *   *

His time in the war had been a different and a separate time, his life then a different life. The memory of it remained always with him, or always near, and yet that time lay behind him, intact and separate as an island in the sea, divided from the time before and the time after.

Returning home from the war, he returned to memory. He returned to the time of his own life that he felt to be continuous from long before his birth until long past his death. He came back to the old place and its constant reminding, awakening memories and memories of memories as he walked in and across the tracks of those who had preceded him. He knew then how his own comings and goings were woven into the invisible fabric of the land's history and its human life.

He was accompanied again, at work and in his thoughts forever after, by people he had always known: his brother, Mart, with whom he lived on in their parents' house, batching, after their parents were gone; his sister, Sudie, and her husband, Pascal Sowers, who were neighbors; the Coulter brothers, Jarrat and Burley; Jarrat's son Nathan and Nathan's wife, Hannah; and then Burley's son, Danny Branch, and Lyda, Danny's wife; and Elton Penn and his wife, Mary. They were a membership, as Burley liked to call it, a mere gathering, not held together by power and organization like the army, but by kinship, friendship, history, memory, kindness, and affection—who were apt to be working together, in various combinations, according to need, and even, always, according to pleasure.

And then, after Andy Catlett's homecoming and settlement near Port William in 1965, because of Andy's cousinship to the Coulters and his friendships from his boyhood with the Penns and the Rowanberrys, Andy and his family became members of the membership and took part in the work-swapping and the old, long knowing in common.

Between Art and Andy there grew, within the larger membership, a sort of kinship, founded upon Art's long memory and his knowledge of old ways, and upon their mutual affection for the Port William countryside in all of its times, seasons, and weathers. They would often be together, at work or at rest, Art talking, Andy listening and asking. Their best times were Sunday mornings or afternoons, when they would travel together on foot or horseback or with a team and wagon, moving at large, sometimes at random, wherever their interest took them. Or they would trace out the now-pathless way, around the hill and up a hollow supposed to be haunted, that the young Rowanberrys had walked to school. Or they would follow the sunken track, long disused, that led from the log house on the ridge down into the river valley where it met the road to town. Or they would pick out other disused ways connecting old landmarks. As they went along, Art's parents and grandparents and other old ones he remembered, or they remembered, would appear in his mind, and he would tell about them: how his grandpaw would tell you a big tale and you could hear him laugh a mile; how old man Will Keith, a saw-logger, who worked a big horse and a little one, would take hold of the little horse's singletree to help him on a hard pull; how Art's own father, Early Rowanberry, never rode uphill behind a team even when the wagon was empty. By then Art's distant travels were long past. On his and Andy's Sunday journeys, having no place far to go, they were never in a hurry. It was never too early or too late to stop and talk. And when Andy needed help, if Art knew it, he would be there. "Do you need anything I got?"

After so many days, so many miles, so many remindings, so much remembering and telling, Andy understood how precisely placed and populated Art's mind was, how like it was to a sort of timeless crossroads where the living and the dead met and recognized one another and passed on their ways, and how rare it was, how singular and once-for-all. When Art would be gone at last from this world, Port William would have no such mind, would be known in no such way, ever again.

Andy Catlett, under the same mortal terms of once for all, has kept Art's mind alive in his own. Some of Art's memories Andy remembers. As he follows and crosses Art's old footings over the land, adding his own passages to the unseen web of the land's history, some of those old ones, who were summoned by reminding into Art's mind, still again and again will appear in Andy's.

And so it is into Andy's thought, into his imagining, that Art has come walking up the hill on that bitter March day thirty years ago. Andy now is an old man, remembering an old man, once his elder and his teacher, with whom he is finally of an age.

Art was wearing a winter jacket, which in its youth had closed with a zipper down the front, but which, the zipper failing, he had overhauled with a set of large buttons and buttonholes, strongly but not finely sewn.

There may have been a time, Andy thinks, when Art was skilled at such work. From his time in the army and before, he had been used to doing for himself whatever he needed done. His hands, hard-used and now arthritic, had become awkward at needlework, and yet he had continued to mend his clothes, pleasing himself both by his thrift and by the durability of his work. When the legs of his coveralls were worn and torn past mending, he lopped off the bottom half, hemmed up the top half, and thus made a light jacket that lasted several more years. When he needed a rope, he braided a perfectly adequate one with salvaged baler twine. He thus maintained a greater intimacy between himself and the things he wore and used, was more all-of-a-piece, than anybody else Andy ever knew.

As he climbed the hill, still keeping to the graveled track, old Preacher still walking behind with his head and tail down, Art watched the creek valley close on his right as the river valley opened on his left. As the country widened around him he breathed larger breaths. And the higher he went, the flatter the horizon looked, in contrast to the alternation of hill and hollow in the view from the creek bottom. He reached a place where he could look out and down over the tops of the bare trees instead of through them. He stopped again then and took in the whole visible length of the larger valley, from the gray, still-winterish slope that closed it a couple of miles upstream to the low rampart, blue with distance, that lay across it down toward the mouth of the river.

He turned presently and went on, the wind pushing him. Soon the track leveled, and he and the old dog were walking along the crest of the ridge. He was walking—as Andy, on his walks with him, had from time to time realized—both through the place and through his consciousness of the presence and the past of it, his recognition of its marks and signs, as his movement through it altered the aspect of it.

He and time were moving at about the same pace. He was neither hurried by it nor hurrying to catch it, his thoughts coming whole as he thought them, with nothing left out or left over. If he seemed to be getting ahead of his thoughts, he stopped and waited.

He was passing a high point out to his left above the river valley. In a certain place out there were what he had known for many years to be the graves of people who lived and were forgotten long before the time they might have been called Indians. He knew what the graves were because, back before the war, on a similar height of ground above Willow Run, a professor from Lexington had come and carefully dug up some graves of the same kind. Art went to see them while they were open, with the remains of skeletons lying in them. That taught him what to look for, and he found these on his own place. The giveaway was flagstones edged up in the shape of a box, hard to see if you didn't know what you were looking for. He rarely spoke of them, and he showed them to nobody. He told Andy about them, indicating with a look and a nod about where they were, but he never showed him. He rarely went near them himself, so as to leave them undisturbed, to leave no track or mark to expose them to indifference or dishonor. Looking at those opened graves, as Andy knew, Art had felt both awe and shame: so long a sleep pried in upon, so old a secret finally told.

The place of the graves now was behind him. They passed from his thought. But he was presently reminded of them again because he was looking into the opening of the Katy's Branch valley where, somewhere in the old woods, all of Burley Coulter that could die lay in a grave formed on the pattern of those ancient ones. This was the sort of thing the elders of Port William were apt to know without knowing quite how they knew it. But Art, with the rest of the old membership, had been in Wheeler and Henry Catlett's law office down in Hargrave the day Danny Branch, Burley's son, returned from somewhere, nobody ever said where, after Burley's disappearance from a Louisville hospital where he had been lying unwakable, kept alive by machines. Though nobody told where Danny had been, in Port William, where people didn't have much that was "their own business," everybody who cared to know knew. And Art knew Danny's mind, as he had known Burley's.

Old Preacher, who still had been walking behind Art, suddenly became young again, bawling and flinging gravel behind him as simultaneously a fox squirrel sprang from the grass, flying his tail like a flag, and just ahead of the dog leapt to the trunk of a fair-sized hickory at the edge of the woods. Art heard the scramble of claws on bark. He followed the dog down through the sloping pasture to the tree.

Preacher, who was a coon hound in fair standing, had a sideline of squirrel hunting that he liked to indulge, to keep in practice maybe for worthier game. He reared against the tree and covered the whole visible world with chop-mouth cries of extreme excitement and longing.

"That's a squirrel," Art told him. "It ain't a bear."

He felt reflexively for the .22 pistol that he often carried with him on such trips, and then realized with a small pang of regret that the pistol was still hanging in its shoulder holster from its nail by the kitchen door. But he did anyhow carefully study the tree, and he found the squirrel lying very still along a branch high up. Preacher stood looking expectantly from the squirrel to Art and back again. His expression appeared to turn indignant when he understood that Art was not going to shoot the squirrel.

"Well, I'm sorry, old dog," Art said. "I know it ain't right to disappoint you."

But all the same he was glad he had forgot the pistol. Though he would gladly have cooked and eaten the squirrel, he discovered, as he more often had done as he had grown older, that he did not want to kill it.

He said to the squirrel, "I reckon you're having a lucky day." And then he said, "I reckon every day you've had so far has been lucky."

Preacher, born again to the life of a hunting dog with important business in the woods, turned and trotted off downhill among the trees. And that was the last Art saw of him until he turned up again at suppertime.

During the little while of Preacher's excitement and then his indignation, that particular slope of the ridge seemed to exist only in reference to the episode of the squirrel. But then the sound of the wind settled back upon it as a kind of quiet. Art looked about and took notice of where he was.

The whole Rowanberry place lay in his mind, less like a map than like a book, its times stratified upon it like pages. He remembered the seasons, crops, and events of the years he had known, of which almost always he remembered the numbers. And the living pages of his memory, as if blown or thumbed open, showed past days as they were, as perhaps they are.

In 1937, in the summer after the big flood, they grew a crop of tobacco on the slope above the hickory where Preacher had treed the squirrel. The summer of 1936, as if to require in justice the terrible flood of the next January, had been terribly dry. The country had been dying of thirst day after day and week after week. All the hard-won product of the farm had amounted almost to nothing. By the spring of 1937, the Rowanberrys seemed to have made it through by luck, if luck was what they wanted to call it. That was the time when Art's father began telling people who asked how he was, "Here by being careful."

But in the late winter and early spring, as people then did, as they had to do, Early Rowanberry and his four sons—Art, Mart, Jink, and Stob—cut the trees from the slope where Art would be standing and remembering in the cold March wind forty-four years later. They dragged off the logs and poles, burnt the brush, plowed and worked the soil, piled the rocks, and in a wet spell in late May, set out by hand the tobacco crop that would have to do for both that year and the year before.

The growing season of 1937 gave them enough rain, and they made a good crop. Art, as if standing and looking in both present and past, saw it in all its stages, from the fragile, white-stemmed plants of the setting-out to the broad, gold-ripe leaves at harvest.

The four sons and their father had kept faith with it, doing the hard handwork of it, through the whole summer. An old man already as they saw him and in fact getting to be old, but never forgetting the hard year before and other hard ones before that, their father drove them into the work, setting a never-slackening pace in the tobacco patch and everywhere else. As if in self-defense, the sons cherished every drink of water, every bite of food, every hour of sleep in fact and in anticipation, and they made the most of everything that was funny.

Just one time, in the midst of a breathless afternoon in July, Jink, who was the hardest of them in his thoughts, cried out, "God *damn*, old man, where the hell's the fire!" It would have been a cry of defiance if Early Rowanberry had been defiable. He might as well have been deaf. He went on. The three brothers went on. Jink himself went on. His outcry hung in the air behind them like the call of some utterly solitary animal.

And then it was getting on toward the noon of a day late in August. By then half the crop had been cut and safely housed in the barns. They had been cutting all morning, going hard, all of them by then moved by the one urgent need to save from the weather, from the possible hailstorm always on their minds, the crop by so much effort finally made. Half an hour earlier Sudie, the brothers' one sister, had brought a cooked dinner in two cloth-covered baskets and had left it in the barn farther back on the ridge. They quit cutting when they saw her pass and began loading a sled with cut tobacco to take with them when they went to the barn to eat.

They were letting Stob, the youngest, be the teamster, driving the horses and the sled as the others loaded. The tobacco they were loading had been cut the morning before and was well wilted. They put on a big load. Their father said, "All right, boys, let's go eat," and Stob spoke to the team.

Standing on the hillside a little behind the sled, Art saw it all as he still would see it when he thought of it in all the years that followed. Stob was sixteen that summer, a well-grown big stout boy who hadn't yet thought everything he needed to think. When he started for the barn he ought to have got on the uphill side of the load. But he stayed on its downhill side, practically under it, walking beside it with the lines in his hands. Maybe all four of the others were ready to tell him, but they never got a chance. All of a sudden the uphill runner slid up onto the ridge of a row, the ground steepened a little under the downhill runner, and the load started over. Stob, who was then stronger than he was smart and too proud of his strength, didn't stop the horses and run out of the way as he should have done, but just threw his shoulder against the load as if to prop it and kept driving. He pretty soon found out how strong he actually was, for the load, the hundreds of pounds of it, pushed him to the ground and piled on top him. The old team stopped and stood unflustered as if what had happened had happened before. The four men were already hurrying.

They unburied Stob, and Art would remember with a kind of wonder how deliberately they went at it. They righted the sled and loaded it again as, carefully, not to mistreat the tobacco, but quickly enough, they delivered Stob back again to the daylight. When finally he rolled over and stood up, as if getting out of bed, he was wetter with sweat than before and red in the face and wild-eyed, his straw hat crushed on the ground and his hair more or less on end.

Art said, "What was you thinking down under there?"

And Stob said, as if Art ought to have known, "I was thinking the air was getting mighty *scarce* down under there!"

Even their father laughed. At every tobacco harvest after that, down through the years, they would tell the story. And they would laugh.

In the wind, in the gray, cold light, Art went back to the ridgetop and the road. His thoughts returned to his amusement at Preacher. He had given a good deal of study to the old dog's character, and the story of the squirrel would stay on his mind. He told Andy about it, and about other events of that journey, for it had been a good one, a few days later. "I reckon he don't have much time for a man without a pistol."

He went on back the ridge, the road passing in front of the old log house, now a ruin, the doors and windows gaping, the hearths long ago dug up by descendants of a family of slaves who had once belonged to Art's family. Those descendants, Rowanberrys themselves since freedom, believed that during the Civil War money and other valuables had been buried under a stone of one of the hearths. Art and Mart told them to dig away, perfectly assured that no Rowanberry had ever owned anything greatly worth either burying or digging up. As they expected, the digging was motivated entirely by superstition, but since then the hearthstones had remained overturned onto the puncheons of the floors. The chimneys too had begun to crumble. All of the old making that remained intact were the cellar and the well. For a long time two apple trees had lived on at the edge of what had been the garden, still bearing good early apples that Art and Mart came up to pick every year. But life finally had departed from the trees as it had from the house.

Art went on to the wire gap into the pasture where they wintered the cows and let himself through. Adjoining at one of its corners the tobacco barn where the hay was stored, the pasture was a field of perhaps twenty acres now permanently in grass. It was enclosed by the best fence remaining on the place, but even that fence was a patchwork, the wire stapled to trees that had grown up in the line, spliced and respliced, weak spots here and there reinforced by cut thorn bushes and even an old set of bedsprings.

The place was running down. Art and Mart were getting old, and the family had no younger member who wanted such a farm or even a better one. After so many years as the Rowanberry place, it was coming to the time when finally it would have to be sold. Mart perhaps already would have sold it, had the decision belonged to him alone. Art so far had pushed away even the thought. He needed his interest in the farm. "A fellow needs *something* to be interested in." He had pushed away the thought of selling, as Andy still supposes, because so far he *could* not think of it. He could not distinguish between the place and himself.

But the place, its life as a farm, continued only by force of old habit.

The two brothers went on from day to day, from year to year, doing only as they always had done. They did nothing new, and as their strength declined they did less. They extended the longevity of fences and buildings by stopgaps, patching and mending, and by the thought, repeated over and over, "I reckon it'll last as long as it needs to."

Their earnings in any year were not great, but they spent far less than they earned. They grew most of their food, or gathered it from the woods and the river. They heated the house with wood they cut and split still as they always had. They were thrifty and careful. Mart kept a pretty good used car and went places for pleasure. Art stayed mostly at home and spent, by the standards of the time, almost nothing.

There were ten cows and, as of that morning, four calves. The cows were Nancy, Keeny, Yellowback, Baby Sitter, Droopy Horn, Brown Eyes, Doll, Beulah, Rose, and Troublemaker. They had their tails to the wind, grazing to not much purpose the short grass. The four calves were lying together, curled up against the chill.

Seeing only nine of the cows, Art set off to find the tenth. He crossed over the ridge to the south side. There, in a swale affording some shelter, he found Troublemaker, afterbirth still hanging, and her still-wet heifer calf uneasily standing.

"Well, look a-there what you've done!" Art said to the cow. "Ain't you proud of yourself!"

He said to the calf, "You're going to make it, looks like."

He didn't go near them. The cow would be ruled entirely now by the instinct to protect her calf. Her long acquaintance with Art would not have mattered. Not to her. She wasn't named Troublemaker for nothing.

"Well," he said to her, "I'll leave it to you." He turned around and went to the barn.

The timbers and poles that framed the barn had come from the nearby woods. The posts, girders, and top plates all had been squared by somebody—Grandpaw Rowanberry, Art thought—who had been a good hand with a broadaxe, for the work was well done. The barn, in its time, had been a fair example of good work with rough materials. Its posts rested on footers of native rock, and it had been roofed originally with shingles rived out of white oak blocks also from the woods of the place.

The only milled lumber had been the poplar siding. Now the barn, like the pasture fence, had become as much a product of the last-ditch cunning of making-do as of the skills that first had built it.

From the hay rick, by now much diminished, Art carried five bales one at a time into the pasture, spacing them widely, cutting the strings with his knife, dividing and scattering the hay, so that even Doll, the timidest cow, would get her share.

Having scattered the hay, he stood a while watching, to feel the culmination of his trip and the satisfaction of hunger fed. Soon it would be warmer and the new grass would come. The time of surviving would be past, and the cows and calves would begin to thrive.

On out beyond the winter pasture, the upland narrowed and then widened again, becoming what they called the Silver Mine Ridge. A long time ago Uncle Jackson Jones, an old man nobody knew much about, had passed through the country, digging for buried money. A number of his excavations were in the Port William neighborhood. Andy Catlett and a few other old men still know where they are, shallowed by time to mere depressions in the woods. The largest was the one on the Rowanberry place. Art's father had worked on that one when he was a boy. Uncle Jackson hired several of the local boys to help him dig. They made a hole long and wide and deep enough to bury a small house or a large corn crib. They had to use a ladder to get to the bottom of it.

While they were digging, Early Rowanberry remembered, another stranger, "a man with a needle," happened by. The "needle," Andy thinks, must have been the arrow on some sort of dial, some instrument of geological divining. The man with the needle took readings round and about. He then told Uncle Jackson that if he would dig a second hole, only a short distance away, he would strike a vein of pure silver. But Uncle Jackson said no, he was after coined money and nothing else. The man with the needle departed and was never seen again. The diggers dug on. But the only silver yielded by their big hole was in the coins paid out by Uncle Jackson to his crew of boys.

Every evening when they climbed out of the hole they left their picks and spades, spud bars, grubbing hoes, and other tools at the bottom. One night a terrific rain fell, collapsing the sides of the hole and burying the tools, which put an end to Uncle Jackson's work at that place.

"After that," Art said to Andy, "it was anyhow a tool mine."

But nobody ever went back to dig for the tools.

"Too much digging for a few tools. And, I reckon maybe, too few tools to dig with."

When the wind, pressing through his clothes, at last laid its cold touch against his flesh, Art turned to face it, buttoned the top button of his jacket, and started back the way he had come. Behind him, the small herd of cows, filling and warming themselves with hay for the night, seemed to him for the time being to have been completed, and he was free to go.

He went back the way he had come, again taking his time, seeing everything now from its opposite side. It was as though he made the place dimensional and substantial by his walking both ways over it, granting it the same interest in going as he had in coming. To his mind it was old beyond knowing and yet new, timeless and yet momentary, so that watching it as once more it opened before him, old as he was, he was renewed.

As the road began its slant downward and homeward, he let himself into the fall of it gladly, for he was tired now, and it was easier going down than coming up.

"If gravity wants to pitch in and help," he told Andy, "I ain't going to be the one to say no."

Going this way, he was looking directly into the long view of the river valley, and he watched it as his passage opened it and then closed it again. And he watched for Preacher, thinking the old dog too might have got tired and decided to head in, but he neither saw nor heard him.

As it turned out, it was better that Preacher had not returned. If he had, the next thing that happened would not have happened.

Art had come down nearly to the bend where the road turned at last directly toward the house. He was looking down, taking care with his steps over the steepening descent, thinking of something he was not going to be able to remember—"of something else"—when a large buck with splendid horns stepped into the road not a dozen feet away. Art stood without moving, downwind as he promptly realized, while the buck walked calmly, looking neither left nor right, across the road and disappeared. That he did not hurry and yet instantly was out of sight made his appearance just barely believable.

"I don't know if he ever even seen me," Art said to Andy. "He must've been thinking about something else too. But I seen him. I didn't make him up."

"If you'd been deer hunting he'd have known it," Andy said. "He wouldn't have come that close."

"Probably not. But if I'd had my shotgun I could a played thunder with him."

"I reckon," Andy said.

Art, however, had not finished his thought. "*But* if I'd a shot him with a shotgun, he might've gone two miles before he died."

And so, for the second time that day, Art was glad not to have had a weapon.

He was sorry, though, to have forgot what he had been thinking about before he saw the buck. Nor could he remember, supposing he had counted them, the number of branches of the buck's horns.

"Maybe I never counted," he said to Andy. "He had more hatrack than most people got hats."

The river valley was out of sight behind him now, the creek valley lying fully open ahead of him. Though the light had weakened, he could still see the house, the barns and outbuildings, the swinging bridge over the creek, at the end of nowhere the center of everything, and the day coming to rest upon it.

He knew he would walk on the earth a while yet, and then he would yield back his body to be with the old ones who had come and gone before him, and of this he made no complaint.

Sold (1991)

It's about all finished now. I took sick in the night back in the fall, past frost. When Coulter Branch came over to see about me the next morning I was down and couldn't get up. Coulter called Wilma on the telephone. He was afraid to leave me to go get her, and she had to come from their house on the tractor, driving with one hand and holding the baby with the other. That's a good girl, I'll tell you. They got me up and fairly dressed and took me to the hospital. The hospital helped me over my sickness, but seemed like I was old after that and not fit to look after myself. And so the place and all had to be sold.

They brought me from the hospital here to the nursing home at Hargrave. Rest Haven they call it, the end of the line. It's all right. I don't complain. But I was the last in Port William of the name of Gibbs.

Before I married Grover Gibbs, I was Beulah Cordle. Annie May Ellis was my first cousin. She was Annie May Cordle Ellis. I was Beulah Cordle Gibbs. Beulah means "a land of peace and rest." A preacher told me that, back when I was young. It made him blush to tell me, and I knew why. But I wasn't cut out to be a preacher's wife, and I reckon he could tell.

I didn't have but one boyfriend, to say a real one, before Grover. But that one didn't last. He was from down at Hargrave. He went off to Tennessee and sent me a postcard that said, "Hoping to be up in your parts by Sunday night." You can't love somebody you've laughed at that way.

I was seventeen when I married Grover. He was twenty-two. We couldn't wait. We ran off to Indiana and waked up a preacher. He stood us in front of the fireplace and tied the knot. When he asked Grover to promise all those things "until death," Grover said, "Would you go over that a little slower?"

That was him exactly. The preacher had to stop and laugh.

By both of us being gone, my folks pretty well knew why. They had some objections, but after while it got all right. And it *was* all right, pretty much, until death.

Well, I reckon you could complain about anybody you've married and lived with a long time. But then they've died and gone from you, and you look back, and you're grateful.

Maybe it's not that easy to tell about Grover. He was good enough at work—better than good enough, I think. But he was not hardly work-brittle. What it was, I reckon, he didn't have what they call ambition, but he suited me. What we both wanted from this world was a living, our daily bread, if that means plenty to eat and a sound roof over our heads. Came a time when we had more, but we knew the more was extra.

Grover mostly never minded being delayed or interrupted. He couldn't finish a day without going off after supper, still picking his teeth, to sit talking in Port William till bedtime. That was the old Port William schedule, you might say. The men would go to town after supper and sit in front of the stores in good weather, or inside somewhere in bad, talking and laughing and carrying on, the way people do who have always known each other and are telling a long story that they all know as far as the night before. Grover did his duty and held up his end of the conversation.

Well, I loved him. I still do. He could be the funniest. You could look in his face, practically all his life, and see that he was just waiting to be invited to have a good time, and that as soon as the invitation came, he was going to accept. He always looked ready to grin, if he wasn't already grinning, even when he thought he was by himself. Because of that, maybe, when he was sad his face would be the saddest you ever saw. But he was always looking for fun, and just about always finding it, until he was almost dead.

When things went to drifting towards what Grover called fun, seemed like Burley Coulter and Big Ellis would sooner or later be into it with him.

It would be hard to tell all the doings they did. And fun lasted them a long time, for after it had happened they'd be years telling each other about it, and the longer they told about it the funnier it got.

As a usual thing, Burley and Grover didn't work together. Burley mostly worked with his family or Elton Penn or the Rowanberrys. But Grover and Big Ellis often would be helping each other, at our place or at Big's. Since they'd married cousins, they were sort of kin, and when one of them needed help the other one would likely go. And since Big Ellis and Burley were neighbors, sometimes Burley showed up too.

When it was just Grover and Big, they talked, probably, as much as they worked. Maybe they'd be in a tobacco patch with their hoes, where I could see them from the kitchen window. They'd hit a few licks and pretty soon stop and lean on the hoe handles. They'd look off at the sky and point and prophesy the weather. And then hit a few more licks. Or I would see Grover lean back and laugh at some outrageousness such as Big was always full of. Like that.

Grover would work as hard to play a joke as for a living. Well, I'll tell you exactly how he would do.

After the pickup balers had been in the country a good while—this was after we had got settled finally on our own place—Grover and Big went in partners and bought a pretty good baler, secondhand. Big was worthless at anything mechanical, so Grover took charge of the baler, always pulled it with our tractor, and did the baling. Grover loved an old tractor. He liked to fix things and he liked to drive.

One summer Big had a field of red clover to put up for hay. He got it mowed, and in a couple of days Grover went over and raked it as soon as the dew dried. After dinner he went back with the baler. Big had got Burley to come to help with the hauling. They were sitting on the wagon, waiting for Grover to bale a round or two before they started to load.

It was a blustery day, and the wind blew Big's hat off. He started after it but couldn't gain on it. When it blew past Grover, he pulled out of the windrow he was baling, put the tractor in a higher gear and cut in ahead of Big. Burley was just paying careful attention to see how it was going to turn out.

So there went Big, stumbling along in his version of running, and there went Grover ahead of him as fast as he could go and stay on the tractor, and there went Big's hat, tumbling over the windrows like it finally had a chance to be free.

Well, it was Grover that caught the hat. He baled it and slowed down and went back to baling hay. He never gave Big so much as a glance. He didn't even grin.

He and Big worked harder when Burley was with them. Burley was tuned up a little different. The people he ordinarily worked with, they went at it pretty lively. Burley was another one maybe not easy to tell about. He wasn't, you might think, all that serious, and yet he was. Time was, this country was full of tales about Burley Coulter. He was a right smart older than me, but I remember him when he was young. He had good looks and ways the women taken to. You'd accuse him of something outlandish you'd heard about him, and he'd say, "If they told it at the store, I reckon it's a story." Or he'd say, "That must have been the day I found myself lost." And he had a way of looking at you. You had to love him. There was a time or two, a night or two.

But he had that seriousness. More and more, I think. He saw his family through their hard times. His friends too. He was a neighbor.

But, Lord, how they did carry on—him and Grover and Big!

Well, them old times are gone forever, but people were neighbors then. Most were. You worked together. You saw each other in Port William on Saturday night, and in church like as not on Sunday morning. Now that I've got mainly nothing to do, I think and think about them all. It just seems natural to me now to expect to see them again over on the other side. I think of us all together, paid up somehow, and complete.

For a long time after Grover and I got married, we were tenants on other people's places, taking half of what we earned from the crops, which I'll say was hard sometimes. I mean you could have a hard thought or two about it. But for people with no land, that was what was possible, and was all right, a chance maybe to get ahead. We got half of the cash money, what there was of it, and back there in the twenties and thirties, there wouldn't be much. But we had our old ways. We had a garden, of course, and milk from our cows and meat from our hogs, and meat and eggs from our chickens, and our patching and mending and making do. And so we had our living.

The place we lived on longest was the old Levers place. Mr. Robert La Vere grew up on that place in the old house that a long time later we lived in. He was known back then as Jappy Levers. But he made a lawyer out of himself, and then he went by J. Robert La Vere. He hadn't been long dead when the tenant before us gave the place up, and we moved there. Run down as it was, it was the best place we'd had, and we stayed on there until my mother died and I inherited our home place.

After Mr. La Vere was gone, his widow, Miss Charlotte, saw to the farm, and I'm telling you! She was something like nothing else. To see her come riding up in the back seat of that big car, wearing her hat and her fur and her white gloves and looking straight ahead through her little specs, you'd have thought she was the queen of Hargrave, which in a way she was.

She was just about the best thing that ever happened to Grover. She couldn't tell a cow from a bull, but she had no end of advice about farming. She would decide the barn cats were too thin, and tell Grover to see they got more milk, or more mice. We would take garden stuff to her when we had extra, we tried to have a little extra for her, and she would wonder if the green beans were ready in March, or roasting ears in November. Grover enjoyed everything she said, and remembered it all, and could talk just like her.

Her driver and man of all work, Willard Safely, would pull up in front of the barn and blow the horn. If Grover was anywhere around, he would pretty soon show up. He would always stand back a ways from the car so she had to roll her window down and stick her head out to talk to him. Her way of doing that completely tickled him, but he would have the soberest look on his face and nod his head and say Yes mam, Yes mam, and memorize it all so he could tell me first thing, and then at town.

The next place we lived was our own. My mother and daddy didn't have but one child that lived, and that was me. By the end of the war my folks were both gone, and we had no good reason to stay with Mrs. La Vere, "Miz Gotrocks" as Grover liked to call her, and so we moved home.

It was not a big or a fine place, a hundred and fifteen acres more or less, some of it steep, but my folks took good care of it and kept up the buildings and fences, and so did we. We were changed by having it, in all the world our own place, more maybe than we were changed by having the children. Grover was Grover, and he'd have been Grover if we'd owned a thousand acres or the whole county. But the hundred and fifteen that was ours made us feel permanent and serious, in a way safe, as we never had felt before.

We didn't change anything much. We kept the best of the things my folks had and the best of the things we had. We stuck to our old ways of doing for ourselves. And we did all right. Grover always felt at home wherever we were, but I got back some of the old at-home feeling I'd had when I was a girl growing up. It was fine for me.

Back in 1920 was when we got married, both of us young but born in different centuries. Maybe that counts for something, but to look at us you wouldn't have known. I'll have to say we didn't waste any time starting a family. Billy was born in nine months, just about to the day. Grover would look at me when I began to show and just laugh. He'd say, "I reckon that must have been *some* night!"

And then in a little more than a year we had Althie. And then I lost a baby. And then six years went by, and then it was Nance, and then Sissy, and then Stanley, named after his grandpa Gibbs and nearly spoiled to death by all the others. And after him, no more.

"Getting 'em's one thing, and raising 'em's another." Grover made a saying out of that. You get 'em here, and then you have 'em to take care of and worry about.

Althie, I'll say, was the best—the best one of us all. The three littlest ones were raised by her as much as by me. She would be carrying them around and looking after them. Playing at being a mother, I thought, sort of doll-playing, but I pretty soon realized that when she was with them I didn't need to worry. She put them first, and was always watchful.

And she hadn't hardly got them of mine raised before she married Tommy Greatlow from down here at Hargrave and started raising her own.

She's getting old herself now, and her health is bad, her heart, but she drives in here every day to see how I am and what she can do for me. Her heart is poorly now, maybe, because she's given it away all her life to anybody that needed it, always *doing* for somebody. She and Tommy are still out there on their good farm in the river valley with the world dug up all around by the sand and gravel company. And they've got one boy, looks like, who'll stick there and go on with it. He's thirty-two, Tommy Junior is, a good boy, good to me.

The others, Althie's and mine too, are gone, long gone, scattered off to city jobs all over the country. When the time came for me to leave the old place, Althie and them of course couldn't take it on, for they already had all the land they could look after, and having to depend on the Mexicans part of the time, as it was. The rest of them, children nor grandchildren, couldn't even think of it. There was nothing in it for them, as they sometimes pointed out to me, nothing anyhow that they wanted.

The worst time in all our family-raising was when Billy was gone in the war. He was wild to fly, and he got into the air force. He was a gunner on one of them biggest bombers. He'd get the pilot, when they was supposed to be training, to fly low over our house and all over the Port William neighborhood, bringing everybody outside to look up, scaring the livestock, looked like almost touching the treetops, taking chances for the fun of it. "Boys!" Grover would say. "That's boys for you!" He said if their brains were dynamite they wouldn't have blowed their hats off. And with a war to fight.

And then they went off overseas into the fighting, taking chances then sure enough, and Billy, you could tell from the little he wrote home, still excited about flying. I wonder if he actually could imagine then, at his age, that he actually could get killed. But I could imagine it, and I did. They were getting shot at, and the fighter planes going at them like the little birds after a hawk. Billy was on my mind, seemed like, even in my sleep, all through the war. And afterwards I realized I hadn't been young since it started.

Grover and I had had, I reckon, our share of troubles before that. Troubles, you know, that will come. And he could make me mad enough sometimes with that grin of his that I could have knocked him in the head with the skillet. But with Billy gone in the war, I saw something about Grover I'd not seen before. I'd be watching him, and I saw the worry and the fear slide across his face behind that grin, and I knew, I knew forever, that without talking about it the way I did he was grieving and afraid, wearing it through, day by day, just like I was. I'd say, "Come here," and he would come, and we would hold each other.

When Billy came back, his head was full of stuff it had never had in it before. He went away to college, and into a suit and into business, and after that was away and away. He set the example, I reckon, for the younger ones. When their times came they went too. I've worried about them all. You can get a plenty of that. Finally you see you've had enough. You've said enough goodbyes. You need one for yourself.

After we decided on the sale, and the children came as they got a chance to see about me, I told them to take what they wanted out of the house, and they did, a few little things, keepsakes. And then I gave the best piece of furniture in the house, an old cherry dresser, to Coulter and Wilma Branch. I just made them take it, because I'd depended on them ever since Grover died, and they'd been nothing but good to me. They'd lived all that time as tenants on the next farm, and I'd pretty much made family of them. All the rest had to be sold, all the farm machinery, all the tools, all the old bolts and nuts and washers and metal pieces that my dad and then Grover had saved in case of need, all the furniture and other household plunder. The cattle that Coulter Branch had been taking care of on the halves, they had already gone off to the sale barn. Everything else, everything that would come loose, was auctioned off the day of the sale. The farm too, it had to go.

The sale was on a bright March day, warm for the season. The children all came home for it. Far off as they were in distance and in mind, they knew, they couldn't help knowing, it was a day that ended something that mattered, at least to me, and so they came. But Althie was the one who looked after me and stayed close, because she was Althie, and was used to me needing her. The others put in the day standing around, looking starched and uncomfortable even with each other, getting recognized by people they didn't recognize or couldn't remember.

Althie got me there early, and led me across the yard—me with my two walking canes, Lord help me!—to the easy chair that they'd carried out with the rest of the furniture and set under the sugar tree in the front yard. That was where they had the wagons that were loaded with household stuff and the hand tools and the odds and ends. When she got me settled in the chair and the afghan she'd brought tucked around me, Althie got one of the straight chairs that had been in the kitchen and sat beside me. All through the sale, until it was over, her hand would always be touching me.

Arnold McCardy cried the sale. He had his loudspeaker and two men to help him and watch for bids. They started the sale out in the barn lot with the farm machinery, and sold their way toward the house and the front yard where I was. I could hear them coming ever closer, Arnold McCardy praising whatever it was he was about to sell, and then his singsong, and then stopping to praise again and plead for another bid, and then the singsong again, and then "Sold!"

And then he would start it all again, a little closer. And I waited, watching the people who were looking at the things for sale, the furniture lined up in rows across the yard and the smaller things, dishes and such, set out on the wagons. And I, who was not going to buy anything, sat there looking at everything that was for sale.

I had sort of got ready to see the household things carried outdoors and laid out to be looked at and sold. What I wasn't ready for was how poor everything looked once it was out of place, so many marks of use and wear, the fretted or shiny places on the furniture where our hands had rested, what I knew to somebody else would be the secondhand look of it all. The cracks and chips in the dishes, seemed like I'd known them so well I hadn't seen them for years, but now I saw them. Everything already looked like it belonged to somebody else.

I was getting spoken to and speaking, some of the women, old friends, neighbors, leaning over to give me a hug, but all the time I was listening. Sold! Sold! Every time I heard it, I knew that, piece by piece, the things we'd all of us gathered there so many years would be scattered and gone. All that had been used to make it a dwelling place, by my folks on back, by Grover and me, by just me with Coulter and Wilma to help me, all the memories of all the *lives* that had made it and held it together, all would come apart and be gone as if it never was.

After while, soon enough, the crowd had shifted into the yard, and Arnold McCardy was selling the furniture, some that went for antiques and brought a pretty penny, some that didn't. He sold the kitchen table, painted how many times, that we bought when we married, when we didn't have hardly anything to put on it. He sold the chiffonier that I think came from my mother's grandmother. He sold the walnut four-poster bed that Grover's dad sawed the posts off of when they moved into a house with low ceilings. Lord, what didn't he sell! He sold a rusty set of firedogs that had been wired to a rafter in the smokehouse as long as I can remember. He sold a set of curtain stretchers that he gave a man a dollar to bid on, and then sold to him for fifty cents.

When he got to the chair I was sitting in and was telling what a fine chair it was, somebody yelled out, "Does the lady go with it?"

And Arnold McCardy said, "No, now, we're selling the chair, *not* the lady."

He sold the chair.

He sold even the doilies I'd crocheted for the stand tables and the back of the sofa.

He sold all the kitchen utensils, all the knives and forks and spoons, all the dishes right down to the sugar bowl.

When everything was sold off of the wagons, and the wagons were sold, and some were beginning to pay for what they'd bought and go to their cars, Arnold McCardy kept his place, standing on the wagon nearest to me. He told about the farm, how big it was, how it laid, the condition of the improvements, and so on. And then he started his cry.

I knew Coulter Branch was going to bid on the place. He had taken good care of it ever since Grover died. He's Lyda and Danny Branch's son, and that's a family that *takes* care of things. Coulter knew the place, knew how to farm it, he wanted it, and he needed it. Lord knows I wanted him to have it, him and Wilma. He was in the bidding from the start, and he stayed in it for a while, and then he had to give it up.

Coulter is a smart man, and thoughtful. He knew pretty exactly what the place was worth as a farm. What I didn't expect, and maybe he didn't, was that to a certain kind of person it was worth more as an investment than it was worth as a farm. And that kind of person, it so happened, was there. "Mr. Gotrocks" I call him, a man from Louisville with, I reckon, no end of money.

I was watching Coulter and trying to think fast enough to pray for him. When his final bid was topped, I saw him walk away with his head down. I'll not forget that. With my last breath I'll grieve over that. I'll die wishing I had just *given* the farm to Coulter and Wilma, but of course my children wouldn't have stood for it. Althie might've, but the others wouldn't.

And I'll tell you what happened then. Althie nor Coulter nor Wilma, none of my loved ones, would have told me. But it was talked about, it got around, and one of the old ones here told me about it.

Mr. Gotrocks hadn't any sooner paid his investment into it than he hired a man with a bulldozer to smash the house and other buildings all to flinders, and push them into a pile, and set them afire. He pushed out every fence, every landmark that stood above the ground, every tree. A place where generations of people lived their *lives*. If they came back now, looking for it, they wouldn't know where they were.

And so it's all gone. A new time has come. Various ones of the old time keep faith and stop by to see me, Coulter and Wilma and a few others. But the one I wait to see is Althie. Seems like my whole life now is lived under the feeling of her hand touching me that day of the sale, and every day still.

I lie awake in the night, and I can see it all in my mind, the old place, the house, all the things I took care of so long. I thought I might miss it, but I don't. The time has gone when I could do more than worry about it, and I declare it's a load off my mind. But the thought of it, still, is a kind of company.

A Place in Time (1938–2008)

When Elton and Mary Penn ran away and got married one night in the October of 1938, he was eighteen and she seventeen. After that, she was to her parents as if she were dead or never born. They were never her parents nor she their daughter ever again. Perhaps the young couple should not have been surprised at this, for they had been warned. Mary had been forbidden to see Elton, who, her parents said, was "nothing." He was a half-orphan boy, educated no further than the eighth grade, who had not an acre or hardly a penny to call his own.

In the year Elton was nine, which was the first year of the 1930s Depression, his father had died. His mother married again—too soon, according to local opinion—and Elton hated his stepfather. When he was fourteen he left home, and from then on, share-cropping and working by the day, he had made his own living. By the time he was eighteen he owned a team of horses, a cow, and a few tools. These possessions made him a little more than the nothing his in-laws said he was, but not by enough certainly to make him a fit match for a daughter of the Mountjoys, a family of aristocratic pretension, with a good farm on the fat upland near Smallwood.

And so Mary and Elton began their life together as outcasts, their very being recognized only by themselves. In hasty preparation for their marriage, Elton had rented from his mother the sideling, rundown little farm she owned on Cotman Ridge, near Port William. Elton and Mary moved there and set up housekeeping, making do with the elderly stoves and the few sticks of furniture that had been abandoned in the house, to which they added the bare necessities they could afford. "Lord," Mary once said to Andy Catlett when she was old, "it looked like it took us forever to accumulate a little kitchen cabinet and a few things to put in it."

The farm offered them no advantages, except that it divided them effectively from Smallwood and the Mountjoys. Smallwood was not far away in miles, but it was out of the orbit of Port William. On the place they had come to there was not a sound building, including the old house itself. Its pastures grew more briars and locust sprouts than grass. The small ridgetop patches that could be cropped had been misused and eroded. It was a place from which too many owners or users had demanded too much for too many years. To Elton and Mary it offered merely a foothold, a chance to survive.

Their good fortune was that the farm lay in a neighborhood of five households that clustered together, with their modest acreages, out there on Cotman Ridge. Elton and Mary's neighbors were Braymer and Josie Hardy, Tom Hardy and his Josie, Walter and Thelma Cotman, Jonah and Daisy Hample, and Uncle Isham and Aunt Frances Quail. The Hardy brothers' wives, the two Josies, were known for convenience as "Josie-Braymer" and "Josie-Tom." Josie-Tom was Walter Cotman's sister. Thelma Cotman and Daisy Hample were daughters of Uncle Isham and Aunt Frances. The Tom Hardys were childless. Braymer and Josie-Braymer had a daughter and two sons. The Cotmans had one daughter. The Hamples were parents already of "a flock" of six, all of them, like their father, so nearsighted "they couldn't see all the way to the ground," and all of them, like their father, born mechanics who "could fix anything by feel for want of sight."

This was an old community. Its middle generation all had grown up together, had known one another "forever," and were closely bound by marriage, kinship, friendship, history, and memory. Almost everything they did, all the long, hard jobs of farm and household, they did together. Sometimes the women worked together apart from the men and the men apart from the women. Sometimes the men and women, and the children too, all worked together. They had, among them, the expectable diversity of knacks and talents. Everybody had always known what everybody else was good at. And so they worked together familiarly, in harmony, and always with a dependable margin, a sort of overflow, of pleasure, for as they worked they talked and their talk pleased them. They remembered and relished everything that had ever happened that was funny. They told and retold old stories along with new ones. They talked and teased and laughed and sometimes sang.

And so at the time when Elton and Mary Penn most desperately needed a community, they had the good fortune to land right in the midst, in the very embrace, of one that might as well have been expecting them.

The women opened their hearts and their arms to Mary. They befriended her, mothered her, gave her freely their companionship. By instruction and example they taught her the arts of farm housewifery, of which they knew, it seemed to Mary, everything. "Everything I know," she would say later, "I learned from those women."

Elton, who still had much to learn, who would continue his eager learning all his life, was already a confirmed farmer, an excellent teamster, and a good hand at anything he tried. The men were glad to include him in all the work they did together, telling him where they would be and when to come. When he needed help, they came to him. The men were to Elton as the women were to Mary. They became his teachers and his friends. And beyond all that they told him, Elton pondered their ways of working, their ways of talking and thinking, their ways even of wearing their clothes. Of them all, Walter Cotman was the best farmer and had the clearest mind, was most fastidious in everything he did or said, was least tolerant of poor work and hardest to please. Elton put himself to school to Walter, watching and questioning him and remembering everything, and Walter did not hesitate to correct him and set him straight even if it made him mad for two days, as it sometimes did.

From every one of them Elton learned something he needed to know. Braymer was the one most likely to know the market value of something and how to get it cheaper. When Elton's old car or some implement needed fixing and he couldn't fix it himself, he took it to Jonah Hample, and then stayed to watch and learn while Jonah figured out what was wrong and put it right. Uncle Isham Quail was a rememberer who had saved up in his mind everything he had seen and experienced and everything he had heard. In his latter years he seemed to live in all the times of that small place back to the original wilderness. Elton learned how to start Uncle Isham's flow of talk, and then he would listen and remember.

The only one of the men whose example Elton finally had no use for was Tom Hardy. By some early learning or by nature, Tom Hardy was a satisfied man, content to be himself, to be where he was, and to have what he had, accepting of every day as it came and went, never asking or arguing for a better. But Elton, probably by nature and certainly by his circumstances, was not a satisfied man, not then and not ever.

Within the limits imposed by Elton's mother's used-up farm, which afforded little scope for their talents and desires, Elton and Mary could not have prospered during their seven years on Cotman Ridge. They had come there hoping merely to survive. But with the help of their neighbors, by their own unstinting work and determination, by taking every opportunity to rent more land or to work for pay, they improved significantly upon survival. They grew strong individually and together.

They grew strong as a couple despite their differences of temperament, and despite the burden imposed upon their marriage by Mary's parents' rejection. The Mountjoys' legacy to Elton was his own retaliatory anger and defiance, preserved all his life by the fear, especially when he was at odds with Mary, that they had been right: that he was, or was in danger of becoming, nothing. To Mary their legacy, in addition to the wound they had given Elton, which she spent all their life together trying to heal, was the wound to herself, assuaged somewhat by the motherly women of Cotman Ridge, assuaged much more by the Christian faith that shone quietly and steadily in her to the end of her days.

It would not be an exaggeration to say that in their years on Cotman Ridge, Elton and Mary grew up. They became responsible and competent in many things. And so when Wheeler Catlett came looking for them in 1945, they were ready.

Wheeler Catlett was Old Jack Beechum's lawyer, his kinsman by marriage, and his friend. He had been raised as Old Jack's neighbor, for the Beechum and the Catlett places lay on opposite sides of the Bird's Branch Road north of Port William. Wheeler knew Old Jack and his place probably as well as he knew anybody or any place. In the late winter of 1945

Wheeler was in the midst of a long and so far unsuccessful negotiation with Old Jack, not as his lawyer primarily, but as his friend and moreover as a family spokesman. This negotiation had begun with an understanding between Wheeler and Mat Feltner, Wheeler's father-in-law and Old Jack's nephew, that Old Jack, eighty-four years old and long-widowed, was too old to continue living alone in his big empty house. He needed to move into the old hotel in Port William where he would be properly fed and looked after by Mrs. Hendrick, who had turned her relict property into a sort of old folks' home.

So far, Old Jack had resisted. In fact he had triumphed. When Wheeler in exasperation had played what he had withheld as his trump card—"We don't want you to die out here by yourself"—Old Jack, returning point-blank the younger man's stare, said, "I can do it by myself." He went so far as to memorialize his triumph with a snort. Wheeler replied only with a snort of his own, partly of delight in the perfection of his defeat.

From the time of his middle years, and according to his principles, Old Jack had been doing his work mainly by himself, when necessary swapping work with his neighbors. As he did not wish to be bossed, he did not wish to boss. He had subscribed to a further principle common enough in the Port William community: "I'd not ask another man to do anything I'd not do myself."

But age and wear and finally arthritis—"that Arthur, the meanest one of the Ritis brothers"—had forbidden him to do himself the work that needed to be done. There followed a procession of tenants or hired hands, who lived on nearby farms or else moved with their families into a fixed-up two-room log cabin that had stood below the barns since sometime during slavery, and whom Old Jack fired always a little sooner than they could be replaced. It began to seem to Wheeler and Mat that they were spending half their time looking for yet another "somebody who might do." What they had to "do" was measure up to Old Jack's standards of work, and one after another they failed.

"You can hire a fellow's body," Old Jack said, "but you can't hire his mind. The mind, if he has got one, has to come along free. Can't you find me somebody can *think*?"

Well, at last Wheeler could, and he did. He found Elton and Mary Penn who, according to available evidence, could think. They could think and do, both at the same time. "They'll do," Braymer Hardy told Wheeler. "They'll satisfy. They're a good pair of young people. You can depend on 'em."

And so Wheeler had understood that they were not going to come as hired hands. He didn't even ask. If they were to come, they would come as tenants, farming the place as full partners, half and half, expenses to be fairly divided. And so Wheeler asked them, and they agreed, provided that Wheeler could get Old Jack to accept them and their terms.

Wheeler laid the proposition before Old Jack that night. It was getting well into February by then. If the thing was going to be done, it had to be done soon.

They talked, sitting in chairs drawn away from the table in Old Jack's kitchen, in the light of an oil lamp with a smoked chimney. He had spurned every offer and promise of rural electrification. Why should he pay for what he already had? His affirmation of certain things had made him good at refusal.

He had been through the motions, as he said, of what he called his supper. Now he sat and merely looked at Wheeler while Wheeler talked. His look did not make it easy for Wheeler to talk, for there was much of doubt and resistance in it. But Wheeler was confident he knew what he was talking about, and he made his case. "This is a good boy," he said, "and he's married to a good girl. They're the right kind. They'll do."

Old Jack reached out with the end of his walking cane and touched Wheeler's leg. "How do you know that?"

"I've looked and I've seen," Wheeler said, allowing himself some emphasis. "Don't you worry about that. And I've got Braymer Hardy's word."

Old Jack said, knowing better, "Braymer Hardy don't know big wood from brush."

"Braymer don't miss much," Wheeler said. "He's got sense, and he's honest."

There was a little while then when nobody said anything. Old Jack's eyes quit looking at Wheeler while he turned his mind's eye upon his thoughts. Finally he looked outward again at Wheeler. "Tell 'em to come on."

And then Wheeler, who had a new trump card, had to play it. "Well, if they come, they're not going to live here in two rooms. They're going to need your house."

Old Jack opened his mouth, and then he shut it again and looked down. To have what he wanted for his place, he would have to leave it. Wheeler, instead of snorting in commendation of his own triumph, had to look away.

When Old Jack looked up again, the burden of defeat and acceptance was upon him, but again he looked straight at Wheeler. "Tell 'em to come on."

In the March of that year of 1945, Elton and Mary Penn moved into the house on the Beechum place, after Old Jack had moved—it was the first and last move of his life—to Port William and the hotel's society of elderly widows.

The Beechum house, a far better house than the one on Cotman Ridge, bore the marks of long inhabitance by an old widower, but Wheeler had attached to it his promise that it would receive the improvements necessary to make it, by the standards of that time, "livable." The outbuildings and the cellar were good. The garden plot was larger and richer than the one they'd had. The electric line finally was installed. The house—even after Old Jack's daughter had come out from Louisville and carried away all the best dishes, silverware, and furniture—still contained furnishings enough, and more than enough, which made Mary happy.

She had come not far in miles from the Josies and the other neighborly wives of Cotman Ridge, but the few miles that now separated them made a difference. They were no longer within an easy walk of one another. There was no more "happening by." Now when they visited it had to be by automobile, and only on Sunday afternoons. Sometimes they would be together in passing on Saturday night in Port William. The women of Cotman Ridge came over one day and helped Mary to make curtains and thus contributed to her "new start," but the easy daily bonds of neighborhood were broken.

Now Mary had for womanly company and comfort mainly Dorie Catlett, Wheeler's mother, who lived across the road. Dorie was of the generation of Aunt Frances Quail—old, old, as she seemed to Mary—but she was, in her abrupt and outspoken way, a kind companion and sometimes truly a comfort to Mary, whom she saw rightly as not only young but hurt and therefore needy. After she had finished her after-dinner housework, and if the weather was good, Mary would often take the shortcut across the fields to the Catlett place, to spend the rest of the afternoon sitting and talking on the front porch with Dorie. Dorie made her welcome, told her things of use or of interest, loaned her books from the glass-fronted small bookcase in the parlor, and listened as Mary told, in bits and pieces, her story. When Dorie had gathered in from Mary, and from Wheeler, the story of the Penns' marriage and its hard beginning, she pronounced her judgment upon the Mountjoys. She turned down the corners of her mouth and said with perfect finality: "Hmh!"

For Elton the old place, new to him, was exactly the chance he had been needing, his chance to prove himself, to exert his mind and his strength. At last, as he said, he could stretch his arms out full length and turn all the way around. In coming to the Beechum place, moreover, he came within the friendship and influence of Wheeler Catlett and of Wheeler's father, Marce, Old Jack's contemporary and friend, and of Old Jack himself. The influence of those men would remain with Elton, a circumstance of his life that was essential and dear, long beyond the deaths of Marce and Old Jack and until Elton's own death.

The neighborhood of the two families soon included Wheeler's boys, Andy and Henry. For Andy Catlett the story of Elton and Mary Penn, from the time he was included in it, became one of the shaping forces of his life. Their example, reduced to instruction, told him this: Grow up. Learn to be a good hand. Learn to be a good farmer. Marry for love. Get a place, a farm, of your own. Shape your life to the needs of your place. So far as you can, without hurting it, shape your place to your needs. Live from it and for it. Always try to make it better.

But to reduce that formative example to instruction is to misrepresent it, for instruction cannot even suggest the passion and the beauty, the difficult requirement and the hardship, of the example. What Andy took from the Penns was not instruction so much as a series of memories, visions, that ruled over his young life and still imposed their attraction and demand upon him when he was old: visions of Elton and Mary delighted with the first ripe tomato from their garden; of Elton plowing in the spring, his mind alight with the thought of the made crop; of Mary and Elton butch-ering their meat hogs, and then of the cured hams, shoulders, bacons, jowls, and the sacks of sausage hanging in their smokehouse; of Elton's best days lived from dark to dark in the excitement of going ahead, leaving a good difference behind him.

Andy's first sight of Elton was from a distance, and it caused a memo-rable, if temporary, twinge to his conscience. On that early summer day in 1945, Andy's conscience was on one of its frequent absences from the neighborhood. He was riding Beauty the pony, and in his left hand he was carrying a bow and an arrow. His grandpa Catlett had sent him to bring in the two Jersey cows for the evening milking, and on that practical level he was functioning probably as well as he needed to. But his mind, which he had stuffed with books and comic books about cowboys and Indians in the Wild West, had more than one level. On a level or two above the practical, he was an Indian hunting buffalo on the broad prairie.

And so when he found the cows resting in the shade of a strawstack, he rode up to them, dropped the bridle rein, and shot the nearest cow with his arrow. The arrow had been cut from his grandma's mock orange and was about as harmless against cowhide as it would have been against steel. It was nevertheless a good shot, the arrow bouncing off the cow's ribs at a point, Andy imagined, very near her heart. But then, allowing him only a second or two for satisfaction, his conscience came flying back to warn him that he might have been seen.

He was, after all, in one of the front fields and on a rise of the ground in plain sight of the road. He saw nobody, no vehicle, on the road. But beyond the road, on the crest of the ridge exactly opposite, he saw a man who had started digging a posthole, but who now was standing with his right hand at rest on the handle of his spade, and he was watching Andy.

Since it was nobody he was kin to, nobody he even knew, though pride forbade him to dismount to retrieve his arrow, Andy untwinged his con-science and drove the cows up to the barn.

Andy—who had just got free of school and who intended to stay with his grandma and grandpa, if he could, until his parents and the school teach-ers forgot about him—already knew the name of the man who had been watching him. He was Elton Penn, of whom he had heard his grandpa say, "Ay God, he's the right kind, and he's got a good woman." Elton and his wife were the new people on the Beechum place.

New people being by far the most interesting items within reach, Andy got on the pony the first thing after breakfast the next morning and went over to see them for himself. At the road, he turned down the hill and then, halfway to the bottom, he turned into the graveled lane that made a long curve along a rock fence covered with moss and lichens and lined with trees. When he came in sight of the house and the yard, the fields adjoining, and the tobacco patch whose neat rows came almost to the yard fence, Andy stopped the pony and looked at everything.

The Beechum place was a good one, as Andy's father had pointed out to him often enough and as Andy by then could see for himself. Old Jack had taken good care of it for a long time. It was a comfort to look at, and this was because the layout of its buildings and fields, even the woods along its steeper slopes and the trees in its fencerows, all fitted rightly together.

At first Andy saw nothing he was looking for. He heard a hen cackling in the henhouse, but he saw nothing stirring. The stillness of the heat of the day had come early, and the place was in a sort of trance. And then, beyond the lilac bush in the yard, he saw a man in a straw hat at work with a hoe in the tobacco patch. The man was young, tall, and slender. He moved with a certain grace, his posture and attitude entirely conformed to the motions of his work.

Andy rode around to a gate and through it to the headland along the yard fence where the rows ended. At the end of the row in which the man was working he stopped the pony again, and again he sat and watched.

If the man was aware of Andy he made no sign. He had not looked up or altered at all the rhythm of his work. He was, as Andy felt then, as later he would articulately know, a master workman, and of no tool was he more a master than the one he was using at that moment. His hold upon the handle seemed to invest the steel of the blade with the sense of touch and an intelligent concern for the well-being of the plants. The hoe did not merely chop the weeds out from between the plants, but conveyed an exquisite attention to them, pulling and lifting and shifting the dirt about. Now and then he would lean down to raise the leaves of a weak plant and tuck fresh dirt gently in around it. He worked swiftly and yet with perfect care. The row as he left it behind him was groomed like a fine horse.

The man did not look up until he had finished the row. When finally he did look up, he looked first at the pony, not at Andy. He had turned the blade of the hoe upward. He held the handle like a walking stick in his left hand. He laid his right hand on the pony's nose and made a gentle downward stroke.

"Whoa," he said. He was a nice-looking fellow who wore his clothes as neatly as he had used the hoe.

When he looked up at Andy he was grinning. He was looking at Andy as he might have looked at writing hard to make out but interesting, also amusing. He reached under his hat to scratch his head. He had black hair that, young as he was, had begun to turn gray. He scratched his head slowly and then settled his hat again precisely as it had been before. He had never taken his eyes off Andy.

He said, "Do I know you?"

"No," Andy said, "I'm Andy Catlett. I'm kin to people around here."

"I'm Elton Penn," Elton said. And he extended his hard right hand that was three or maybe four times as big as Andy's.

They shook hands. It was clear to Andy that Elton had expected him to be Andy Catlett, just as he had expected Elton to be Elton.

Elton had now crooked his right forefinger around the headstall of the pony's bridle just above the bit, and he was still grinning at Andy. He still had the studying look in his eyes.

He said, "I saw you shoot that cow."

Andy did not think of anything to say. He only sat there on the pony, twiddling one of his shoes in a stirrup and grinning back.

When it was clear that Elton had said all he was going to say for the time being and was just going to stand there grinning and watching, Andy, who was getting embarrassed, said the next thing that came to his mind:

"They won't let me have a rifle. You've got one, haven't you? Maybe you'd take me hunting with you sometime. Maybe we could go to the woods down yonder along the creek. There's some *big* trees down there. A lot of squirrels. Maybe you'd let me shoot one."

"If you shot a cow with a rifle, it *might* hurt," Elton said.

Again Andy could think of nothing to say.

The door of the screened back porch opened and a slender young woman carrying a basket of wet clothes stepped out, heading for the clothesline, and the door banged shut behind her. She saw the two of them and stopped. Her hair was the color of a new copper penny, except that the sun shone all through it and made it even brighter.

"Mary," Elton said, raising his voice only a little and not looking away from Andy, "this is our neighbor, Mr. Catlett. Mr. Andy Catlett."

Mary said, "Hello!" and she laughed. She laughed maybe because Elton was so clearly enjoying himself, and maybe because Andy was so unabashedly looking at her, getting his eyes full.

"You notice she's got red hair?" Elton said. "You've got to be mighty careful around a redheaded woman."

And Andy said, "Oh, I will!"

On the Beechum place Elton and Mary Penn came to a new beginning. This was a new beginning also in the lives of Andy and Henry Catlett. If the Penns had been interesting as new unknown people, they were far more interesting and more exciting too when they were known. The boys, so to speak, were kin to both the Catlett place and the Beechum place and had always had the run of both. But after the Penns had come, a new path was worn across the fields between the two houses.

When the mood was on him, Elton was a comedian. He could be immensely amused at himself, at the things he invented to say, at the foibles and oddities of the boys, at the world's plentitude of foibles and oddities. He was a good mimic of people's expressions and gestures, their ways of talking and walking. As the boys followed him about at his work for their own amusement and for his company, they grew from merely trying to help to being actually helpful. Elton would hire them then and instruct them and pay them a wage. Working with him, they got to know him better, and Elton was a man there was plenty to know about.

As they discovered soon enough, you could not work day in and day out with Elton and not get crossways with him on some days. He could not hide his feelings or keep from speaking his mind. Free as his laughter was in his times of exuberance, when he was in a mood for condemnation his judgments were sudden and harsh. Andy would realize eventually that Elton's condemnations were likely to involve self-condemnation. He could get into moods in which he was dark and self-obscured, his caustic pronouncements flying out in all directions, so that some of them fell inevitably upon himself. It would be as though that never-forgotten sentence of the Mountjoys, "He is nothing," began to close upon him, and he strove for air and light.

For of course Andy and Henry knew the story of Elton and Mary and the Mountjoys. They heard it from their grandma Catlett, from their parents, and, as time went on, from Elton and Mary. It was one of the legends of the boys' childhood and growing up. It was a love story lived against the dark background of a hate story. It was a comprehensible story lived against an incomprehensible one. Elton and Mary were attractive people. Who, knowing them, could think it strange that they had fallen in love, or that they had married with nobody's permission but their own? But who could understand her parents' anger, so unrelenting for so long, so apparently final?

From the time Elton and Mary got married and moved to Cotman Ridge, their story was one of the stories of Port William. Everybody knew it. It became in the end a legend of the place, according to which Elton, to prove his worth and to fling success and defiance into the faces of the Mountjoys, worked himself to death. But this explanation of Elton's too-early death Andy Catlett, among others, strongly doubted. It was too simple. There are always people who, taking for themselves every precaution against working themselves to death, are comforted to believe that somebody else has done so. Andy knew, on the contrary, that beyond the poverty that certainly drove Elton in the early years of his marriage, and beyond his undoubtable need to disprove the judgment of the Mountjoys, Elton was driven also by a passion for farming as great as that of Jack Beechum and Marce Catlett, both of whom lived long enough to become his teachers. Elton loved the use of his mind that revealed the possibilities within places and showed him the work that needed to be done. He loved offering himself to the work. He loved the knowledge of what one man's skill and strength could do in a day. He farmed as a lover loves.

And so not all of Elton's angers came from the old wound that was his legacy from the Mountjoys. They could come also in response to offenses against his devotion and his standards.

There would be a day when Elton and Andy would be in the young tobacco with their hoes. This was work that Elton liked. He accepted, was even beyond, its difficulty. To Andy it was a hardship always, but on some days more than others. It made large and clear the differences between the two of them. In Elton's mind this job, which he considered "pretty work" in itself, took a comeliness and a larger sense from the patterns of the farm and the year's work into which it fitted. To Andy, who still was inclined to understand work only in relation to himself, it fitted no pattern and so was all the more a trial. Elton, besides, was in the prime of his strength, whereas Andy, who was still growing, was weedy, dreamy, and awkward, not to mention slow—"barely able to stand up by himself," as Elton had the delicacy not to say until years later, when Andy himself could think it was funny.

It was the summer of 1949, and Andy was a few weeks shy of fifteen. Often, when just the two of them were at work, Elton would position himself between his own row and Andy's. From time to time he would work a little in Andy's row, so that Andy could keep up and they could talk. Sometimes the talk would help, and for Andy his misery would take on an overlay of pleasure.

But that day, though Elton was helping him along, they were not talking. The weather was hot and humid, without a breeze. Elton had simply remarked, with a gesture at the sun, "Old Hannah's laying it on us today, ain't she?" and had gone ahead, apparently not minding. But Andy was stopping from time to time to pull out his bandanna and wipe the sweat from his face, and from time to time he expelled his breath in a sigh.

If he had been paying attention, he could have told by looking that Elton was running out of patience. Andy's sweat-wiping and sighing were putting forth an opinion with which Elton did not agree. But Andy was not paying attention, at least not to Elton. He was paying attention to how hot and weary he was and how much he would like to be somewhere else.

Elton worked fast and accurately. He never missed a weed and he never cut off a tobacco plant. He worked with a steady rhythm and forward motion. Andy, faltering along, would occasionally snip off a plant, as on that day he finally did. Through the hoe handle he felt the little resistance of the stem as he cut through it. That did get his attention, and he was instantly aware that Elton was watching. He knew instantly also the track that Elton's mind was on. Elton was thinking that Andy was working poorly because he could afford to do so, because somebody else would pay for his mistakes. Elton, when he was Andy's age, had paid for his mistakes himself, and this was another difference between them.

"I'm sorry," Andy said.

And Elton said, "Too late."

With Elton, Andy was always ready to accept blame and apologize, and often enough Elton would say, "Don't worry about it," or "Well, it's all right," or, at worst, "I reckon you couldn't help it."

But Elton was not always so forgiving. He could also see, and at times he could see only, that all apologies come too late, and he would require Andy to see, likewise, that apologies do not undo mistakes, and you can't improve bad work by being sorry for it.

Andy did not look back at Elton. He went on working, but he could feel Elton watching him.

Elton said, "It *might* help if you'd *think* about what you're doing. What do you charge for the use of your *mind*?"

When that failed to provoke a reply, Elton said, "And take hold of your hoe the right way. It's not a *broom*!"

And then Andy, already fuming with self-justification, got mad. He said, "I reckon the damn world depends on how I hold a damn hoe!"

Elton gave Andy a look then that he seemed to poke at him to make sure it went all the way. He said, "Not just you."

From then until quitting time, Andy saw nothing of Elton but his back.

There were occasionally and inevitably days like that one, days when discord built to a momentum that could be checked only by the day's end. But there were days also that were exceptional for their goodness, when Elton and the Catlett boys, either or both, worked together in sympathy and harmony that were joyous.

The boys' grandpa Catlett died in 1946 and Old Jack in 1952. Elton had studied them closely in their latter days, just as he continued to study Wheeler. He had thought long about their devotions and their ways. He would quote them in their own voices at appropriate times by way of instruction or correction to the boys. He seemed to call the absent into presence and they spoke through him.

It would be Marce Catlett: "Mind what you're doing, baby." Or: "Ay God, I know what a man can do in a day."

It would be Old Jack: "If you're going to talk to me, you'll have to walk." Or: "Ready *hell*! I *been* ready!"

Or it would be Wheeler: "Put 'em to work! Make 'em do it right!" Or: "Honey, wait a minute. Hold on a minute."

Much of the knowledge of their elders passed to the boys through Elton. Sometimes it seemed that a current of love traveled among them and joined them to one another, to those who were absent, to the old times, to the land and its creatures.

In the Penns' second year on the Beechum place, Elton bought a large secondhand tractor. In their fourth year, he bought a small new one. Elton's horses continued to be used, by him or the Catlett boys, for the lighter jobs or as an "extra tractor," until Elton pensioned them off. He kept them, out of loyalty and gratitude, until they died. From about 1949, Elton cropped on the Catlett place as well as the Beechum place. For a while after he bought the big tractor, tractors being still rare in that country, he did custom work for neighbors. Andy, staying at the Catlett place, would sometimes wake in the night and hear Elton's tractor off in the distance still at work.

After Old Jack died, bequeathing to Elton a sum meant to be a down payment on the farm, and to Wheeler Catlett a most urgent plea—"See the boy has his place"—Elton and Mary, by Wheeler's intervention and help, did buy the Beechum place in the late winter of 1953. They bought it at what Elton thought was too high a price. But then, his own boss at last, and doing better economically than he had feared he would do, Elton gradually shaped the place to his own vision of it. He rebuilt the fences. He repaired the old buildings and built new ones. He and Mary, working on one room at a time, made the old house a comfort and a pleasure according to their needs. In 1958 they bought a second farm, an adjoining place long neglected and rundown.

* * *

As Elton went about his work day after day and year after year, the Beechum place came to a new order and beauty around him. After they bought the second farm, it too came to life and throve. Doing their own work, each helping at the other's work, Elton and Mary were making a life together, and lives for each other. Together they were coming substantially into existence, Mary from her death to all she had known and been before their marriage, Elton from the nothing her parents had judged him to be. They were making a success, even a triumph.

This accomplishment of the Penns stood among the other good things of the early life of Andy Catlett like an illuminated page. He had seen firsthand what they had done and how they had done it. They had taken what had been given them and what had been available in the time and place, and they had brought it to abundance and the luster of a new thing.

After they had come to the Beechum place and had got their feet under them, Mary and Elton had two children, first a daughter, Martha, and then a son, Jack, named for their old benefactor. As Andy and Henry Catlett grew up, they grew into friendship with Martha and Jack Penn, whom they played with and teased and helped to look after when they were small children, and whom they loved and bore in mind after Martha had become a schoolteacher in Cincinnati and after Jack too, having farmed for a few years following Elton's death, had gone away.

The story of Mary and Elton Penn was included in the story of Port William, which was included in the stories first of the Depression and then of the War, and then of the mechanization of farming and the disintegration of country life that began almost immediately at the end of the War. The old life of home farms and frugality and neighborhood and care-taking held together until the end of the War because it had to, there being until then no alternative. After the War, with the application of war machinery and chemicals and military-industrial thinking to agriculture, farming began to give way to an economy that was alien to it.

Andy would come to think of the fifteen or so years immediately following the War, which were the crucial years of the Penns' rising into prosperity, as a time unique in the stresses and contradictions that bore upon it. It was a temporary suspension or standoff between the last supports of the old agrarian economy and the forces, eventually dominant, of the economy of industrialism. It was a time when the farmers' self-sustaining household and neighborhood economies were still in place, when prices were generally good, and when for those reasons, though only for a little while, industrial equipment could serve at a reasonable cost the effort of a young farmer such as Elton.

The Penns' story, then, was a story of the gathering up of a small, brief coherence within a larger, longer story of disconnection and incoherence. Even as Elton and Mary were making themselves whole, in their marriage and in their place, Port William and its neighborhood were coming increasingly into the story of cheap fuel, speed, and the fire-driven machinery of disintegration. By the time of Elton's death in 1974, the balance had tilted against such a life as he had aspired to and lived. The economy of industry had prevailed. The land and the people who did the land's work were to be used, and used up, by the measures of mechanical efficiency and corporate profit. Greed was replacing thrift as an economic virtue. All was to be taken, nothing given back. In his last years, Elton saw that this was happening, and he raged against it. It was again a reduction to nothing, this time not just for him, but for him and his kind. When he died, the world as he had known it, and for a while had helped to make it, was ending.

As time is reckoned in the modern age, Elton's death already is long ago. The Penns' kind and their kind of life are nearly gone from the Port William neighborhood and from the whole country. As Andy Catlett looked back on it, their story, in addition to all else it was, came to seem to him a sort of lens. When he looked backward through it, he could see the lives and ways of Marce Catlett, Jack Beechum and forebears dead before he was born. Looking the other way, he saw farmers never out of debt, resorting to town jobs, working at night and on Sunday to stay even, and always fewer of them as they died or gave up or failed to meet their payments and were sold out. After they were gone, there were always fewer to remember them. It is hard to remember one world while living in another.

In the Port William neighborhood as elsewhere, there would remain a few throwbacks, dissenters, oddities, who would be rememberers, conscientiously loyal to an old membership. Andy Catlett was one of these. The story of Elton and Mary Penn survived in his memory and mind, in the fabric of his life, and in his conversations with his family and a few neighbors. As the story receded into the past and the light of more and more days fell upon it, it changed and grew larger and clearer in its aspects and in Andy's understanding. But always unchanged in its background were the dimensionless, legendary figures of Mary's parents, the old Mountjoys, whom Andy never knew and rarely had even seen.

Andy had now lived longer than both Elton and Mary. In his aging thoughts of them, he saw how young they were when their story began. They had been a boy and a girl, not long from childhood. He saw that what they did was rash enough, a bad surprise, surely, to her parents, to whom it might have been a bad surprise even if Elton had been heir to a fortune. But Andy saw too, as he always had seen, that when the marriage was made, it was as finally made as any marriage. Elton and Mary would not have submitted to its undoing any more than they had submitted to the judgment that preceded it.

Because he had been young himself, Andy understood how the marriage could have come to be. Because he had known Elton and Mary, he understood the finality of what they had done. Because he had children and grandchildren of his own, he understood Mary's parents' grief and disapproval. What he could not understand, and could not imagine, was their rejection of their daughter, which had been exactly as final as the marriage: "until death."

Over all the accumulating years, and in spite of the distance that separated them, Andy's old friendship with the Penns' daughter Martha was still intact. They would sometimes meet and talk when Andy would happen to be in Cincinnati, or Martha would stop to see him on one of her visits to her parents' graves in Port William. Now and again one of them would telephone the other, and they would talk a long time, exchanging news, and always speaking of the days they had known in common.

One night, seventy years after her parents were married, Martha called Andy and they spoke, as often before, of the circumstances of that marriage, of the Mountjoys and their long resolve. And then Martha told him something he had not known.

"After I moved up here," she said, "my grandmother tried to get in touch with me. She called my school and left her number. I never called her back."

Andy was not surprised that Martha had not returned the call. They were grandmother and granddaughter, but also they were strangers. Supposing that Martha had decided to call the old woman back or even write to her, what could she have said? Did our language afford the possibility of circumventing the years of silence by which the Mountjoys had kept to their decree that Mary Penn was dead to them and that Elton was nothing? Or supposing that, by some remarkable inspiration, Martha had thought of some cordiality with which to reply, would not that cordiality have been in effect a betrayal, a treason against her parents? Could any slightest acknowledgement of her granddaughterhood have surmounted the long dishonor paid out year after year to her mother's daughterhood? Or, supposing that Martha had returned the call, what could the old woman have said to her? What language known to us might have encompassed a wrong so old, an atonement so long delayed, to speak to a young stranger an acceptable acknowledgment of kinship?

And yet old Mrs. Mountjoy, by that phone call of years ago, had conveyed at last to Andy a possibility he had not thought of before: Suppose she was sorry.

That thought could not have borne heavily upon Martha, who had dismissed it by an instinct undoubtedly proper, who was even under obligation to do so. But upon Andy, who had been a participant in the story but by then was merely a witness to what he had known and what he now knew, it fell with a palpable weight.

Suppose she was sorry.

On that night of his conversation with Martha, Andy may have been more than usually vulnerable to such a thought. He was, for one thing, weak and in discomfort from an illness. For another, the great industrial empire to which he and his family perhaps helplessly belonged, was again at war, imposing its will by the deaths of helpless old people, women, and children, and by the torture of prisoners. The imperial economy, based upon nothing but the overconfidence of the greedy and the gullibility of victims, was disintegrating, justly, but with unjust consequences to the misled and the helpless. It was this gigantic economy, incorporating gigantic oblivion and gigantic failure, that had laid waste the world that Marce Catlett and Jack Beechum and Elton Penn had stood for and hoped for, the world that they had offered to Andy's heart and his thoughts half a century and more ago, and that he had accepted. After night had fallen, the suffering of the time and the world had drawn close to Andy, and his illness and dejection seemed to him merely a fit response.

And now the thought that, years too late, old Mrs. Mountjoy had been sorry, had repented of the hurt she had given and wished to take it back, and that her old husband also may have suffered the same too-late sorrow—that thought came to Andy as a command he could not refuse, for he had in the same instant obeyed it. He had begun to suppose. Until that moment such a possibility had been hidden by his assumption that to her death Mrs. Mountjoy had been steadfast in her anger. Until then she had been to him a wicked old woman in a tale learned in childhood. And now suddenly she was removed from legend and had become, in his imagination, only human, a fellow sufferer with Mary, her disclaimed child, and with Elton, her declared enemy. And all too late. "Too late," Andy could again hear Elton saying with the blunt finality of the world's mere truth.

As he sat on in the silence after he had hung up the phone, it seemed to Andy that the floor of creation had opened beneath him, and he had dropped into a limitlessness of heartache: of second thoughts too late, of the despair of undoing what had been done, of some forlorn hope, even, that could not be undone by despair or numbed by time.

Andy had often proposed to himself that joy, the joy of love or beauty or of work, could so abound in this world that it would overflow all of this world's mortal vessels. But that night he was thinking of sorrow, filled suddenly with the apprehension of such hurt and sorrow as might overflow the capacity of the world, let alone that of a mere life. That there had been an immeasurable joy in the story of Mary and Elton Penn he had long known. But now its suffering also had been made present to him in an amplitude beyond the reach of his mind. He would never know even the extent to which its suffering had been unnecessary.

It seemed to him almost a proof of immortality that nothing mortal could contain all its sorrow. He thought, as we all have been taught to think, of our half-lit world, a speck hardly visible, hardly noticeable, among scattered lights in the black well in which it spins. If all its sorrow could somehow be voiced, somehow heard, what an immensity would be the outcry!

In the silent, shadowy room in the great night he was thinking of heavenly pity, heavenly forgiveness, and his thought was a confession of need. It was a prayer.

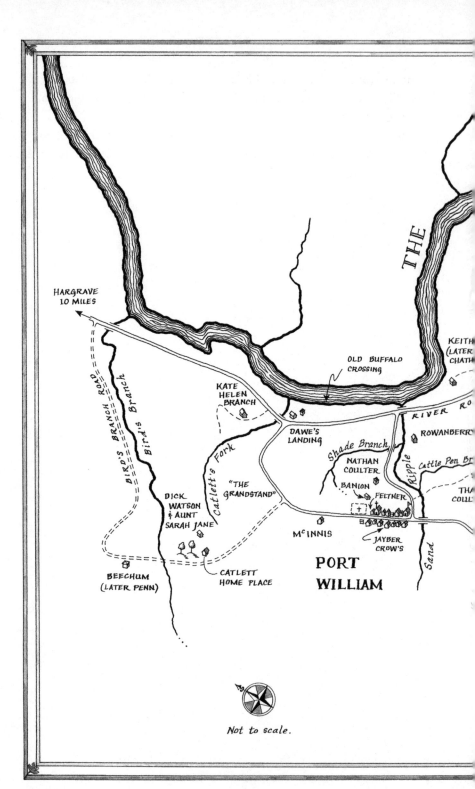

HARGRAVE
10 MILES

THE

KEITH
(LATER
CHATH

OLD BUFFALO
CROSSING

KATE
HELEN
BRANCH

RIVER RO

ROWANBERRY

DAWE'S
LANDING

Shade Branch

Cattle Pen Br

BIRD'S BRANCH ROAD

Bird's Branch

Catlett's Fork

NATHAN
COULTER

BANION

THA
COULL

FELTNER

DICK
WATSON
& AUNT
SARAH JANE

"THE
GRANDSTAND"

JAYBER
CROW'S

Mc INNIS

Sand

PORT

BEECHUM
(LATER PENN)

CATLETT
HOME PLACE

WILLIAM

Not to scale.

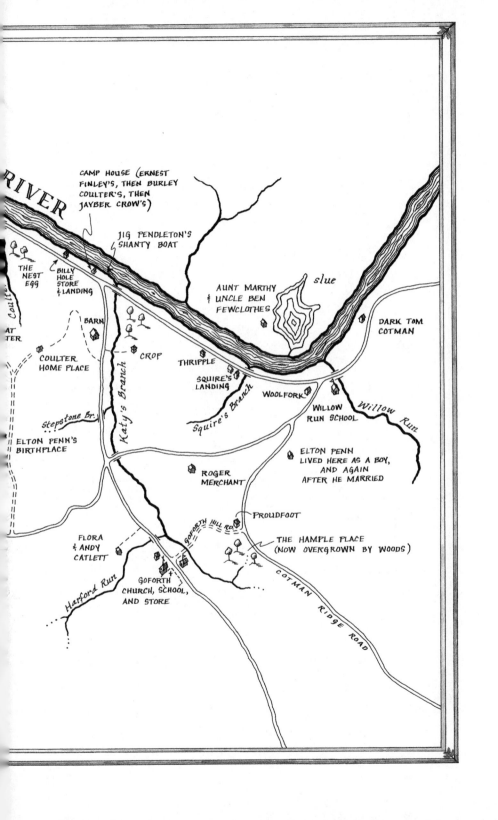

RIVER

CAMP HOUSE (ERNEST FINLEY'S, THEN BURLEY COULTER'S, THEN JAYBER CROW'S)

JIG PENDLETON'S SHANTY BOAT

Coulter

THE NEST EGG

BILLY HOLE STORE & LANDING

AT TER

BARN

COULTER HOME PLACE

CROP

Katy's Branch

THRIPPLE

SQUIRE'S LANDING

Squire's Branch

AUNT MARTHY & UNCLE BEN FEWCLOTHES

slue

DARK TOM COTMAN

WOOLFORK

WILLOW RUN SCHOOL

Willow Run

Stepstone Br.

ELTON PENN'S BIRTHPLACE

ROGER MERCHANT

ELTON PENN LIVED HERE AS A BOY, AND AGAIN AFTER HE MARRIED

PROUDFOOT

FLORA & ANDY CATLETT

GOFORTH HILL RD.

THE HAMPLE PLACE (NOW OVERGROWN BY WOODS)

Harford Run

GOFORTH CHURCH, SCHOOL, AND STORE

COTMAN RIDGE ROAD

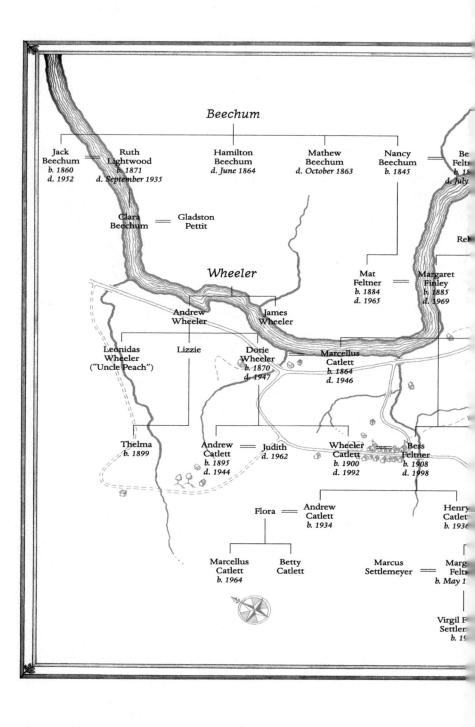

Beechum

Jack
Beechum
b. 1860
d. 1952
= Ruth
Lightwood
b. 1871
d. September 1935

Hamilton
Beechum
d. June 1864

Mathew
Beechum
d. October 1863

Nancy
Beechum
b. 1845

Be
Felt
b. 18
d. July

Clara
Beechum
= Gladston
Pettit

Re

Mat
Feltner
b. 1884
d. 1965
= Margaret
Finley
b. 1885
d. 1969

Wheeler

Andrew
Wheeler

James
Wheeler

Leonidas
Wheeler
("Uncle Peach")

Lizzie

Dorie
Wheeler
b. 1870
d. 1947

Marcellus
Catlett
b. 1864
d. 1946

Thelma
b. 1899

Andrew
Catlett
b. 1895
d. 1944
= Judith
d. 1962

Wheeler
Catlett
b. 1900
d. 1992
= Bess
Feltner
b. 1908
d. 1998

Flora = Andrew
Catlett
b. 1934

Henry
Catlett
b. 1936

Marcellus
Catlett
b. 1964

Betty
Catlett

Marcus
Settlemeyer

Marg
Felt
b. May 1

Virgil F
Settler
b. 1

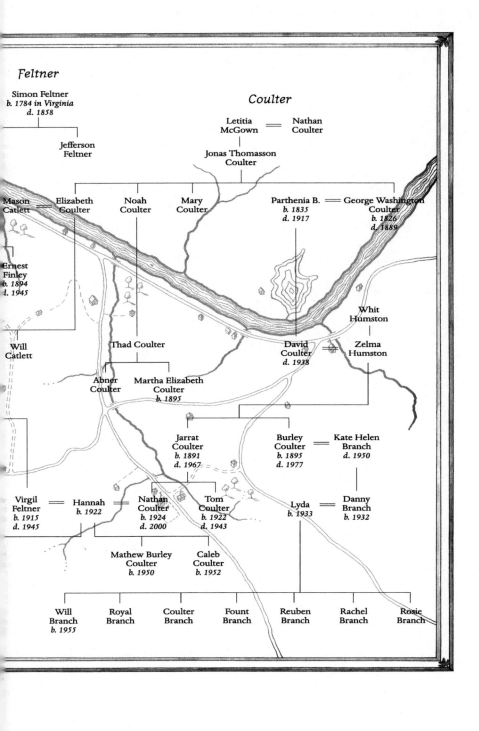

Feltner

Simon Feltner
b. 1784 in Virginia
d. 1858

Jefferson
Feltner

Coulter

Letitia
McGown ═══ Nathan
Coulter

Jonas Thomasson
Coulter

Mason
Catlett ═══ Elizabeth
Coulter

Noah
Coulter

Mary
Coulter

Parthenia B.
b. 1835
d. 1917 ═══ George Washington
Coulter
b. 1826
d. 1889

Ernest
Finley
b. 1894
d. 1945

Will
Catlett

Thad Coulter

David
Coulter
d. 1938

Whit
Humston

Zelma
Humston

Abner
Coulter

Martha Elizabeth
Coulter
b. 1895

Jarrat
Coulter
b. 1891
d. 1967

Burley
Coulter
b. 1895
d. 1977 ═══ Kate Helen
Branch
d. 1950

Virgil
Feltner
b. 1915
d. 1945 ═══ Hannah
b. 1922 ═══ Nathan
Coulter
b. 1924
d. 2000

Tom
Coulter
b. 1922
d. 1943

Lyda
b. 1933 ═══ Danny
Branch
b. 1932

Mathew Burley
Coulter
b. 1950

Caleb
Coulter
b. 1952

Will
Branch
b. 1955

Royal
Branch

Coulter
Branch

Fount
Branch

Reuben
Branch

Rachel
Branch

Rosie
Branch